ROAD TO MASTERY
VOLUME 1

WRITTEN BY
VALERIOS

ART BY
HEITOR AMATSU

AETHON BOOKS

vault

ROAD TO MASTERY
VOLUME 1

WRITTEN BY
VALERIOS

ART BY
HEITOR AMATSU

EDITORIAL
ADRIAN WASSEL – CCO & EDITOR-IN-CHIEF
DER-SHING HELMER – MANAGING EDITOR

DESIGN & PRODUCTION
TIM DANIEL – EVP, DESIGN & PRODUCTION
ADAM CAHOON – SENIOR DESIGNER & PRODUCTION ASSOCIATE
NATHAN GOODEN – CO-FOUNDER & SENIOR ARTIST

SALES & MARKETING
DAVID DISSANAYAKE – VP, SALES & MARKETING
SYNDEE BARWICK – DIRECTOR, BOOK MARKET SALES
BRITTA BUESCHER – DIRECTOR, SOCIAL MEDIA

OPERATIONS & STRATEGY
DAMIAN WASSEL – CEO & PUBLISHER
CHRIS KANALEY – CSO
F.J. DESANTO – HEAD OF FILM & TV

ROAD TO MASTERY, VOLUME 1, MAY, 2025 COPYRIGHT © 2025, VALERIOS. ALL RIGHTS RESERVED. "ROAD TO MASTERY", ROAD TO MASTERY LOGO, AND THE LIKENESSES OF ALL CHARACTERS HEREIN ARE TRADEMARKS OF VALERIOS, UNLESS OTHERWISE NOTED. "VAULT" AND THE VAULT LOGO ARE TRADEMARKS OF VAULT STORYWORKS LLC. "AETHON BOOKS" AND THE AETHON BOOKS LOGO ARE TRADEMARKS OF AETHON BOOKS, LLC. NO PART OF THIS WORK MAY BE REPRODUCED, TRANSMITTED, STORED OR USED IN ANY FORM OR BY ANY MEANS GRAPHIC, ELECTRONIC, OR MECHANICAL, INCLUDING BUT NOT LIMITED TO PHOTOCOPYING, RECORDING, SCANNING, DIGITIZING, TAPING, WEB DISTRIBUTION, INFORMATION NETWORKS, OR INFORMATION STORAGE AND RETRIEVAL SYSTEMS, EXCEPT AS PERMITTED UNDER SECTION 107 OR 108 OF THE 1976 UNITED STATES COPYRIGHT ACT, WITHOUT THE PRIOR WRITTEN PERMISSION OF THE PUBLISHER. ALL NAMES, CHARACTERS, EVENTS, AND LOCALES IN THIS PUBLICATION ARE ENTIRELY FICTIONAL. ANY RESEMBLANCE TO ACTUAL PERSONS (LIVING OR DEAD), EVENTS, INSTITUTIONS, OR PLACES, WITHOUT SATIRIC INTENT, IS COINCIDENTAL. PRINTED IN USA. FOR INFORMATION ABOUT FOREIGN OR MULTIMEDIA RIGHTS, CONTACT: RIGHTS@VAULTCOMICS.COM

Table of Contents

Ch. 1	Apocalypse Day	1
Ch. 2	Jack vs. Goblin	13
Ch. 3	Hello World	23
Ch. 4	Big, Aggressive Prison Mates	33
Ch. 5	Beating the Shit out of Stuff	41
Ch. 6	The High Goblins	49
Ch. 7	Challenging the Ice Pond	59
Ch. 8	The Last Monster Group	69
Ch. 9	Fighting a Hobgoblin	77
Ch. 10	Serial Bonker	85
Ch. 11	Racing a Bear	95
Ch. 12	The Jack-Goblin War	103
Ch. 13	Punching a Boss	111
Ch. 14	Class Time	123
Ch. 15	Beary Strong	133
Ch. 16	A Summit of Kings	145
Ch. 17	Jack Rust vs. Bear King	153
Ch. 18	King of the Ring	161
Ch. 19	Crossing the Pond	169
Ch. 20	World of the Waterfall	179
Ch. 21	The Strongest Monkeys	187
Ch. 22	Boxing a Gorilla	197
Ch. 23	Calamitous Punch	207
Ch. 24	Monkey See, Monkey Do	217
Ch. 25	Breaking Through	225
Ch. 26	Exploring the Dao	233
Ch. 27	Wolf Hunting	241
Ch. 28	Between Life and Death	251
Ch. 29	Meteor Punch	261
Ch. 30	Reaping the Rewards	269
Ch. 31	Brock the Monkey	279
Ch. 32	Entering Civilization with a Bang	293
Ch. 33	Seeking Revenge	309
Ch. 34	Ar'Tazul the Merchant	319
Ch. 35	Challenging an Entire Faction	329
Ch. 36	Triumph	337

Chapter 1
Apocalypse Day

Jack Rust gazed at the mouth of a cave, black like the night and barely wide enough for a grown man to push through. He clicked a button, and his flashlight burned to life, shooting a wide beam of light into the darkness, dispelling it.

Only rock walls met his sight. This place was a shallow slit in the hillside, but he knew that wasn't entirely the case—another researcher had stumbled upon it and called on Jack to look.

Of course, he thought. By all means, have me explore the dark, dirty cave. I love it.

Jack was an average-built man. His dark-haired head rose six feet from the ground, but he lacked the musculature to intimidate anyone. At least his younger years of sports left him with a slim, athletic build, though he didn't exercise anymore.

His body shape, along with his green eyes and kind smile, made him slightly handsome if you asked most people, or not at all if you asked girls named Maria, of which he had a particularly nasty streak.

It also made him quite suitable to investigate narrow, rocky crevices, which is why he was here instead of a person of lower seniority. He didn't like it, but alas—job called.

Still better than spending the entire day in a cramped lab full of smelly undergraduates.

Grumbling, Jack made sure the pockets of his cargo pants were secured. He surveyed the rocks, mapping out the sharp ones jutting out of the walls, then ventured forth. His body went sideways, eyes glued before him, watching out for errant spider webs or multi-legged annoyances.

Though he could fit pretty easily, the rocks wound tight around him. He felt trapped.

Fortunately, claustrophobia wasn't enough to stop Jack. If not, he wouldn't be here.

He was aware of the precautions. He'd rehearsed them mentally while crossing the nature reserve. If anything felt off, or if the crevice got dangerously narrow, he would go back. He prayed for that, actually; it would make this excursion a paid field trip.

Unfortunately, that didn't happen. A few feet ahead, the crevice opened into a cave fifteen feet across and nine to the side. Jack took out a device from his right pocket and let it inspect the air—it beeped twice; all clear.

Damn, he thought, but smiled. At least he'd make headway. If he discovered even a single female viper caterpillar here, they could mate it with the one they already had and create enough specimens to last. Plus, the cave looked pretty clean, as improbable as that sounded.

APOCALYPSE DAY

He also checked his featureless gray T-shirt. It appeared fine; hadn't been caught in any rocks, thankfully. Though simple, it was his favorite shirt.

Jack then swung his flashlight across the walls. If there were carapaced insects skittering around, he couldn't see them. It didn't matter. He'd only be here for a little while, and poisonous varieties weren't indigenous to this area.

He set his flashlight on a rock, letting it illuminate half the cave. He then removed a pair of gloves from his pocket, put them on, kneeled beside a patch of moss, and stuck his hands into it. As he idly ran his fingers over the rock, sensing nothing through the gloves, he released a sigh.

What am I even doing?

He was shuffling through moss in a tiny, dark cave in the middle of nowhere, trying so hard for something he didn't care too much about. Not that he didn't like his job. Being a biologist could be fun at times, and he even had a PhD—almost. He was financially set for life and with a job more interesting than most.

However, at the end of the day, it was just that—a job—and, if he was being honest, it didn't fill him. Not at all. It wasn't the life he dreamed about.

Jack had followed the yellow brick road. He'd done well at school, done well at university, then proceeded to get a PhD—well, almost. He'd taken all the expected steps and still ended up trapped. It was such a shame.

Maybe it was youth's boiling blood talking—the one he wasted every day. The clock kept ticking and would never go backward.

He shook his head. Unfortunately, the world was what it was. His thoughts were only pipe dreams brought forth by the novelty of exploring a small cave in the Greenway Nature Reserve. He had to survive, somehow, and having a job he didn't dislike was already better than most. There were bright sides. That was reality.

As the professor would say, everybody had to slave away, so why not do it at something interesting?

But he couldn't shake off the fantasy. Was this all life had to offer? Was he doomed to spend forty years of his life doing such tiny things, doomed to constantly suppress his inner desire for... something? Anything?

Jack was just a regular guy, and that brutal reality grained on his soul. It wasn't the rock walls that trapped him—it was everything else.

But there was nothing to be done. He understood that, and at the same time, hated it.

A bump on his fingers brought him back. A little green thing squirmed to escape, and like a hawk, he grabbed it. It was helpless in his hand.

Nice! he mentally exclaimed, raising it to take a better look. *A viper caterpillar!* Going by the color patterns, it was a female one, too. He'd found it.

Whistling in joy, he lowered the caterpillar and dropped it in a small jar he'd been carrying, twisting its lid closed before the little insect could escape. He then wiped his gloved hand on a nearby rock. He smiled. The trip here had taken a while, but it was worth it. At least the searching part had been short.

How long did it take me? Five minutes? Wow. There have to be more of them.

A conscientious worker would keep searching. Jack took one look at the upturned moss and shook his head. Maybe it was due to his previous, morose thoughts, but he didn't feel like doing anything. *We'll just wait a couple days for them to breed.*

APOCALYPSE DAY

He focused on the caterpillar in the jar. It was tiny and trapped. Just like him.

"What am I even doing..." he muttered, sighing. He didn't want to look for caterpillars in dark caves, just to return to his lab. He wanted to feel alive.

It was the millionth time he had that thought, and the millionth time he wasn't going to do anything about it. This time, the universe responded.

> Sapience located. Starting Integration...
> Branching Immortal System...
> Welcome to the New World!

A shiny blue screen snapped into existence in front of Jack's face. He backpedaled—the screen followed—and accidentally stepped on the glass jar, breaking it under his boot. The caterpillar escaped. Jack's elbow met a sharp rock.

"Woah!" he shouted, more surprised than hurt.

A blue screen appeared in the air. That couldn't be right.

Before he could consider the issue further, the world shook. Rocks rumbled and groaned; the earth moaned underfoot. Jack paled. An earthquake was the worst thing to happen in a cave. He dropped to his knees and huddled around them, covering himself under a seemingly sturdy protrusion of the walls. The shaking intensified instead of stopping, and a bright cyan light blinded him again, making him hug his knees, pray for his life, and hope for the best.

A few rocks fell from the ceiling, but fortunately, not on him.

It felt like hours before the shaking stopped, though it couldn't have been more than a minute. When everything stood still again, as caves were supposed to do, Jack opened his eyes and met an impossible sight.

A small pond now lay where the far cave wall used to stand, along with a short waterfall sprouting from the rocks behind it. The water was so cold he could feel it even from a few steps away, but there was no ice on its surface. His flashlight had tumbled into the water—he could see it—but he didn't need it because the pond itself was shining. And had the cave grown larger?

Jack gaped. His mind failed to process the sight. *I'm in a dream*, he concluded. *This is where I wake up.*

But he didn't wake up. Instead, the blue screen kept rolling in his sight, spitting out line after incomprehensible line.

> **Terraforming complete.**
> **Overseers informed.**
> **Immortal System initiated.**
> **Think 'Status' to access your status screen.**
> **Creating dungeons...**

Status?

> **Name: Jack Rust**
> **Species: Human, Earth-387**
> **Faction: -**
> **Grade: F**
> **Level: 1**
> **Physical: 4**
> **Mental: 7**
> **Will: 6**

What... the... fuck...

Jack was a smart guy, as were most scientists. Unfortunately, no amount of mental muscle could prepare him for what was currently happening.

He struggled to put things in order.

I am fully aware. If this was a dream, I should have woken up by now, but I haven't. What the hell is happening?

Too many emotions warred inside him. Fear of the unknown, confusion, helplessness, and finally, an inexplicable relief he couldn't deny. He was drifting in a new sea, and, for some odd reason, he suddenly felt alive. He studied the blue screen in his face, the one apparently called 'status.'

This is like a videogame, he realized. Did AI finally conquer us?

He looked at the pond that shouldn't be there, wondering about a bunch of things. The blue screen obliged.

> **Ice Pond (E-Grade)**
> A hidden resource of the Forest of the Strong. The piercing cold of the Ice Pond can heal and forge a cultivator's body. The deeper you go, the more painful the cold, and the more effective the forging.

There were so many unknown words, Jack's head spun. The status screen before, the levels, the attributes... Had his world turned into a game?

One thought pushed all others apart. *Am I going to get magic? Fuck yeah!*

Every child dreamed of becoming a wizard. If reality suddenly malfunctioned or was altered by advanced nanobots, why not let him shoot fire too?

Relief and excitement flooded him again, even harder than before. He had no idea what was happening, completely lost in something that didn't make sense, but he didn't reject it. Without even knowing what was going on, Jack instinctively hoped it was true, that the world really had turned into a game and nothing made sense anymore.

Because, if that happened, he would be *free*.

The child inside him awoke. A grin spread on his cheeks, and he neither could, nor wanted, to stop it. Whatever was happening was dangerous, unknown, and something he could thrive in. His escapism fantasies had turned real.

Assuming this *was* real, he needed to rush to understand it. Thankfully, he was good with deciphering complex information. All he needed was time.

The world shook a second time. His vision swam for no reason. Odd smells suffused the space, bringing in mind a clean, strong breeze and fiercely swiping grass. New blue screens sprouted before him, and Jack felt an increasing need for them to fuck off. He'd had enough already.

Unfortunately, they did not fuck off.

**1,111 dungeons created.
Monster spawning schema complete.
Integration complete.**

Transmitting message from assigned Overlords, the Animal Kingdom (B-Grade):

Welcome to the System world. If your planet did not have magic before, it does now.

APOCALYPSE DAY

Monsters and dungeons have spawned everywhere. You have been assigned attributes and Levels, and you have the capability to rise in strength by slaying strong creatures or deeply understanding the world. We understand you are in a state of shock. Do not worry. Everything will be alright in the end. It is expected that your society will collapse soon, if not already, but you will be fine. We, the Animal Kingdom, will take care of those things.

For now, you should focus on becoming individually stronger. Hunt monsters, conquer dungeons, sink your mind deep into the world, and you will attain power greater than you can dream of. Embrace the new reality. The first step to that power is the Integration Tournament, which will be held in twenty galaxy days (note: fifteen Earth-387 days) from now. Comprehend even the tiniest corner of the world by then, and endless possibilities will open up for you.
Good luck, Animal Kingdom

You have entered the Forest of the Strong (F-Grade) Dungeon.
Forest of the Strong (F-Grade): A forest where only the strong survive. There are three monster groups, each holding a unique resource and representing a unique challenge. Slay the leader of a group to despawn them.

This Dungeon is in conquer-or-die mode. Defeat the Dungeon Boss to exit or die trying. We applaud your bravery for entering and wish you the best of luck.

...*What? Aliens?*

Jack scanned over the screens, barely understanding half of what he read. He was completely lost, so he grabbed onto the few things he knew. He was familiar with games. He knew how dungeons worked—they were special places teeming with monsters, where players could enter at great risk and accordingly great rewards.

Apparently, this new state of the world—the New World, if the blue screens were to be believed—shared many game-like elements, including dungeons. They'd probably spawned around the world.

Except...

We applaud your bravery for entering—Motherfucker! A dungeon spawned around me!

Jack was livid! As if he didn't have enough on his plate. He now had to kill some Dungeon Boss or die trying.

"This is a mistake!" he shouted. "I didn't enter on purpose. Let me out!"

Unfortunately, neither the blue screens nor the walls replied. Jack was left staring at the ice pond.

He crossed his arms. "I don't like this. At least give me magic."

Faint blue light coalesced out of nowhere by the lake. Jack was relieved—he might have been sabotaged, but at least, he was given magic!

As the light expanded and solidified, his hopes were dashed. This wasn't magic—well, it was, but not his. A short, green, humanoid creature with long ears appeared out of nowhere. It barely reached his chest and was fully naked, as well as skinny and bald. Jack thought it looked like a child.

It then turned around, and he almost screamed. This was no child.

Its mouth was unnaturally wide and filled with sharp teeth. Its nose was long like a finger, its hands sported short claws, and its yellow eyes were filled with malice. It grinned, while Jack could only stare.

> **Goblin, Level 2**
> *Goblins are weak, primal humanoids who move in large groups. They are barely intelligent enough to cook their food, and they often derive pleasure from torturing their victims. Cultivators are advised to kill them on sight.*

"Kekeke..." the goblin chuckled in a high-pitched, grating, evil-sounding voice. "Weak, tasty human... I will eat your legs first, kekeke..."

A myriad thoughts ran through Jack's mind. He was terrified of this creature. It wanted to eat him alive. He had to escape.

At the same time, a different part of his brain, the analytical one, couldn't help noticing how this System manipulated him. It spawned a man-eating monster right in his face, made it clear they were enemies, and said it was okay to kill it. Moreover, it gave the monster an ugly, terrifying visage, as well as opening lines that served to squash any doubts in his mind.

Jack had a PhD—almost—in biology. He knew how evolution worked. Nature was brutally efficient, not comically evil.

This creature was not natural. It was engineered. Fake. A target for him to kill or die trying. He didn't know why the System acted like this, but these were unarguable facts, because he'd spent half his life studying nature and the other half playing video games.

These thoughts snapped like firecrackers in his battle-addled brain. It took less than a second for all the connections to be made, and then came the realization that they were worthless.

He could only fight.

Now would be a good time for magic, he thought, but nothing came. He scanned around—no sharp rock for him to use. He carried no knife. His car key was electronic.

There were no weapons. There was also no time.

He got up and clenched his fists. The goblin pounced.

Chapter 2
Jack vs. Goblin

The goblin rushed in, and Jack rushed back. It was faster. Claws raked Jack's forearm, which he raised to defend, drawing three thick lines of blood. He groaned—the pain shot fire into his nerves, jolting his entire body. The feeling was immediately subdued. Instincts he didn't even know he had kicked in, dulling the pain, translating it into fuel to push him forward.

He grabbed the goblin's wrist and tossed the entire creature away like a ragdoll, but it only took a few steps before regaining itself. It jumped right back into the fray.

Jack gritted his teeth as he surveyed the space around him. There was nothing he could use, not with a cursory glance. No rock, branch, or even a stick. And his flashlight was buried under the pond.

MAGIC! he screamed to the blue screens. If they could summon a goblin out of thin air, they could certainly give him the ability to shoot fire. Unfortunately, nothing happened.

The goblin was upon him again. Jack panicked, swinging wildly and missing, only clipping its shoulder. The impact was enough to push the little fucker away, but it returned with renewed force, and this time, its claws raked across his upper chest, barely missing his throat.

Jack paled. As the goblin jumped at him, sharp teeth about to tear him apart, time slowed. He was growing weaker. His heart shivered and the world closed in on the goblin—the little green ball of hatred that was going to kill him.

The realization settled in: *I am going to die.*

Suddenly, the world flared. Jack's entire potential as a human was unleashed and directed towards survival. His body surged with power, power he was already using but wasn't conscious of. He'd thrown the goblin many feet aside. He was strong, and it was just a little green ball of claws.

As death approached, something clicked in Jack's mind. His primal instincts stepped in and took the wheel. His thoughts rolled by themselves. He didn't care about injuries. So what if he bled? It was acceptable as long as he killed the goblin and lived to see another day.

The irrelevant disappeared. Jack got serious. He clenched his fist, and the raw power shocked him. His body outputted strength he couldn't even fathom. He felt fast, incredibly strong, and inexhaustibly tenacious. His pupils dilated. His skin tingled. All his muscles buzzed with electricity. The cold terror in his heart became a fuel that drove him. Fear gave way to ecstasy.

He was ready to fight. Jack became a beast.

He didn't know how to punch, but his body did. His fist smashed into the goblin's face, cracking its long nose and throwing it back before it could reach him—he possessed the longer arms, after all.

Jack became intently aware that his fist was in massive pain. Correction: his body didn't know how to punch, either. That didn't matter though.

Just as the goblin got its footing, he pounced. He would kill it.

He fell on it like a wild animal. He didn't care about the scratches he received, the pain, the blood. These all washed away into the back of his mind. He balled his fist and drove it into the goblin's face again, smashing it hard into a wall. It screamed, but the sound only gave Jack hope. He tried to pin the wily beast to the rocks, but it slipped under his grasp and jumped aside. Claws raked him again, cutting his belt—didn't care.

He stared at the retreating goblin, whose eyes were filled with hatred and fear, and charged after it, grinning. He didn't know what he felt, didn't need to. Everything was easy. The violence was rising from inside him, and he was its conduit.

There was something cathartic about violence, about the silence as every fiber of your being focused on a single task. Jack had never felt so complete, so happily monolithic. There were no worries or fears, only a body that brimmed with ecstasy and a cold, calculating mind that inspected everything at impossible speed.

Jack's shoes tilted to perfectly hug the uneven stone, and his body turned with impeccable balance. The goblin threw a feint, but Jack saw through it. As it turned, it didn't find a target, only a fist getting planted hard into its face.

The goblin flew off its feet and into the wall behind, losing its balance, and Jack was there. He pinned it to the ground and pummeled it, channeling the entirety of his newfound strength into repeatedly driving his fist into the goblin's face as hard as he possibly could.

Bones cracked and groaned—some his, some the goblin's. Every punch came in heavy, every strike devastating. The goblin resisted for a while before going still, yet Jack punched a couple more times and only then stopped.

Absentmindedly, he noted he was out of breath, in terrible pain, and several parts of his body felt wrong. His brain calculated everything with cruel precision. It reviewed his situation, then scanned his environment for solutions. His belt and pockets carried nothing of significance. He had to patch up the big wound on his forearm, where blood was flowing, and he had to do it now.

He tore his sleeve—how easy it was—and wrapped the fabric, tightening it so hard it hurt. His shirt was wet with blood at places, so he just removed it. There were more wounds on him, mostly insignificant—the goblin had missed all major arteries.

He was stable, and the enemy was dead. He was fine.

A single fluttering of relief filled Jack's heart, and his battle mode receded as quickly as it'd come. He was left shivering, cold, and breathless. The pain came in warm waves, and kneeling as he was, he failed to stifle a cry.

"FUCK!"

What the hell just happened?

The wretched sight of the goblin corpse entered his vision. He bent to the side and retched on the stone, the hot bile's burn accompanying the ones on his limbs and chest.

He cried.

It took a long time for Jack to regain himself. The pain receded, and the blood stopped flowing. Jack was left sitting on a rock, holding his head between his palms, and trying not to stare at the mangled goblin corpse.

He hated what he'd done. No—he wasn't sure what he felt. Trying to get his thoughts in order was futile.

So many things had happened, and in such a short timeframe. Blue screens had appeared, magic everywhere, a pond formed out of nowhere, a magically-spawned goblin tried to kill him, and he'd punched it to death.

Jack had a steady mind. He could comprehend the blue screens and their magic, or at least accept them. By now, he was aware it wasn't a dream. The world had changed irreparably. Be it aliens, AI, something else, or everything at once, *something* happened, and it had altered the course of his life forever.

He could work with that. He could fit it into the frame, somehow. Could even accept the fact that a dungeon had spawned around him, filled with goblins and who knows what else, and that he had to slay a so-called Dungeon Boss to escape.

Those were all things he could comprehend.

However, the version of himself he saw... That wasn't easy to swallow.

Those feelings saved him, but they'd come from somewhere deep inside him, a place he couldn't even perceive. They flooded him out of nowhere, and he had no control—they were part of him, and at the same time, weren't.

It wasn't a bad thing—he survived, after all—but he never before realized how deep the lightless region inside him was. How much control it could have over him.

Were those things part of him, or dark passengers?

Jack didn't know. His mind had been ravaged by an unknown companion, and its effects were still there. Even as he sat, away from immediate danger, he remained aware that more goblins could show up at any moment.

Whatever was happening, he had no time to lose, and the callousness permeated his mind even now. His eyes were hard as he stood. He had to survive.

He took in everything again. The goblin corpse no longer upset him now, at least to a degree, and he had things to consider.

So, no magic. The world has become a video game, and I'm trapped in a dungeon. OK. What now?

An exclamation mark was blinking in the lower left part of his vision, and he willed it open.

> **Level Up! You have reached Level 2.**

That was it. No acknowledgment of his bitter struggle against the goblin, no words of compassion or comfort, no explanations. Only cold information.

Of course... He shook his head before proceeding.

> **First Kill Bonus: Fistfighting (I) skill!**

That gave Jack pause. Skills were a common element in games, and the System seemed to follow those conventions pretty faithfully so far. Was it a coincidence, or something deeper?

And, at the end of the day, had the world really turned into a game? Had he been drawn into one? It didn't make sense, but it was hard to disagree with the goblin corpse in the corner. He couldn't ask anyone else either—his cellphone didn't have signal in the cave, and he sure as hell wasn't going out there unprepared.

He could only depend on himself.

Fistfighting... Curiosity sprang inside Jack. He reviewed his status screen.

> **Name: Jack Rust**
> **Species: Human, Earth-387**
> **Faction: -**
> **Grade: F**
> **Level: 2**
> **Physical: 4 (+)**
> **Mental: 7 (+)**
> **Will: 6 (+)**
> **Free points: 2**
> **Skills: Fistfighting (1)**

His level was 2, indeed, and it was clear the level up gave him two free points. He could add those in any of his stats, as indicated by the plus marks.

If this really was like video games, adding those points would make him faster or smarter. Taking a step further, he could make himself a better warrior or an... intellectual? Wizard?

Probably wizard.

He refused to believe there wasn't magic—he just didn't have it.

In video games, it was better to focus on one path. Better a master of one rather than a jack of all trades, even though his name was Jack. Given his current stats, coupled with his knowledge of himself, Jack was clearly more gifted in mental endeavors than physical ones. It also worked with his desire—and childhood dream—to one day wield magic.

Unfortunately, the fact remained that he currently possessed no magic or promises of getting it anytime soon. The only thing he had, besides the promise of more goblins, was the ice pond, an E-Grade natural resource, whatever that meant:

> **Ice Pond (E-Grade)**
> *A hidden resource of the Forest of the Strong. The piercing cold of the Ice Pond can heal and forge a cultivator's body. The deeper you go, the more painful the cold, and the more effective the forging.*

Even this pond only spoke about the body.

It was starting to dawn on Jack that he couldn't follow the path of magic. He needed something to defeat the Dungeon Boss and escape, and that something could only be his fists—or, even better, some weapon.

Before committing to anything, he focused on his only skill, Fistfighting. If this really worked like a video game, he could—*Aha!*

> **Fistfighting (I):** Grants basic knowledge of fistfighting. While fistfighting, slightly enhances the user's physical attributes, reflexes, and kinetic vision.

It was promising, also ominous. If this skill's description was true, the System could mess with his entire body and brain... Jack didn't like that, though at this point, it was expected.

At least the skill was good. He clenched his left fist, confidence growing—he understood why he'd almost broken his right one on the goblin's face. He adopted a fighting stance—another gift of the skill—and punched the air, boxing against his shadow in the ice pond's glow.

He felt different. Stronger. Aware. He was like an amateur boxer—not really a master, but familiar with the movements alongside his body. Though it wasn't a stunning difference, if he met the goblin again, he was confident in demolishing it—well, more easily than before.

He chuckled darkly. How quickly I adapted...

There simply was no choice. He needed to adapt. Something was happening, and even if he didn't know what, it could kill him—*would*, if he let it.

I must get stronger.

This new skill was a great boon to his survivability—not just because it increased his attacking power, but mostly because it gave him better control over his body and awareness of the situation. He could avoid injuries, which was essential to his survival.

The only downside was that it required fistfighting, which meant he couldn't use a weapon... He didn't have one, anyway. He would fight with his fists, for now, and reconsider the issue when he found—or made—a knife. Any inferior weapon was incomparable to the fighting experience the skill offered.

That done, Jack returned to the issue of his stat points. Which was a no-brainer.

With a sigh, he allocated both points in Physical and a cold current, like a massive shiver, rose through his body. He tensed up, then realized this was his new normal. He was stronger, faster, and harder than before. He flexed his fist, and it felt steadier than ever.

It was impressive.

Being an expert in biology, Jack didn't have the slightest clue how this could happen. Just made no sense. If this improvement was what it promised—or rather, what his video game knowledge promised—it was a feat completely beyond the reach of modern science.

This System would somehow have to alter both his DNA and body structure, as well as spontaneously create a bunch of extra cells to fill in the gaps. All of these were impossible, and extremely worrying, because it meant the System had complete control over his body and, most probably, his mind.

It was a grim thought—almost grimmer than the goblin in the corner.

Chapter 3
Hello World

Jack finally managed to process all the information. Not completely, but enough to proceed. He'd also killed a goblin, though he didn't like to think about that.

Gradually, a plan formed in his mind:

Leave the cave; Explore the natural reserve; Find water, shelter, and food, in that order; Survive until someone found him or kill the Dungeon Boss to escape.

A good plan, assuming everything really was game-like. The largest doubt he had was about the environment outside.

Before the Integration, as the blue screens called it, Jack had been in a small, hidden cave in the middle of the Greenway Nature Reserve. The System had called the dungeon Forest of the Strong, and given that the natural reserve was a forest, it was reasonable to assume the entire reserve had been dungeonified.

On one hand, that was good, because Jack had been here many times. On the other, it was a dungeon. Even the best of dungeons sounded worse than, say, his house.

Regardless, Jack now had his bearings, a way to fight, a basic awareness of the situation, and a plan. He was ready to survive harder than anyone ever survived before.

There was just one last thing to do. He set his sights on the ice pond. It promised a forging of his body, which sounded suspiciously nice. If he was going to fight for his life, he couldn't let this opportunity go. Moreover, it mentioned something about healing, and his entire body was still in pain and sore from the goblin fight. His right fist was also bruised and bloated.

Jack reached the pond in two steps. It was nine feet wide and stretched fifteen feet back, by Jack's estimation. A short waterfall was at its end, supplying cold water from a crack between the rocks.

From this distance, the chill was staggering. Jack could've been standing by a glacier. The water was still and extremely clean, letting him easily make out the rock bottom. He could even see his green eyes staring back at him from the surface.

Jack gulped. The smooth incline of its bottom made it inviting, but the cold was forbidding.

What if I get pneumonia? What if this water is full of bacteria?

Many doubts crossed his mind, but at the end, he was in a game-like situation. Mundane things like pneumonia were distant and inconsequential. The goblins were a much more immediate danger, and the pond could help him live through it.

He took a deep breath and removed his clothes, leaving on only his underwear to feel safe. He then stepped into the pond with his right foot.

And instantly thought he lost it. All feeling disappeared, leaving only a numbness and ten thousand frozen needles. His instinct screamed to remove his foot, which he did, and the cave's humid air was heavenly compared to that blitzing cold.

"Holy shit..."

Jack took a few breaths to regain himself, then inspected his foot. It was fine—no, more than fine. It was rejuvenated and sturdy as if brand-new.

Such an odd sensation. One he could only equate to taking a comfortably cold shower, except the rejuvenation was far more intense, and so was the cold. A magical equivalent of a cold shower.

Clearly the System hadn't lied—this was healing and forging—and Jack, having recovered from the cold, decided he had no choice.

"Fuck me."

He decisively stuck one foot into the lake, this time enduring the cold. He waited, and the feeling gradually receded, stabilizing to a level that was cold enough to be painful but not enough to be harmful.

It was safe.

Taking another deep, trembling breath, Jack put his other foot inside. When he got used to the cold again, he kneeled in the water to submerge more of himself. His teeth were clattering. He didn't dare sink any deeper, as he remembered the System's warning that the cold increased the farther he went. There was already a freezing current coming from the depths of the pond. A single step would increase the cold substantially, and he was already at his limit.

Jack's body spasmed. The cold was so piercing it caused him physical pain. His body demanded to get away, but his will resisted, holding himself steady. He could tell it was safe, at least for a little bit, and told himself it wasn't *too* cold.

The frigid temperature spread from his legs to his entire body. He was pale, but he could also sense a new sturdiness seeping in, enhancing him. His skin, flesh, and bones were filled with that cold, all shivering in pain and anticipation.

Finally, the cold settled and he got used to it. Through gritted teeth, he took a deep, deep breath. He couldn't help grinning. This pain was so self-improving it was almost addictive.

Almost. He'd gotten what he ought to.

Save for one thing. He stuck his right palm into the water, the one he'd injured against the goblin's soft bones. He couldn't stifle his scream. The cold assaulted his injured hand as if alive, surrounding it and submerging it in wave after wave of freeze.

Jack instantly lost all feeling, and this time, it felt dangerous. He had to pull away *now*.

He jumped back outside the lake, losing his footing by the drastic change in temperature and fell on his butt. His hand was slightly blue, but the bloating was already receding. It was much better.

Jack let his back meet the ground as he exhaled in relief, closing his eyes. The cave's relative warmth was massaging his entire body, the sensation so euphoric it nearly made up for the pain of the lake.

As he eyed the water, he shivered at the thought of entering again, but he had to. He briefly considered investing in Will at his next opportunity to handle the cold better and decrease the pain, but discarded the notion. How far he could go into a lake like this was dictated by how much cold his body could handle—meaning, his Physical. No matter how strong his willpower got, it wouldn't affect his bodily limits. Plus, he'd already locked his points into Physical—he'd just have to bear through the pain.

When his body grew more resilient, mostly through level-ups, he could go deeper into the lake and reap more benefits... Of course, that's if the lake lived up to its System description.

> Ice Pond bonus: +1 Physical

It was a short message of great significance. Jack reviewed his status screen.

> Name: Jack Rust
> Species: Human, Earth-387
> Faction: -
> Grade: F
> Level: 2
> Physical: 7
> Mental: 7
> Will: 6
> Skills: Fistfighting (1)

His Physical had increased by one sixth by simply stepping into a lake. One point didn't seem like much, but Jack had a mathematical mind—it was actually humongous!

Since his initial stats were 4,7,6 for the three stats respectively, he assumed the average was 5. Now, he was as strong as he was smart.

If I put those free points in Mental, would I be smarter than the Professor? he wondered idly, then chuckled and shelved the thought. *No way.*

Then again, my Physical started at 4, but it couldn't be below average. I'm a healthy young man. Is the average not 5? Or does it include other things besides humans? Is it not built around averages to begin with, and the human average would be 3.689 or something random like that?

Jack shook his head. It didn't really matter.

He then jumped upright, surprising himself. His body was vastly superior to what it used to be, and he even had the Fistfighting skill to augment him. Compared to when he met that goblin, he was a completely new person.

He eyed the tunnel leading upward, toward the surface. The world up there could be filled with monsters, terrors, and nightmares... but Jack was ready. He grinned.

Prepare yourself, world. Here I come!

Jack peeked his head out of the cave. "Gah!" he said, blinded by the sunlight. He rubbed his eyes and tried again.

A rocky surface stretched to his left and right—the hill over the cave. His front was occupied by interspersed trees and bushes, dense enough to be called a forest, but sparse enough for people to walk in between. The trees reached from nine to eighteen feet into the air, their trunks a dark brown and leaves a bright green. The bushes were paler in color, and mostly filled with annoying sticks and spikes.

There was the occasional berry hanging down, maybe the rare fruit, too, but the nature reserve was pretty empty overall.

That is, unless the System had anything to say. Jack hoped it wouldn't.

His current shelter was a crack in the rock, seemingly shallow but actually leading to a hidden cave. Not an easy to find place. Maybe that's why the System put the ice pond inside it. A hidden bonus, of sorts, for those willing to explore—a bonus that would save Jack's life.

With that comfort in the back of his mind, it was time to see the outside world.

The first thing he did was take out his cellphone, an old Samsung model, and give it a shot—there was no signal at all. *Yeah, thought so. Like the System would let me call the police.* After placing it, his electronic car key, and his wallet in a hidden crevice of the rocks, he looked around.

Seeing no animals or goblins nearby, Jack took a tentative step outside, then another.

The air smelled the same as always—wet grass and crisp breeze. The grass parted easily under his feet, and the tree barks were uneven under his hand. Insects buzzed in the air, animals yelped from afar, and leaves fluttered in the wind—one even flew to his chest. Everything was as he remembered.

Was it all a hallucination? he wondered. *Did the earthquake release gasses in the cave?*

A blur shot past his line of sight, darting from bush to bush. Jack caught a glimpse of its bushy, orange tail and triangular snout.

> **Fox, Level 1**
> *Foxes are mostly harmless omnivores that inhabit forest areas.*

Not too talkative now, are we?

Compared to the goblin's description, the fox's was tiny. It was clear the System either didn't know or didn't care about them—probably the latter.

Regardless, even this bit taught Jack many things.

His communication with the System was still on. It was aware of the local wildlife. And, most importantly, foxes were level 1—or somewhere around there. This was interesting, because understanding the level classification was crucial to Jack's survival.

The goblin was level 2 and could threaten an adult human. The fox was level 1 and could possibly threaten an adult, but not quite as much as the goblin. Then, were adult humans between levels 2 and 4, with the average at 3?

Sounded elegant. Of course, for every problem, there was a solution that was simple, easy, and wrong.

Jack himself had been level 1 when he beat the goblin, but that couldn't be accurate. He'd been stronger than it—not by much, but stronger nonetheless. It didn't make sense for the goblin to be higher-leveled than him.

Am I on a different scale than everything else? Is it because I can level up while they can't? Or, maybe, everything can.

He shook his head. The more he considered the issue, the more questions came up—which was good, because that's how knowledge was supposed to work. If he could see through the System at a glance, it probably wouldn't be a good System.

Thankfully, he didn't need to know much right now.

After my power-ups, I can fight level 3 creatures and should probably run away from level 4s. I need more samples to understand the power curve, though.

Insects and a squirrel didn't trigger the System's response, giving at least a good estimation about the lower bounds of level 1. Armed with that knowledge, Jack set out to explore.

Well, explore was a generous term. He had to find water, shelter, and food. He already had the second. As for water, the reserve had plenty of creeks to choose from. It wouldn't be too difficult.

First on his agenda was seeking a path to escaping the nature reserve—or, at least, confirm that dungeons were as inescapable as they sounded. If he stayed here for a month and someone came and said, "oh, why didn't you just walk away," Jack would feel like an idiot.

Angling himself south, the closest edge of the nature reserve that probably overlapped with the dungeon, Jack set out. In the process, he kept his eyes open, not only for goblins but also for everything else. The wildlife was abundant in the reserve, letting him make several observations.

First, plants didn't register with the System. The weakest animal he found at level 1 was a big crow, and the strongest a boar he spotted from afar at level 4. He was getting a hang for what levels meant, though it wasn't easy to set in stone.

Thankfully, his forest experience came in handy. It allowed him to cross the terrain stealthily, not raising the ire of any creatures. He knew when and where to hide, which animals were aggressive, and which weren't. There weren't any natural predators in the reserve, at least not for humans, so it was smooth sailing.

Being a biologist had its perks. Jack focused on insects, of course, the testbed of evolution, but he knew a bit about everything.

Excluding goblins.

Luckily, he could get to know them quickly enough, as three were approaching. He could hear them through the bushes.

Chapter 4
Big, Aggressive Prison Mates

Jack held his breath and kept himself low, hiding in a bush. The grating voices were approaching—three of them—and he could tell from their wicked cackles they were up to no good.

"Kekeke, me bite."

"Me bite too!"

"The leg is mine!"

"No, mine!"

The goblins weren't just ugly and in bad taste, they were also exceedingly stupid and stealthy like elephants. They were crossing the forest as if they owned it—which they might, for all Jack knew—speaking freely and paying little to no attention to their surroundings. Said attention was reserved for the bloodied fox carcass they carried, from which they occasionally pinched pieces of meat to devour, fur and all.

Their sharp claws tearing through the flesh and sharp teeth chomping with gluttony, his distaste for these goblins only grew. They were repulsive beings, an affront to any possible concept of beauty. His stomach turned, but he held it in until they disappeared, completely oblivious to his presence.

Poor fox... he thought, shaking his head. Nature had its ways, but nobody deserved to die to such distasteful creatures. The fact he'd almost suffered the same fate didn't escape his notice.

The goblins had been levels 2, 2, and 3 respectively. He could probably take each of them individually, just not all at once. Though Jack was coming to understand his plan moving forward—or rather, the rules of the game.

The goblins were weak, stupid, and hateful. They were the perfect grinding stone for a lone human trapped in the dungeon. He could hunt them down for levels relatively easily and without many moral setbacks.

Jack didn't for a moment believe this was a coincidence. Everybody had an agenda, which probably included alien systems or whatever this was—and that's without even mentioning how blatantly engineered these goblins were. They were the perfect mobs.

That left Jack with a question. The dungeon description mentioned three groups of monsters and a Dungeon Boss. If goblins were one group, what about the rest? And what about the Dungeon Boss?

If I really have to fight this dungeon, I should scout the other groups before making a move on the goblins. Information is power.

Right now, the goblins didn't appear to be on to him— how could they? Moreover, going by game patterns, the other two groups would be of similar strength. He should research before committing to something.

Again, information equaled power.

Jack's cave was in the southern part of the Greenway Reserve, slightly to the west. Since the goblins were heading south with their prey, that was probably their headquarters. Therefore, Jack changed his previous plan and headed west instead of south. Reaching the edge of the reserve that way would take a little more time, but it was better than running through a bunch of green-skinned man-eaters.

No other goblins appeared as he made his way through thin trees and wide bushes. The only notable thing was the impossibly wide, impressively futuristic, shimmering blue wall that rose from the ground where the reserve ended, stretching to the sky and fading after some point. It extended as far to the right and left as Jack could see at an almost imperceptible curve, presumably enclosing the entire reserve.

"Fuck me..." The blue thing was opaque too, so he couldn't see outside. "I really am trapped... unless I can go through."

He grabbed a stone and tossed it at the blue wall. It bounced off. He threw another stone, harder, and it was catapulted backward with such force, Jack barely managed to pull his head out of the way. The stone zoomed past and buried itself in an unlucky bush.

"No escape, got it."

His gaze traveled up again, to where the blue wall faded away and only air remained. It must have been at least sixty feet high.

Can planes go through, then? he wondered. *Can birds? Can Superman?*

He did his best to throw another stone that high up. He succeeded on the third try, then watched the stone bounce against a patch of blue that solidified out of thin air. It fell back down with a small thud, and when Jack grabbed it, the stone was hot to the touch.

"Only looking, no touching... No way out, then."

He considered touching the wall, but the System had already informed him he was stuck here until he got the Dungeon Boss. Calling its bluff sounded like a terrible idea.

I'm trapped. Suddenly, his chest tightened, and panic welled up inside him. He forced it down. *Deep breaths,* he repeated several times to himself. *I'm trapped. I have to fight and level up until I can beat the boss, no matter what it is. Either that or die trying. So, fight now, existential crisis later.*

Jack steeled his resolve and forced himself to focus on the here and now. What were his next steps?

Right. Scout out the other monster groups. Maybe they'll be easier than the goblins.

With the goblin headquarters likely in the south, the other monster groups would be to the north and... east? Unless they were all jumbled up, of course, but Jack doubted that. It didn't mesh with the game mechanics he was familiar with.

I'll be on guard, in any case.

Therefore, Jack turned his back to the wall of his new prison and moved deeper inside the reserve, where he'd come from. He could have followed the wall, of course, but its sight upset him greatly. He wanted nothing to do with it.

After the blue wall disappeared in the tree branches, he turned north, keeping his eyes and ears open for any change. Crossing the entire reserve would take hours on foot, and there were monsters out there trying to kill him. He would be damned if he let them.

While traveling, he wondered how he'd adapted so quickly, how he'd accepted magic, goblins, and reality becoming a game. Had the System messed with his mind?

He didn't think so, though it'd already proved to clearly possess the power. Something inside him just latched on to the change, a part of him desperately hoping for his smothering reality to crumble. Maybe due to how trapped he'd felt in his life; or, maybe, because of how many times he'd fantasized about similar scenarios as a teenager. The world had just gone to shit, everything he knew was thrown out the window, and though there possibly were dull, realistic explanations refuting magic, deep in his heart, Jack wished this was all real.

He didn't fear the danger. He simply felt alive. Like this was how things were supposed to be.

He didn't have much to lose, anyway. His friends could probably handle themselves, and he had little family. He was only worried about the professor, but... she would manage. She was smart. If anybody could find a way to survive in a new world, it would be her, even despite her old age.

As for himself, there was nothing holding him back. If everything returned to normal, he only had a dull life to look forward to. He would get his PhD, work his ass off as a researcher for thirty-five, forty years, then retire. At least he liked biology, but it didn't fill him. It wasn't enough.

This was. Stalking goblins through a forest.

Life is so weird... He shook his head, refocusing. He wasn't safe here. He couldn't afford daydreams.

It was only a moment later that a faint growling reached his ears. Jack froze. Nothing in this forest was supposed to growl. His mind went through all possible animals before settling on one.

Slowly, as quietly as he could, he got on the ground and crawled inside a bush. It scratched him, but he couldn't care less. Inwardly, he prayed the creature would move away. He'd made a mistake. The other monster groups weren't as weak as the goblins. The System had cheated.

An animal made its way into his field of vision. He could barely make it out through the branches—a brown behemoth, putting tremendous weight on the ground with each step. He also caught sight of yellow flashes on its fur, but he was too far away to discern them. Not that it mattered—a bear didn't need magical enhancements to maul him.

> **Earth Bear, Level 15**
> *Bears are omnivorous creatures that stand at the apex of most food chains. Earth Bears, in particular, are a stronger, highly territorial variant. They can use very limited earth magic, and the rocky parts of their fur can be used to craft F-Grade weapons and armor. Earth Bears are most commonly found in the Ursus Forests of planet Ursi.*

It wasn't heading directly toward Jack at least, but the mere sight of a bear froze him solid. He couldn't even shiver or breathe.

If it sees me, I'm dead.

That would be the end of it. There was almost no way to escape a bear in the forest. The wise song came to mind:

If it's brown, lie down. If it's black, fight back. If it's white, goodnight.

Well, this one is brown, but also magical. I guess if it's magic, fucking fantastic.

Jack's thoughts screeched to a halt when the bear stopped and raised its snout to sniff the air. He panicked.

I'm sweaty; can it smell me? Did the bush scratch me? Can it smell my blood? It probably can. Oh, God, I'm so dead.

He considered bolting, but again, he couldn't escape a bear in the forest. They could even climb trees—at least, the non-magical variant could, and he wasn't willing to test this unless he had to.

His mind worked at great speed developing plan after plan to somehow survive. His entire body trembled with tension.

Eventually, the bear lowered its head and kept going. Jack couldn't believe his luck. When it disappeared and the sounds of its growling faded, Jack was left panting and terrified.

I'm trapped in a forest with bears.

This brought everything under a new perspective. Not only was there great danger, the bear wasn't even the Dungeon Boss. The level range of this dungeon had just risen precipitously. There had to be level 20 creatures at the very least, and that's assuming this particular bear was the leader of its group, which didn't seem too likely.

Plus, there was still a third monster group, which could be even stronger than the bears. That seemed unlikely, but so what? For all Jack knew, the System could have spawned kung-fu tigers in the northeastern part of the reserve. Even risking a glance at the third group felt idiotic.

Sweat pooled out of him until he drenched the soil. Escaping this dungeon now seemed impossible, and even surviving until someone rescued him was unlikely. His arrogance was stomped to the ground and shit on.

I have to survive.

Jack headed back. In this game-like environment, there was a clear path forward. He no longer cared about how premeditated these goblins were, or what the System's agenda was for guiding his actions.

There was only one way to survive, and it was called "kill a shit-ton of goblins."

Chapter 5
Beating the Shit out of Stuff

Jack Rust sat on a branch, waiting. Strips of fabric were wrapped around his fists and knuckles, courtesy of his now-ruined shirt, so they wouldn't break or bleed.

He'd considered making a weapon, but the Fistfighting skill's enhancements were too good to pass up. A spear was only nice until you tripped and impaled yourself. Plus, his fists were more than enough for the task.

Below, his victims approached, unaware of the human predator eyeing them.

They were green, ugly, and wickedly stupid. The three goblins were arguing over a piece of wood—a club, probably, though it looked like a fallen branch.

They had no idea what was coming.

As they passed nine feet below Jack's perch, he took a deep breath and fell on them.

The sight of the earth bear and the ramifications it implied sharpened Jack's resolve. He was on fire now, in a race against time. He couldn't afford to hesitate.

The nine-foot fall was long, but Jack broke it on the back of an unsuspecting goblin. His fists were clenched, and his Fistfighting skill helped him make the landing, though he had to roll once—that wasn't the skill, he could always do it.

Jack and the goblin collided with a heavy thud, and the poor greenskin was driven into the ground hard enough to break its neck. Jack rolled, stood, and grinned.

One down, two to go.

The other two goblins were surprisingly quick on the uptake. Before their comrade had even stopped moving, they were already screaming and pouncing at Jack, claws extended.

> **Goblin, Level 2**
> **Goblin, Level 3**

He grimaced. The goblin he'd just killed had also been level 3. Unfortunately, he didn't have time to observe them fight beforehand. He assumed the level 3 goblin would be faster than its brethren, which was true, but he completely underestimated the world of difference.

The fucker was *fast*.

The attack was almost instant, claws blitzing to tear him apart. Jack defended by punching back. His reach was significantly longer, given that the goblins were child-sized, so he should win this exchange.

Unfortunately, the goblin was slippery. His Fistfighting skill only provided basic familiarity with the movements, and the goblin slipped under his punch to enter his guard. Jack panicked. His battle mode activated in full throttle. His veins were filled with steel, and his entire body felt on fire while his mind turned ice-cold. His eyes widened to take in everything. The world slowed down.

The goblin remained fast.

A set of claws raked his chest, while another went for his eyes, only narrowly missing. The chest attack hit dead-on, but no blood came out. With a grin, Jack's knee rose to meet the goblin's face and catapulted it backward.

This time, he was prepared to fight—and, though he couldn't use a weapon without sacrificing the skill's bonuses, he could wear armor. A layer of bark decorated the inside of his half-torn shirt, protecting against the goblins' short claws. They could have seen it if they weren't stupid.

The second goblin arrived as soon as the first went flying. It screeched, grabbing his leg before he could knock it away. Its claws pierced skin and drew blood, and it refused to let go when Jack pulled his leg back, intent on maiming him. It opened its jaws wide and lunged in for a bite.

That wasn't a very good idea.

Jack's fist bashed onto the goblin's head like a meteor, smashing its mouth shut. It stumbled, still weakly holding onto Jack's leg right under the thigh, but a brutal punch to the face threw it back, forcing it to let go. Thin bones bent under Jack's fist. The goblin didn't stand back up.

Thankfully, it had missed the major artery in his thigh.

He turned around with an elbow already striking out, trying to hit the other goblin before it surprised him, but it wasn't there. A hard strike to the back of Jack's head brought stars to his eyes. He fell forward, instinctively rolling to the side and avoiding a second attack.

Motherfucker...

The level 3 goblin, bleeding from where its long nose had been broken, was now wielding the branch-turned-club. It lunged at him again, shouting a grating "Kekekeke!"

Jack, still on the ground, blocked with his forearm and it cracked under the impact. He growled, seeing red. The world was swimming, he was in pain and deadly danger, yet his heart was filled with rage. He gave in to the beast, letting violence take over.

The goblin smashed its club down again, and Jack defended with the same arm, sensing it crack further. He lunged at the goblin before it could retract its heavy weapon and grabbed the top part of its face. Twisting around with the goblin in hand, he put a leg behind its knees and smashed its head into the ground. Hard.

The club left its hand as the goblin screamed, and Jack screamed back, right in its face. Sharp jaws bit his palm, ripping a piece of flesh—he didn't care. When the goblin tried to rise, he drove a left punch into its face. Its head bounced off the ground, but its level wasn't for show.

Despite the heavy hits, it was still kicking and clawing. Crimson lines appeared on Jack's arms, along with a thin one on his cheek, right below his eye. Jack remained relentless. If he stopped now, the goblin would stand back up.

He braced through the claws and kept pummeling. He roared like an animal. His fists rained on the goblin's face, each punch jolting its head to the left and right. The goblin's throes weakened—and then, with a tremendous burst of strength, it rolled under his feet and jumped upright beside him.

It tried to run away, but Jack couldn't let it. If even one goblin escaped, the entire tribe would learn about him, and he would die.

Even as it tried to run, Jack grabbed its ankle and pulled it back—the beast was light. With a massive roar, he raised the entire goblin over his head like a club and smashed it head-first against the ground.

The head exploded, painting the dirt red and decorating it with brain matter.

Jack plopped to the ground, staring at the dead goblin with horror. As the battle fever died down, he realized what he'd done. It was necessary but so madly brutal...

I did this.

He puked. *I did this*, he kept thinking, spiraling into guilt and disbelief. *I did this...*

It wasn't about killing the goblin. It wasn't even about the brutal way of doing so. These were all necessary, and Jack had already come to terms with it before attacking.

No, what terrified him was the mad rush of satisfaction he felt while doing it. Fighting these goblins, he was *alive*. When he let go of everything, the increased brain activity and awareness, as well as the feeling of omnipotence his body gave, were almost ecstatic. When he smashed the goblin like an octopus, he wanted to roar in triumph.

These were the same feelings he'd experienced against that first goblin in the cave. Only, back then, they'd been overshadowed by the fact he'd killed something and all the new information he received. Now, these feelings were laid bare, and he had to face them.

At least his injuries weren't too deep, and his enhanced body was quick to stop bleeding.

Jack stayed there for a while, struggling to get his thoughts in order. An increasing panic and a desire to run away threatened to spill over, but he forced himself to calm down. Eventually, he succeeded, at least to the extent where he could think and operate as normal.

He stumbled away and back to his cave, then sat near the entrance. He took a few deep breaths.

Transitioning from a researcher to a forest killer wasn't easy.

Jack was in control though. The emotions were too many to comb through quickly, but he wasn't overwhelmed after the initial onslaught. The same drive that pushed him to survive no matter what, now helped him put himself in order.

He'd known this was coming. He could handle it. He just needed a bit of time.

The minutes ticked by for Jack, turning into hours. In his mental self-healing state, time had lost its meaning as recovery took priority. His entire being was focused on digesting the brutal reality that the modern world didn't let people experience.

Now, Jack was speed-running it. The experience was harrowing but necessary—and, thankfully, he could handle it.

No, not just handle it. He would *thrive* in it. He could feel it in his bones. This was where he belonged. This was him.

Transitioning wasn't easy, but he would get there.

Jack kept comforting himself until the sun hung low in the sky. He was better, and all at once, terribly thirsty. The back of his head hurt like hell, and his stomach was empty enough to burn.

Shit! I forgot to find water!

He had shelter—his cave—but water was the single most important resource. Without food, he could survive for weeks. Without water, not even a couple days. It just hadn't crossed his mind before.

There was a creek nearby. The water wasn't too potable, but it would do—stomach and intestine problems were better than dehydration. He would even drink his own piss if he had to.

The only thing he wouldn't drink—besides saltwater, the only fluid that doesn't help dehydration—was the ice pond. He suspected it was something more than simple water—something magical—and that its freezing cold would persist inside his stomach, destroying him from the inside out.

At least, he wouldn't take the risk unless he had no choice.

He could always capture a small animal and experiment, but... Jack had his bottom lines. Killing man-eating goblins was fine. Torturing innocent animals was not. At least while he could help it.

He stood up to head to the creek, but before that...

> **Level Up! You have reached Level 3.**

Another cold announcement, product of an unfeeling System that pitted living creatures against each other. Jack shook his head, then opened his status screen and put both free points into Physical, raising it to 9. He intended to invest in Mental as well—it should help with everything, including his unstable mental state—but not yet. Not when he almost died every time he battled.

The familiar surge of power passed over his body. He was stronger, faster, healthier. By now, he was already at the level of a professional athlete, if not past that, and all it took was four goblins...

His status screen reminded him of how many things he didn't know yet. What were factions? Grades? He'd seen F before in the dungeon description, and the ice pond was an E-Grade resource, but what exactly did that mean?

More importantly, his species was referred to as *Human, Earth-387*. This clearly implied the existence of multiple Earths, possibly multiple intelligent species.

Was the System really alien? Did it refer to a galactic empire or an inter-dimensional one, where many variations of Earth existed? Maybe that Animal Kingdom? Then again, if intelligent species existed on other planets, why wouldn't they name their planet Earth? It literally meant dirt. It could be the most common planet name in the galaxy.

But yes. Water. Then, Jack would revisit the ice pond to try and get extra bonuses—after his level up, he might be able to take an extra step—and then, goblin-hunting.

By the end of it, he would be a superhuman killing machine. The thought should have been terrifying.

Why did he feel excitement instead?

Chapter 6
The High Goblins

The goblin tribe was a bundle of misshapen wooden huts, ugly green forms, and burnt animal carcasses. Just placing it in a forest was an affront to nature.

Jack squinted from the bush he hid in. After reaching level 3, healing himself, and satiating his thirst, he'd decided to gather more information before launching his anti-goblin campaign. There was some time before nightfall, anyway.

He'd located a goblin squad—it wasn't difficult—and followed it to the tribe. After cresting a hill, the ugly visage greeted his sight, and there were many things to notice.

First, there were many dozens of goblins. These guys had a full-on village going.

Second, there weren't just goblins. Jack spotted a few off-green forms, paler and larger than their goblin brethren. These were the size of short humans, had dark hair—goblins were bald—and walked with a sharpness that belied intelligence.

> **Hobgoblin, Level 6**
> *Stronger, meaner, and smarter than normal goblins, hobgoblins are an evolved version of the same ugly monster. It is advised to kill them on sight, but they should not be underestimated.*

The System's description was short as always, filled with details Jack could already discern. The only real information was their level. After scanning all hobgoblins within sight, Jack determined them to be level 6 or 7. Normal goblins ranged from level 1 to 5.

In Jack's most recent estimation, he could fight a level 4 goblin head-on, maybe even a level 5 if he was lucky. Hobgoblins should be outside his reach, so he was glad they weren't participating in the hunter squads.

In short, Jack was incredibly weaker than the goblin tribe.

Moreover, the largest problem wasn't the hobgoblins, but their leader.

> **Goblin Shaman, Level 9**
> *Goblins aren't always stupid. Some of them are born intelligent, and when that happens, they often develop shamanic powers. Goblin Shamans can lead small tribes of goblins and hobgoblins, though they're usually seen as elite soldiers in larger tribes.*
> *This Goblin Shaman is the group boss.*

THE HIGH GOBLINS

The leader of the tribe wasn't a hobgoblin, but a goblin dressed in ruined robes. It cackled like the rest of them, but even the arrogant hobgoblins made way for it—the flames that danced on its fingers brewed respect.

Moreover, its eyes carried a cunning glint that was hard to miss.

Jack admitted that fire-slinging enemies challenged his current experience. Goblins were fine. Hobgoblins would also be fine, eventually. However, this shaman would prove to be a pain in the ass; he just knew it.

"Fire in the forest?" he whispered with a tsk. "So much for an omniscient, omnipotent, intergalactic System. Can I get a refund, please?"

No reply came his way. The System wasn't the most talkative of partners.

However, there was one thing that was even more impressive than the shaman. The goblins were high. Not tall—*high*.

A wide, short bush stood in the middle of the tribe, sporting long, thin leaves. Some goblins were gathered around it, chatting and cackling without making much sense, while occasionally snapping off a leaf to chew on. They weren't eating it, just licking it before dropping the remainder on a big pile.

The eyes of these goblins were completely red, they toppled over whenever they tried to stand, and wouldn't stop laughing. On closer inspection, many goblins were carrying a few of those leaves or munching on them, just measuredly. The ones falling all over themselves were probably on their day off.

> **High Speed Bush (F-Grade)**
> A resource guarded by the goblins of the Forest of the Strong. Commonly found in the wet jungles of planet Peruvian, the leaves of this bush can enhance a person's reflexes, dexterity, and agility. They can also make you high as a kite.
> The stat increase is a one-time bonus.

I just knew things couldn't be simple... Damn you, System. Can't you at least destroy my planet with decency? Did you need to drag weed-licking goblins into this?

The System, again, didn't reply, and Jack could only keep observing the goblin camp. There wasn't much else to see—he already had more than enough.

He slowly made his way back, keeping an eye out for guards—which were non-existent, as the goblins apparently felt safe. On the way, he processed all the new information, as he often did lately.

The goblins aren't just strong, they have intelligent leaders... Which means if I keep picking them off, they'll catch on. Therefore, I must get as many of them as possible before they're on to me. I can't afford to take it slow.

However, when they do catch on, will I be strong enough to face them? Probably, if it comes to guerilla tactics. If I can reach level 6 or so, I should be able to handle hobgoblins, especially if I set up an ambush... but they'll eventually get me.

This sounded like a pickle, but Jack recalled the dungeon description—any previous blue screen could be willed into reappearing, apparently.

> **Forest of the Strong (F-Grade):** A forest where only the strong survive. There are three monster groups, each holding a

THE HIGH GOBLINS

> unique resource and representing a unique challenge. Slay the leader of a group to despawn them.
>
> This dungeon is in conquer-or-die mode. Defeat the Dungeon Boss to exit or die trying. We applaud your bravery for entering and wish you the best of luck.

The last paragraph's sarcasm aside, there was one important clue hidden in there.

Slay the leader of a group to despawn them... So, if I kill the shaman, all the goblins will simply go poof. That's almost too good to be true.

On second thought, it wasn't. It was a double-edged knife. Monsters—in this case, goblins—were dangerous, but they were also walking bags of levels. An equilibrium was shaping in Jack's mind: the later he assassinated the shaman, the more danger he would face, but the more goblins he would be able to kill before they disappeared.

After all, there was no way the System would reward him for the creatures he despawned. It wasn't that kind.

Jack needed the levels. There were level 15 magical bears in the forest, along with their group leader and a third group of monsters which could, potentially, be even stronger than the bears. There was also the Dungeon Boss, an existence undoubtedly stronger than anything else.

If Jack wanted any chance against them, he needed levels, he needed wits, information, and battle experience—the only thing he had so far was pants. The goblins could provide most of those. He couldn't afford to take it easy. He had to gamble.

Jack would try to drag on the conflict as long as possible, and when things got insufferable, he would assassinate the goblin shaman. Certainly risky, perhaps too risky, but it was the only long-term plan he could come up with.

He could also just hide and hope for someone to save him, but he somehow doubted the System would let him escape that easily.

Therefore, Jack made his decision. He would wage war on the goblins—possibly a genocide, too. Was he evil for thinking that way? Maybe. Was he justified? Probably, since they clearly wanted to eat him too. Was it necessary? Absolutely fucking yes.

Jack Rust refused to die.

But, before waging his war, he needed to find food.

Jack held the rabbit carcass tenderly. It pained him to kill an animal like this, but he had to eat something…

At least he'd killed it painlessly. He'd found a den under a tree soon after night fell, then dug behind it to scare the occupants. As soon as the rabbits rushed outside, he grabbed one, and before it could understand what was happening, snapped its neck. It was easy, like snapping a twig, and Jack grew forlorn at his new power and the way he used it.

When he killed the goblins in heated battle, he felt triumphant. This time, he was empty… Still, hunting was a part of nature, and it was more ancient than compassion.

Jack shook his head to clear it. This new reality was grim, but he had to accept it.

He was currently standing over the ice pond, holding the carcass. He was going to light a fire and roast it, but he thought that maybe the lake's body forging properties could be transmitted through food. It was a theory he needed to test, as he couldn't afford to let anything go to waste.

Besides, the freezing cold might have a purging effect on harmful microorganisms. It was magical, after all, so why not? The cold didn't stick to his body when he left the lake, so it probably wouldn't stick to the rabbit's, either. If it did, he'd just have to go hungry.

He gently dipped the rabbit into the water, feeling the numbness on his fingers. Nothing happened, except for its fur turning slightly whiter, and that was it. When he withdrew it, the rabbit was cold to the touch, but no other difference could be seen.

He let it sit for a while and confirmed that the cold was seeping out. That was good, because it meant he wouldn't freeze to death, and bad, because it meant his body wouldn't be forged. He shrugged.

Well, good to know.

He went outside, a ways off the cave entrance, and lit a fire under the moon—he'd prepared tinder beforehand. He wasn't particularly familiar with cooking rabbits on campfires, but he had cooked a lot in his life, so he had some ideas. If he messed up, his 9 Physical would hopefully pull him through.

In the night, the fire's smoke couldn't be seen, so he only worried about the firelight itself attracting unwanted visitors. The goblins were already gathered at their tribe when night fell, and bears weren't nocturnal—and, even if they were because of magic, they had no reason to be in this area.

That left the final monster group, but Jack didn't believe they would turn out to be nocturnal wanderers. Nocturnal, maybe, but not wanderers—and, if they were, he'd just face them. He had to cook at some point. Doing it now was certainly better than doing it mid-day when the goblins could easily spot his smoke and come knocking.

Jack cooked for a while, enjoying the night sky in silence. It was beautiful. Maybe the System had magically removed all air pollution and shut down the lights, but Jack could see the sky as his ancestors did. Stars shone everywhere, ten thousand sparkling dots, and a long river of light stretched between them—the galaxy—farther and larger than the mind could comprehend.

It wasn't just beautiful, Jack corrected himself. It was breathtaking. He was sitting under the infinite cosmos.

Is this what the ancients saw every night... he wondered, and its beauty was so striking that, for a moment, Jack wondered whether the System's arrival was a good thing.

He idly realized that, against such a night sky, his smoke was visible, as it hid the starlight behind it. He shrugged. If the goblins made the connection and came over, let them.

Time passed with only the crackling of fire and the sizzling of juices on the burning logs keeping him company. The forest was quiet, most nocturnal animals still shivering in fear from the arrival of the monsters, and only some birds dared squawk, undoubtedly in confusion from everything that was happening.

The smell of cooking meat flooded Jack's nostrils like a delicacy from another dream.

He may as well be the last person in the entire world, and for a moment, he was crushed by heavy loneliness and despair. He felt primal. In his element. Also alone, scared, and in pain.

Was he having fun?

Jack gazed at the stars, the same ones he always saw and a million more, and found no answer. Of course he didn't. He was alone.

He closed his eyes and endured the heavy emotions that darkness bred. It wasn't his first tough night, not even close, and it certainly wouldn't be the last—unless he died.

That was a sobering thought, and he chuckled as he pulled the skewer of rabbit meat off the flames. *The last man in the world... Take that, Maria. Heh.*

He then bit on the rabbit, savoring the taste. It was disgusting. And, at the same time, it was the most heavenly meal he'd ever had.

Chapter 7
Challenging the Ice Pond

The Integration happened on the 19th of September, 2024. A day later, on the 20th, the world was nowhere near adapting. Millions had died and the rest were busy organizing into small communities that could protect their members. The bravest had already defeated a monster or two.

On the morning of that day, Jack Rust waged war on a goblin tribe.

The goblins didn't know it, of course. He didn't walk in with a war declaration and his head on a silver plate. All they saw was an increased number of hunters failing to return.

Jack stalked them from the high branches, hid in bushes, sprang from under the dirt. His fists dealt swift death, and where he passed, only broken goblin corpses remained.

Each kill made him stronger, his fists harder, and his battle experience greater. His Fistfighting skill let him fight above his level, and Jack gradually began to internalize the knowledge. When the margin between success and failure was razor-thin, he understood why his skill made him move in exactly the way it did.

He knew what did and didn't work, to an extent, but he gradually understood why. At the same time, his increased Physical attribute gave him better awareness and control over his body.

His fighting skill kept rising. Unbeknownst to Jack, this constant life-or-death pressure was the perfect grinding stone.

A goblin squad passed by a bush, yapping about something. The bush exploded, and a human jumped out, wearing a pair of tattered shorts and nothing else. His shirt had long been torn apart or cut into bandage-like strips, and after a point, he didn't need shoes.

In their eyes, *he* was the monster. Caked blood and filth covered his skin, he smelled, but his eyes were the hardest, sharpest things they'd ever seen.

The three goblins screamed. Before they could react, a fist smashed into one's head and burst it apart. Another fist buried itself in a goblin sternum, breaking bones and sending its entire body flying backward. The last goblin recovered in time and made a mad dash for safety. Before it could take two steps or shout for help, a hand firmly grasped its throat.

Jack squeezed and the neck snapped. He let go, and the goblin's body collapsed to the forest floor. He stared at his hands.

I am a killer...

For the past two days, he'd been hunting and annihilating the goblins. They couldn't offer resistance anymore, only stand there and die. The only thing restraining his carnage was the time needed to locate new goblin squads—there weren't too many left.

Am I a monster? he wondered idly. Or am I justified?

The gruesome sight didn't bother him anymore. He'd gotten used to corpses, to death, to blood and brutal violence. He'd gotten used to the way his soul fluctuated when he went in for the kill, sparking crimson, to the feeling of breaking bones with his bare hands.

He'd come to peace with his path. This was reality. In this dungeon, it was him or the monsters—the goblins, in this case—and they would gladly devour any humans they found, they would wreck nature and rampage on innocent people.

He would kill them first. Between himself and monsters, he chose himself, even if it meant becoming a cold-blooded killer—which, in all honesty, wasn't the worst of things. When the initial social conditioning wore off, he managed to acclimate. It wasn't easy or pleasant—but not too terrible either.

Jack looked aside, where the notification waited.

> **Level Up! You have reached Level 5.**

The leveling difficulty didn't scale too much. It took him one goblin to reach level 2, three for level 3, nine for level 4, and another nine for level 5. Of course, these last ones were higher-leveled—either the goblins had gotten scared, or they were leveling up as well.

He'd tried to keep his numbers low to delay the inevitable. So far, he was okay—the squads were still made up of three goblins each, and he hadn't seen a hobgoblin outside the tribe. That was bound to change, eventually, but by then, Jack planned to be strong enough.

Another factor that kept his number of kills low were injuries. He was steamrolling them now, but at the start, every fight hung at the edge of a knife. Each ambush was a hard-fought battle that left him with heavy injuries. One time, he even almost died.

Forced to crawl back to his cave after each battle, enter the ice pond and endure the torturous cold that assaulted his injuries. As he grew stronger, he had to go deeper for the healing powers to take effect, and the cold only grew worse, but at least, so did his stat bonuses. The lake had given him another three points in Physical, the equivalent of a level and a half.

Jack's life had become a cycle of looking for goblins, killing them, healing at the lake, and repeating. It was a fine life.

He assigned the free points from his most recent level up to Physical, then took a look at his current status.

Name: Jack Rust
Species: Human, Earth-387
Faction: -
Grade: F
Level: 5
Physical: 16
Mental: 7
Will: 6
Skills: Fistfighting (I)

By now, his physical prowess was approaching superhuman levels. He possessed three times the strength of a normal pre-System human—or maybe more—along with a vastly sturdier body, lightning-fast reflexes, crystal-clear kinetic vision, and agility that would put cats to shame—not that he had any to check.

CHALLENGING THE ICE POND

He was possibly exaggerating, but the ease with which he dispatched the goblins confirmed his hypotheses. He was like a martial arts champion.

The gradual enhancements of level-ups intrigued him. Just how high could they go? Would he eventually become strong enough to break mountains or run faster than cars? Was there an upper limit?

The F-Grade part of his status screen, along with the E-Grade ice pond, implied the existence of D, C, B, and A Grades, but even the earth bear had only been level 15, and it was in an F-Grade dungeon. The Dungeon Boss, which could be level 25, was also F-Grade, unless Jack had misunderstood something.

Just how far away were those other grades? What was the limit? Was there one?

A sense of progression infiltrated Jack's psyche and took over. Constantly improving yourself by such tremendous amounts was addictive—and familiar, too. He'd been addicted to video games once, and this felt similar, though a hundred times better.

He clenched his fists. He wanted to grow stronger, as strong as he could. Then, he could finally take control of his life and be free.

Power was the foundation of everything.

And, luckily, Jack had more than one way to get it.

The sun was setting, so he walked back to his cave. He had explored the surrounding territory well by now and knew exactly where he was.

The crack in the rocks was still there, untouched, as was the cramped passage that led deeper in. Jack took the familiar steps, weaved around the rocks and into the small cavern he'd come to call home.

He was welcomed by the ice pond's familiar glow, a soft white light that now accompanied his sleep. The cold was condensed, thankfully, so he could rest comfortably on the other side, where he'd taken to sleeping on a patch of flat rock.

However, Jack didn't plan on being comfortable tonight. He'd met his goblin quota early. Now, he planned to once again challenge the pond.

He'd already done that a few times, and understood how things worked.

From the shore to the small waterfall at the back, the pond was only fifteen feet across. Fifteen short steps. For every step he took, the cold would augment his body by a single point of Physical.

One point wasn't much for the current Jack, but, if his calculations were correct, the pond had the potential of fifteen points, which was massive. Moreover, he suspected the waterfall hid something more.

Unfortunately, the pond wasn't a free lunch. Each step was harder than the last, and even now, Jack had only managed to take four steps. Today, he would go farther. He was determined to test his limits.

He took off his clothes and stepped in the lake with resolve. The cold assaulted him, traveling up his legs and around his body, but he was familiar with the feeling now, and his body was stronger than it used to be. This cold couldn't faze him.

He stepped forth. The temperature dropped further, sending long, sharp pins through his calves, but he persevered. Another step. The freezing current licked his legs. He shivered and clenched his teeth—he still had a ways to go. If he let the third step stop him, how could he defeat the Dungeon Boss?

The fourth step. The water level reached his knees, and his legs felt encased in ice. It was clearly water, but it was hard, requiring effort to move. By now, the cold was

CHALLENGING THE ICE POND

downright painful, and this was his current record. Jack was resolved to keep going. He had to take at least the fifth step.

That was easier said than done. His body was stronger than the last time he'd been here, but the crippling fear still ate at him at the thought of the next step. He took a few moments to get used to the cold before proceeding. He had to be careful.

Finally, he was ready—as ready as could be. He took a step.

He instantly lost feeling in his legs. They were completely numb, and the cold that reached his chest was so painfully piercing, it felt like someone was knitting with his bones. For a moment, he was paralyzed from the waist down. Jack was in terrible pain. His skin was turning blue.

> **Ice Pond bonus: +1 Physical**

The bonus came as the cold finished permeating him. It was a slight respite, but nowhere near enough. Jack's body screamed at him to turn back, but through the cold and crippling pain, his eyes were fierce. He only stared at the waterfall, so close yet so prohibitively far.

It mocked him. The waterfall was *mocking* him. A fire burned in Jack's heart, fighting against the ice, and his mind was taken over by an unbreakable resolve. Moving farther would be dangerous, something bad could happen to his body or he could really lose control of his legs and collapse in the pond forever, but in that moment, he refused to retreat. He would make it. Never again back.

He took a step.

He was in a frozen hell. His entire body was encased in ice now, not just his legs. He lost feeling everywhere. His pale skin was truly blue now. His legs spasmed, and it took

all his concentration to stay standing despite not feeling them.

His head hurt so bad it was about to break, and his heart struggled to keep beating, almost stopping. Jack's pain tolerance was swiftly expiring, and he released a muffled roar as he was unable to open his mouth, eyes bulging out as if someone were squeezing him to death.

Jack's entire body screamed to return to shore. This time, he didn't dare say no. If he stayed here any longer, he would die. He'd gone too far.

Except his legs weren't moving. They were as solid as rocks. Trying to move them was as plausible as trying to fly.

Jack panicked.

Is this how I die?

Suddenly, a blue exclamation mark flashed in the lower part of his vision, and the cold got a tiny bit easier to withstand. Jack's eyes bulged again with effort. His entire mental capacity was squeezed into making *his fucking legs move*. They shivered.

Jack fell backward. His back splashed into the water that swiftly moved to embrace him. Despite its freezing cold, it was also warm compared to the freezing hell he'd just endured.

He still couldn't move. He lay completely still under the water, gazing at the clean surface just above his eyes.

Am I going to drown? he wondered. Fear, panic, bitterness, spite—it all threatened to overwhelm him. His body caught on fire. With a tremendous pull of will, Jack used his hands to turn around, then crawled forward through the water. Every moment was torturous. The end was near, both literally and metaphorically.

He'd only taken six steps into the pond. As he fell back, his head was very close to the edge. He just had to crawl a tiny bit before his breath ran out. His lungs burned. So did his arms. He kept pushing.

With a final tug of will, his head broke the surface of the water and rested on the cold rock, which felt heavenly. He could breathe—and, as he'd pulled himself away from the center of the pond, the cold was receding. He managed to crawl out completely and lay on the stone, shivering, panting, and thanking every god he knew for making it out alive.

FUCK! he would have screamed, if not for his incessantly clattering teeth.

> **Ice Pond bonus: +1 Physical**
> **Feat of Will performed: +1 Will**

He wished he could chuckle.

He'd almost fucked up real bad... but at least he'd made it. He'd gotten the extra stat point, another one, too, and even proved to himself what he was capable of. He could push himself to the very limit. He could make it out of this fucking dungeon.

He was Jack Rust. And no matter what the world threw at him, he would survive.

He would thrive.

Chapter 8
The Last Monster Group

The goblin tribe originally had seventy-two members, including the one that spawned in Jack's cave. Five were hobgoblins, and one was their leader, the goblin shaman. On the first night, seven hunters failed to return—three had been killed by Jack. On the second day, the goblin squads went out as usual, but a whopping thirteen goblins never returned.

On the third day, nine more went missing—the goblins had learned to avoid the other monsters. They couldn't have lost nine goblins naturally. Something was hunting them.

Of the seventy-two goblins, only forty-two remained, and that alarmed their leader greatly. He didn't know what they were facing, but something was after them—something that didn't dare attack the tribe, choosing to pick off hunter squads.

That night, the goblin tribe echoed with whispers of the Hunter.

When morning came, seven squads left the tribe. Each was led by a hobgoblin or a level 5 goblin, and each numbered five goblins instead of three. The leader would have liked to further condense his forces, but they still had to procure food for the entire tribe. This would have to be enough.

Crap... Jack stayed in his bush and let them pass by. This squad had five members, one of which was an evolved version, a hobgoblin. *They're onto me.*

It was bound to happen. He'd already killed a total of twenty-two goblins, including the one in the cave, so if they hadn't caught on yet, they would be extremely stupid.

It's okay. All good things must come to an end.

Jack let this squad go, wagering he probably couldn't take them yet. However, since they were bound to reach this stage, he already had a plan.

The first order of business was to scout out the last monster group. Now at level 5 and with multiple bonuses from the pond, he was confident he could either beat, escape, or hide from most things. If the System gave him kung-fu tigers, well... that would just be playing dirty.

He had to take the risk at some point, and since the goblin squads had just gotten dangerous, now was a good time. Depending on what he met, he would just brave the risks to keep attacking goblins or switch to the new group.

Jack receded into the shadows. His destination was northeast, approximately where the final monster group would lie, according to his calculations.

He also hadn't met the Dungeon Boss yet, having no idea where it could be. His best assumption was the big rocky hill at the center of the reserve, because why not, so he took a roundabout route. His cave was in the southern part and just a bit to the west, so he circled around the center to the northeast. No other goblins crossed his path—there were too few squads now.

Jack was careful, the journey taking two hours.

As he approached the northeastern part of the Greenway Reserve, his suspicions proved correct. The forest was different here. Wilder. Silent.

The trees rose higher, reaching up to thirty feet at places, and their foliage was thicker. The System clearly messed with this part of the forest, as such vegetation had certainly not been here before. Moreover, despite the forest's silence, its floor was strewn with shit as if suffused with wildlife.

His previous thought about tigers crossed his mind. It had been a joke then, but now...

Could it be true?

Jack hesitated. If there really was a strong, fast enemy here, proceeding might be a mistake. He'd already spent two hours to reach this area—four, including the return trip. Was it such an ugly risk?

He decided to keep going. His pace slowed to a crawl, and his eyes constantly surveyed the overgrowth. As he snuck from hiding place to hiding place, the distant caws of birds made him jump. He bit his lip and steadied his heart—he shouldn't be nervous.

He continued for another hour. Gradually, he relaxed, not meeting any enemies. Only some random forest critters got in his way, but they all disappeared quickly enough. Jack's eyes never left the overgrowth, and that's why he saw it.

A small dark shape left the higher branches of a tree and flew his way. It was a projectile of sorts, but that's all Jack had time to see. He moved his head so fast his neck cracked and barely dodged it, rushing behind a tree.

At the same time, the forest around him came alive. Screams and bangs filled the air, and the creaking of branches was clearly audible. Jack counted many voices, and as soon as he recognized the animal they belonged to, he peeked from behind his tree in shock.

He barely had time to scan the creature before a dry, brown thing smacked him right in the nose.

> **Gymonkey, Level 7**
> *A primate variant from planet Green.*
> *Gymonkeys inhabit all forest biomes and move in packs, defending their territory with flying poop and great muscles. Their unique name comes from their habit of lifting heavy things to increase their strength.*
> *While not particularly aggressive, they are highly territorial.*

The poop smacked Jack's nose and fell to the ground with a plop. His brows shivered in irritation.

Did they really throw poop at me?

A pack of monkeys screamed at him from the branches—but these weren't any normal monkeys. They had short, off-brown fur, and were bulky, way bulkier than monkeys had any right to be. It was a miracle the branches even supported them.

Their saliva-filled jaws were intimidating, but nowhere near as much as their stunning pecs. These monkeys had thick biceps, low body fat, even six-packs! They could probably snap a human in two with one hand. It was like the System got a bunch of body builders and turned them into monkeys.

There were five altogether, and they were using their humongous muscles to hurl poop at Jack. One was already reloading, its face covered in an evil grin.

The analytical part of Jack's brain, the one dedicated to biology, wondered just how these monkeys managed to evolve like this. What kind of ecosystem could push them toward strength? Maybe predators that were fast but weak? Was it a mating thing? And did the conscious act of exercising hint at intelligence, or was it just completely ingrained into their DNA?

Every other part of his brain was just pissed they threw poop at him.

However, Jack's annoyance switched to fear when their levels registered. His surprise and disbelief evaporated. These were five level 7 creatures. He couldn't handle them.

At that moment, a deep roar came from farther inside the monkey territory, making Jack blanche. He knew about monkeys.

They have a gorilla!

He wasn't going to sit around and wait for the monkey-daddy to arrive. He entered flight mode, and his entire body erupted with power as he ran for his life. His bare feet thundered on dirt and roots even as a rain of poop whistled around him. A few even hit his back, some more recent—and wetter—than others.

Jack didn't know whether to curse or scream in fear.
THIS IS UNFAIR, SYSTEM!

He ran with all he had, and the monkeys chased him for a while, content to pelt him with their poop from a distance. They were strong, but luckily, they were also slow. Jack could outrun them.

Coming this deep had taken him an hour, but it took less than three minutes for him to fly out of their area, still zigzagging amidst flying poop. They didn't harm him, but they were annoying, and the force of the impact was enough to make him trip a couple of times.

Even when the poop stopped coming, Jack kept running for another minute before he dared look around. Then, he stopped. The monkeys watched him from the far-off trees, threat in their eyes and fresh poop in their hands. He wasn't welcome there.

Jack also glared at them. He'd been pooped! The dishonor! The humiliation!

"I will remember this, monkeys..." he said through gritted teeth. He couldn't defeat them now—but soon, he might, and then he'd get revenge. He'd make them eat their damn poop.

Ridiculous! Goblins and magic bears, and then poop-hurling monkeys? He fumed on his way back to familiar ground. *It took you this long to show your true face, System? Fuck you! You will not make a joke of my death!*

He spent the entire trip hurling insults—mental poop—at the System before he could calm down enough to think. He'd been so high-strung lately that seeing something even remotely funny had completely riled him up.

In the end, he was lucky. Maybe the monkeys were annoying, but they hadn't tried to harm him, only kicked him out. That was a good thing—and, at the same time, a bad one.

He couldn't afford good monsters. They had to be evil, like the goblins, to justify killing them and turning them into level material. Those gymonkeys—what an awful name—didn't want to harm him, just to be left alone. They were animals, not monsters.

Had the System lied? Weren't all monsters evil? Or had he only assumed that?

Jack didn't enjoy that train of thought.

Whatever, he concluded. *For now, I'll keep fighting the goblins—I can't handle the monkeys or bears, anyway. When the time comes, I'll revisit the issue.*

He used to hate how manipulative the System was for engineering the goblins and making them such easy to kill creatures. They were weak, ugly, clearly evil, and exceedingly hostile—the perfect humanoid enemies for someone unused to violence.

Now, he understood their utility. If the System wanted him—and all humans—to dive head-first into a world of violence, goblins were, indeed, a good solution. He was thankful for that. Because if he had to kill a more peaceful species while dealing with this change, he might have been in such harrowing confusion, that he'd end up dead.

He still hated the System with a passion, but he acknowledged it was good at its job.

What's the end goal, though... he wondered, walking *through shrubberies and undergrowth. Are they training us to fight a war? Are they broadcasting our struggles as a tv show? Is this simply a form of torture? Since the System can clearly enhance us, why demand we level up instead of simply augmenting us to the point of superheroes?*

These were difficult questions, and unfortunately, he didn't have the information to answer them.

Maybe the goblin shaman will know more. If possible, I will capture it, he resolved grimly. He hadn't captured a goblin yet or even exchanged words with them, fearing it would make him soft. He acclimated to this new world and its law of the jungle, but he didn't want to give himself the opportunity to regress.

The forest around him became familiar. He'd reached his area, his territory, and that meant he was ready. He had scouted out all monster groups and could determine a plan of action.

Kill the goblins. Kill the bears. Kill the monkeys. Dodge the Dungeon Boss for as long as possible.

It was simple and clean. The bears came before the monkeys because they were solitary, according to his earthen knowledge. Even if they were strong, he could ambush them and hopefully deliver a blow strong enough to swiftly take them out. He could start from the weakest bears and slay them one by one.

The monkeys wouldn't be as easy. When—if—he did attack them, he would need to be a one-man army.

"Oh!" he exclaimed, the pattern now obvious. *The goblins are many but weak. The bears are strong but few and solitary. And the monkeys are something in between.*

It was only a hypothesis, but it checked out—and, even if it wasn't done on purpose by the System, it still held.

Now, Jack was ready to continue his war against the goblins, and he would do so by killing his first hobgoblin.

He cracked his knuckles as he slid into the shadows. He was the hunter. And he was coming.

Chapter 9
Fighting a Hobgoblin

The goblins rested in a clearing.

There were five in total, including the hobgoblin, arrayed in a loose circle so that all angles were covered. The corpses of a boar family rested between them, while only one goblin appeared lightly injured.

The hobgoblin was clearly much more skilled in warfare than its lesser brethren. The scene Jack currently saw was a far cry from the distracted, disorganized, inefficient hunting squads he'd fought before.

That made things difficult. Half his success was based on goblin stupidity, and that weakness was now covered. It only enhanced his decision to start with the hobgoblin—which was level 6. He'd met another squad but ignored it as their hobgoblin was at level 7.

The hobgoblin had to fall first, or it might rally the other goblins into an organized attack, which would end badly for Jack. Moreover, there was no visible tell about its strengths and weaknesses. If it was fast, as goblins tended to be, he couldn't escape unless he killed it.

As he watched from a distant bush, while they rested before returning to the tribe, he focused on the hobgoblin. It was a male of average stature, with long dark hair done in a ponytail. Its body was slightly taut, and its seemingly empty eyes took in everything calmly. Jack had no doubt the hobgoblin was on guard. He only dared inspect it from the side.

Moreover, it carried a weapon. A shortsword. And that was really bad news because Jack had no idea how to deal with a shortsword. His basic Fistfighting skill didn't cover that.

At least it was unarmored.

I must kill it before it draws that weapon, he concluded.

The goblins were in a solid formation, so there was no way to lay an ambush. He did know which forest path led to their tribe, so he lay in wait on a branch they would have to pass under. The leaves hid him well, so even if the hobgoblin looked up, it was unlikely he would be spotted.

Time went by. Soon, far-off cries resounded—the goblins were ready to return. He couldn't see them, as any glance risked his stealth. He could only watch under his branch and wait for the hobgoblin.

Footsteps and hushed yapping drew closer. Jack's body was almost shivering from the tension, but he kept it in check. His eyes sharpened. His breath grew deeper. His fists were clenched and ready to draw blood.

As his tension reached its climax, a green form passed below him. He almost lashed out on instinct and barely held himself back. One goblin walked past, carrying a little boar in each arm, followed by another. The hobgoblin was third in line so it couldn't be easily attacked.

A smart plan. Unfortunately, it hadn't accounted for Jack's tree-climbing genius.

The moment Jack saw the hobgoblin, he rolled around the branch and fell on its head. At the same time, likely having heard a rustle of leaves, it looked up and only saw a fist.

Jack channeled his entire falling momentum and Fistfighting skill into this single punch. He turned his body and ignored the landing. His punch smashed right into the hobgoblin's raised face like a meteor from the sky, with enough force to almost break Jack's hand and completely break the hobgoblin's face.

The sound was sickening, and its neck released a crack, barely holding. Jack fell to the ground and rolled amidst the goblins, which were too slow to react. The hobgoblin, blinded by pain and shock, similarly didn't react in time.

He jumped up and nailed a punch into its sternum, then another into its falling throat. The hobgoblin was already stumbling, but it possessed admirable tenacity. Despite taking the hits head-on, it still stood.

Jack grimaced. The weakness of Fistfighting was that it couldn't easily deliver critical strikes—or, at least, he didn't know how.

The hobgoblin's hand was already grasping for its shortsword, so Jack had no choice. He pounced on it like an animal, pelting it with bone-cracking punches. It screamed.

The other goblins came to their senses. Seeing their strong leader helpless and injured, their first reaction was to shout, "THE HUNTER!" and run away. That saved Jack's life.

He kneeled on the hobgoblin's body and punched with every fiber of his being. Each hit was strong enough to reverberate through its bones, and his knuckles bled through the fabric strips—the goblin's body was hard. Level 6 wasn't a joke.

Deep in its pain, it reacted instinctively. It kicked out and punched at Jack, slamming him with the full power of an evolved goblin, and his eyes swam for a second. That was enough.

The hobgoblin drove a fist into his ribs and rolled with it, escaping under Jack's legs and turning to face him. Its face was a mask of blood. One hand grabbed its shortsword handle. The other reached for its eyes to wipe them.

Jack wasn't an idiot to let it.

Ignoring his burning ribs, he fell on the hobgoblin again with all the force of a desperate, cornered man, not letting it wield the shortsword properly.

He was in deep shit. This fucker had prodigious defense, and the other goblins would catch on eventually. If he couldn't finish this off quickly, he might be finished himself.

The shortsword handle dug into Jack's belly and he released all air, but had escaped the blade. The two rolled on the ground, each struggling to come out on top. Jack held its wrist firmly.

This close, he could tell the hobgoblin was struggling to stay conscious. It just needed a little push to go over the edge.

That push came in the form of its ponytail. Jack stepped on it with a knee and the hobgoblin's head jolted sideways, letting Jack have the upper hand. He positioned himself, then drove a devastating jab into the back of its neck while still holding the ponytail down.

The hobgoblin's neck finally snapped with a sickening crunch, and its lifeless body crumpled.

Jack didn't stay to watch. He turned to find the goblins, some of which were about to group up against him. When they saw him kill their leader, they froze, then scattered and ran for their lives.

> **Level Up! You have reached Level 6.**

Through the pain, Jack's eyes remained sharp. He'd known some would escape. His goal was to kill the hobgoblin and as many others as he could. So what if they ran? Any goblin he let go now would become another grunt to face in the future. Mercy at the enemy was cruelty at oneself.

Jack wouldn't make that mistake. He put both points in Physical in the blink of an eye.

He pounced, landing one punch at the back of a low-level goblin's head and killing it instantly before turning to another—

—and then he stilled. Completely.

There was no goblin there. What met his gaze was a dark-furred wolf larger than any he'd seen before. Its snout was only three feet away from him, chewing on a just-slain goblin. Its teeth crumpled the body like paper.

The wolf was completely calm. Jack met its eyes and felt true despair. This wasn't the panic of an ambush going awry. This was the hopelessness of a predator he could never, ever escape. If this wolf wanted him dead, he was dead. Simple as that.

> **Black Wolf, Level 49 (Elite) (Dungeon Boss)**
> *Black wolves are mostly solitary creatures. They are also territorial, proud, aggressive, and infamous for being a scourge at the peak of F-Grade. If a Black Wolf is spotted, experienced hunter squads should be dispatched quickly, or all big game of the surrounding area will disappear.*

Jack averted his eyes, not daring to move a muscle, so as not to be seen as a challenger.

The black wolf chomped down hard three times, then swallowed, and the goblin was gone. It then turned to survey Jack.

His mind raced. His newfound confidence disappeared, replaced with fear. It wasn't just the level. He could *feel* the difference between him and the wolf. He was helpless, hopeless, thoroughly and utterly fucked.

Left without options, Jack fell to the ground and bowed to the wolf. It was all he could do. The System description said the wolf was proud—perhaps, if he showed subservience, it would spare him.

The goblin beside him—not the dead one—followed suit in a moment of genius. It fell to the ground next to Jack, its butt quivering. The other goblin, the more distant one, chose to run.

Jack didn't even see how the wolf moved. A blur crossed his eyes as fast as a blink, and the wolf was no longer there. It was now chomping on the goblin that tried to run. It screamed once, then the wolf's jaws closed around its head, killing it without any resistance whatsoever.

For the goblin beside Jack, that was the straw to break the camel's back. Its entire lifetime of smartness spent on its

FIGHTING A HOBGOBLIN

previous decision, it now stood and ran like the stupid shit it was.

Jack held his breath and lowered his head even farther. Unexpectedly, the sound of the goblin's footsteps didn't stop. He could still hear them, tapping against the ground and slowly getting farther and farther away.

He dared raise his eyes. The wolf was still devouring the previous goblin. Then, without turning around, it simply walked away.

We are insects to it... Though this thought should have been terrifying, it lit a howling bonfire inside him. The wolf didn't know this, but it was Jack's designated enemy. He had to kill it to escape. There was a target on its back, and though Jack was currently too weak to even stand in its presence, that would change eventually.

Then, it wouldn't ignore him.

As the wolf walked away, Jack didn't dare move just yet. It was only after the sound of its unsuitably light footsteps had disappeared that he raised his head, gazing in the distance.

He'd survived. And, where there's life, there is hope. He quickly brought his thoughts in order.

A goblin had escaped, but that wasn't too important. He'd expected it. The tribe would know of him, but he would handle whatever they threw at him. In Jack's mind, the goblins were only stepping-stones to reach that wolf.

level 49... He shuddered. The highest level he'd seen so far was the earth bear at level 15, but the wolf was so much higher than that. It didn't make sense. How would he get that high? With the goblin weed bush?

Are you trying to kill me, System...

He chuckled. Of course it was, and that was okay. The odds might have been against him, but so what? Jack would find a way—or gather food, block the entrance to his cave, and hide in there until more people came from outside the dungeon. Such a scenario was bound to happen. He couldn't be the strongest person on Earth.

For now, his hope was that the System would form a level ladder for him to follow. The goblins could maybe take his level to the tens, then maybe the bears and monkeys would be hiding a soft incline of levels deeper in their territory. Maybe there were a bunch of gorillas at level 30—how would he know?

If yes, he could take things slow, or at least slower than jumping from level 15 to 45.

Jack refocused. The wolf's seemingly unreachable level hadn't just terrified him, it also fueled his resolve to go higher. Night was falling. He would sleep, and come morning, he would keep hunting goblins. They had to eat, so they would send out squads, and now that he knew what hobgoblins were capable of, he could craft a better plan against them.

It would all work out.

His fingers tightened around the hobgoblin's shortsword—a halfway-decent shiv—and stuck it under his belt. He wouldn't use it as a weapon—he had no idea how to wield it, and his fists were effective enough—but it could help with skinning the rabbits or other practical tasks.

Plus, after using his fists to fight for so long, using a weapon now would feel hollow. Muted. Distancing himself from the thrill of the fight. *What the fuck is wrong with me...* he wondered, though he didn't stop grinning. *Is the constant fighting turning me insane? Is my brain adapting to cope? Or am I simply unearthing what was always there?*

Why do I feel so alive?

That night, he dreamt of dark wolf jaws tearing him apart, over and over. He didn't sleep well.

Chapter 10
Serial Bonker

Unfortunately, the goblin leader was not an idiot. When he learned about Jack, he stopped sending goblins out to be killed. The next day, only one hunting squad left the tribe, and it was made up of three hobgoblins.

They weren't only hunting prey, but Jack too, and he scrambled to avoid them. He didn't even dare come close. The hobs were brutally efficient, constantly wary, and fiercely intelligent. Even beating one was difficult, let alone three. Moreover, the three hobs were so good at hunting, they secured enough food for the entire tribe—what was left of it, anyway.

In light of those facts, Jack decided the goblin shaman had outplayed him. He couldn't fight these goblins, and he was far from able to storm the tribe itself. That left only one option.

And that was how Jack Rust found himself stalking a bear.

Man, I've come a long way... he thought, shaking his head. Four days ago, I was looking for slightly brighter caterpillars. Now, I'm trying to kill a bear with my bare hands. That's life for you.

What happened to that caterpillar, I wonder? Wait—I don't care. Hah.

Jack's mind returned to bear hunting.

His fighting style was set in stone by now. He fought with his fists like a boxer on hard drugs. He didn't have time to learn something else from scratch.

However, his almost-failed ambush on the hobgoblin had taught him that fists, for all their power and versatility, couldn't easily assassinate someone. Therefore, Jack now carried a big-ass stone hammer, which he planned to smash into a bear head with all his power.

Fisting time would come after that.

He'd channeled all his inventiveness to create that hammer. He'd found a young tree and hacked it into two pieces with a big, sharp rock. Then, he made the lower part into the hammer's handle, and the top part into twine. Another unlucky tree fell at this point, as the twine wasn't enough. He got a rock bigger than his head and used the twine to tie it to the handle. It wasn't too steady, but that was okay. He only needed it to hold for one strike. Then, he could easily remake it.

Armed with resolve and what made humans the planet's apex predators, Jack set to the hunt.

The majestic beast prowled through the undergrowth. Sticks snapped under its heavy paws, and branches bent where they met its head. Its fur was riddled with yellow patches that glinted in the afternoon sun, indicating their rock-like hardness.

> **Earth Bear, Level 13**
> *Bears are omnivorous creatures that stand at the apex of most food chains. Earth Bears, in particular, are a stronger, highly territorial variant. They can use very limited earth magic, and the rocky parts of their fur can be used to craft F-Grade weapons and armor. Earth Bears are most commonly found in the Ursus Forests of planet Ursi.*

Jack had spent the morning scouting the bears from a distance and managed to spot a few. Based on his observations, they ranged from level 13 to 17, though there could be stronger specimens or variants deeper in their territory.

For now, he'd singled out the weakest bear he could find, extrapolated its path through the forest, and hid on a branch it would pass under. It was a tried and tested method which minimized the risk of missing its mark—except bears didn't follow predictable paths. This was his fourth attempt at ambushing the bear.

And it remained the best plan Jack could think of, so he stubbornly clung to it. He'd already invested all afternoon. He might consider retreating and trying something else if this attempt failed too, but he was in luck.

The bear ambled below him, not looking up. Strangely, Jack noticed that the bears were constantly wary of their surroundings, scanning left and right for danger, which made his task harder. He didn't know what they had to be afraid of assuming that the wolf boss liked to hunt in this area. That would explain why he hadn't met it so far.

Unfortunately for the bear, though it constantly scanned the distance, it didn't expect a predator from above. Jack fell from a high branch, swinging his stone hammer that he struggled to carry despite his 20 Physical. The bear sniffed the air and looked up, a tendency that, apparently, most things shared when ambushed from above.

The heavy stone hammer, the twelve-foot fall, and Jack's entire physical strength combined to smash the bear's head so hard it broke open on the spot.

> **Level Up! You have reached Level 7.**
> **Level Up! You have reached Level 8.**

Just like that, a level 13 earth bear had been slain.

Jack had rolled and sprung up ready for a fight, only to realize what had happened. He stared at the headless corpse, unable to believe himself, then broke into frenzied laughter. The System thought it was being funny with poop-throwing gymonkeys, but *this* was funny.

For once, things were going well! His struggles were paying off!

"Hooray for human intelligence!" He laughed, scaring a pair of birds on a nearby branch. "Who needs goblins? Bears are so fucking easy!"

Succeeding so effortlessly on a task that seemed herculean was surreal.

Of course, it hadn't actually been easy. Jack had gathered information, prepared carefully, and spent a lot of time to set up the perfect ambush. That was the main reason he succeeded, along with his great strength, which allowed him to use the hammer, and his agility, which let him swing accurately from such a difficult position. Moreover, if he failed in the original strike, the risk was tremendous.

But he'd prevailed. Water under the bridge.

Now, Jack had four free points to allocate, and he considered the issue. Physical had been his go-to stat for a while now, and would likely continue being so, but this last battle reminded him of humanity's greatest weapon, the one that allowed them to rise above animals and become the rulers of the world—their intelligence.

He already felt pretty smart, but now that he had points to spare, maybe it was time to test what Mental would do. More brains never hurt anybody, and at this point, one or two points in Physical hardly made a difference. He allocated two points in Mental.

The world brightened before his eyes. Patterns of movement emerged in the floating leaves, Fibonacci sequences everywhere. For a moment, he felt like the God of Math—or maybe Albert Einstein.

At the same time, his grasp over the world's workings solidified a bit. He was more aware of himself and others, could decipher and use the patterns that his heightened intelligence unearthed.

In short, he'd become smarter and wiser—but, while the difference was clear, it felt a bit useless.

Jack was a smart person to begin with—his starting Mental was 7. He'd also spent a lifetime studying and polishing his mind. He already had the foundation to navigate this dungeon situation and come up with plans that were close to optimal.

The Mental increase was welcome, of course, but it would only be useful if he returned to his lab. It was unnecessary to the current him, in the same way that extra

Physical would be unnecessary to a scientist—how much strength did it take to turn doorknobs and open jars?

The only useful thing was his increased insight into himself, which helped him deal with this ongoing modern-to-primal transition, but mental health paled in importance when compared to not being eaten by wolves.

In the end, Jack had done his experiment, as he should, and concluded he should focus on Physical for now. As he liked to say, better a master of one than a jack of all trades—even though his name was Jack.

He allocated the remaining two points in Physical and inspected his status screen.

> **Name: Jack Rust**
> **Species: Human, Earth-387**
> **Faction: -**
> **Grade: F**
> **Level: 8**
> **Physical: 22**
> **Mental: 9**
> **Will: 7**
> **Skills: Fistfighting (I)**

Not bad, not bad at all.

He'd stopped looking for a normal-world equivalent of himself. He was at least four and a half times more fit than a pre-System normal person across the table. He was roughly as strong as a professional weight lifter and as fast as a professional sprinter, while also having the endurance of a professional marathon runner and the durability of... Well, he wasn't sure there was an equivalent for that. A brick wall, maybe?

In any case, Jack was pretty sure that, if the current him was in the pre-System world, he could steamroll any decathlon competition to ever exist.

Presently, he was using his power to steamroll bears and goblins, but to each their own.

The takeaway was that Jack was a total badass, and that felt damn good after twenty-seven years of barely making ends meet in a life he didn't like much. Even his appearance was improving—muscles were beginning to bulge under his bare chest and arms, and he had hints of a six-pack.

Physical was great.

Snapping back to the present, Jack looked at the bear corpse, then at the sky. Hunting monster bears was his new shortcut to levels—unfortunately, it was a time-consuming hobby, and the sun was already setting.

Though he was uninjured, he had to retreat and come back tomorrow—but, on the bright side, he was uninjured. With his recent level-ups, it was time to get an extra stat point or two from the ice pond. So what if there was hellish pain?

Could it be worse than death or losing the one opportunity he ever had to shine?

Night came and went. Jack managed to go one step farther into the pond. The difficulty wasn't linear, it rose exponentially the deeper he went. The waterfall was less than ten steps away now, and he estimated he'd need to reach the twenties in level before getting there, maybe more.

Not that he could complain. The pond had already granted him the equivalent of three levels in points and a little more, and it wouldn't stop anytime soon. It was the gift that kept on giving. Jack's lucky star.

Come morning, the hobgoblins were scouring their territory again, and Jack considered attacking them but didn't. He might have, if there were only two, but there were three. The goblin shaman was proving its intelligence. It would rather go hungry for a bit than lose more of its people. It had ramped up the difficulty too much at once, and Jack's leveling speed couldn't cope—for now.

Fortunately, the bears weren't as smart. They probably hadn't even noticed yesterday's assassination. Therefore, Jack, in his endless generosity, would give them more opportunities to notice.

Morning found him hiding in branches and hoping for his target bear, at level 14 this time, as he hadn't found a weaker one, to pass under him. It didn't. And after four such failures, Jack got irritated.

He kept himself in check. Arrogance could get him killed. He didn't have the strength to fight bears head-on yet, so he could only take things slow.

After five hours of stalking the same bear, he finally managed to pull off his ambush.

Bonk!

> **Level Up! You have reached Level 9.**
> **Level Up! You have reached Level 10.**

Jack smiled. He put all four points into Physical, raising it to twenty-seven, and kept on with his merry hunting. His progression was so fast these days, he'd almost gotten addicted to the dings that accompanied level-ups.

He carried his bloody hammer through the forest until he spotted another bear, this one at level 14, too. He then employed his signature move, hiding in branches and waiting for the unsuspecting bear to cross underneath.

However, the moment it appeared under him, the bear sniffed the air. Its head whipped up, eyes meeting Jack, who was only starting his fall. He froze in midair. Panic took him over. He hadn't realized this, but he was looking a fucking bear in the face.

What gave me away? he thought, and instantly, he knew. *The hammer! I never cleaned the blood!*

Far too late for regrets. At this point, Jack had to go all-in. He swung and gloriously missed as the bear moved its head.

Its yellow eyes now glared at Jack from only a few feet away, and its entire body tensed up to attack. It growled, spitting on him and exposing large, sharp teeth. The yellow patches on its fur glowed.

Jack paled. *Shit!*

Chapter 11
Racing a Bear

Jack stared at the bear. The bear stared at him. It growled. He jumped.

"Shit!"

The bear wasn't one to waste time. It lunged at Jack, swiping a large paw, and he narrowly dodged the strike. The claws dug thick lines on the tree behind him.

Jack caught on fire. The now familiar fight or flight instincts kicked in, taking control and giving him greater power than his body could wield. A thousand synapses fired in his brain all at once.

Fight or flight?

As if in slow motion, he considered the issue. One hit from the bear could incapacitate him. At the same time, it wasn't particularly agile. He could dodge everything. Maybe he could make it.

The bear swiped again. Jack ducked under the blow, letting his stone hammer fall as he clenched his fists. His Fistfighting skill kicked in, further heightening his fighting awareness. As he dodged the claw, he rotated his body and shot a hard hook into the bear's belly, throwing all his weight behind it.

His fist met rock-hard fur. The impact was so strong that, despite his augmented body, his knuckle bled and almost cracked. The bear, on the other hand, only bent its body a bit—a yellow glow had appeared on the point of impact and absorbed most of the damage.

Jack remembered its description. *Limited earth magic. Fuck.*

He jumped back—avoiding a set of sharp jaws so close the heat of its maw curled against his skin—and turned around in midair. He was faster than the bear, but the damage he dealt was minimal. It would catch him, eventually. He couldn't afford this fight.

Flee.

Decision made, Jack's entire body lightened as his legs hummed with power. They smashed into the forest floor, throwing dirt and stones all around, shooting him forth at tremendous speed. A patch of bushes practically zoomed past his vision.

A roar and four heavy thuds indicated the bear would give chase. Of course it would.

And so began Jack's first race.

Humans cannot outrun bears. However, that only concerns pre-System humans. At 27 Physical, Jack had already outgrown that entire civilization—but had he outgrown a bear?

There was only one way to find out.

His bare feet smashed the ground hard enough to break it. His body was slanted forward, riding the air resistance to stay upright, and his hands frantically moved back and forth. The bear's roar was approaching. Jack accelerated.

Running for your life was a unique feeling. Everything disappeared, all thoughts went silent, letting the running become your entire life.

Jack was one with the air, one with the forest. He wasn't a human, but a movement, a gale crossing through bushes and over roots. His high Physical made the forest's terrain easy to traverse. He zoomed left and right, purposefully passing through narrow parts to slow down the bear. In a straight line, he couldn't match its speed, but this was a forest.

Where he only had to duck, the bear had to plow through fallen branches and hollow logs. It wasn't only the roars that indicated its position, but also the breaking of wood and uprooted vegetation.

Despite all that, it was still gaining ground. A claw fell only inches behind his back. Jack's eyes sharpened as he went all-out.

He jumped over logs, swung from branches, and stepped on trees to make his turns sharper. The terrain became his ally, not an enemy. Though he'd only tried parkour once or twice before, he imagined this was how pros felt.

The bear was close. He spared a glance its way just as it emerged from an exploding bunch of logs, splinters flying everywhere but unable to penetrate its fur. It galloped at full speed, heedless of any obstacles in its way. Only trees could slow it down, but those, too, were snapped in half occasionally.

Jack gritted his teeth. The speed he was moving at was superhuman. He'd run before, of course he had, but he only possessed 4 Physical then—before the System. Now, he'd claimed 27. The difference was stunning. Trees and bushes momentarily snapped into his vision before disappearing. His body reacted beyond what his conscious processes could pick up.

He was sprinting at the top of the world, and the bear slowly, slowly began to fall behind. Its roars became hollower, the sound of its crashes duller.

And sprinting like this was beginning to take its toll on Jack. He was growing tired. His lungs burned, his legs were made of lead. He caught himself panting.

He hadn't tried out his running abilities, except when escaping the monkeys, but he was focused on them, then. Now, he could take in the changes of his body, and they were majestic.

His surroundings were changing. He began to recognize things. That crooked tree, this malformed bush, the perfectly round clearing. He'd left the bear's territory and entered his own, where the hobgoblins prowled, but he had a big-ass bear on his back. Stealth be damned.

As he jumped over a fallen log, he saw them. Three hobgoblins, each standing slightly apart from each other as they gaped with surprise that quickly turned into fear when the log behind him exploded and an enraged bear flew through, galloping wildly.

Jack didn't dare lead it at them. He was only barely outrunning the beast as it was. The slightest complication would doom him.

He kept running, filled with the mad desire to flee, and as he did, a wondrous feeling took over. His exhaustion disappeared. His strength grew. His senses sharpened.

His feet now hammered even harder against the ground, pushing him forward so fast the air screamed in his ears.

Exhaustion turned into fuel, into ecstasy. Jack now loved running. He could go on forever, and as he thought that, he accelerated, surpassing his previous limit.

The bear didn't. Its tired panting was evident through the growls, the creature was slowing down, and he grinned. In the animal kingdom, humans weren't sprinters, they were endurance runners. Since the bear hadn't caught up yet, victory would be his.

Confidence swelled inside him, enhanced by the euphoria of being one with himself. He felt fast, strong, invincible, that he could take on everything the world threw at him. He controlled this entire forest. He could grab the ground and stop Earth's rotation, then spin it in reverse.

He almost stopped and turned to face the bear before catching himself. That unmatched arrogance disappeared as quickly as it had come, but the euphoric confidence remained.

He kept running, savoring the feeling. At some point, the thuds and growls had disappeared. The bear had given up.

Jack stopped, too, taking a look at the empty forest behind him. How long had he been running alone? It didn't matter. He was still full of energy, full of vigor and strength, and though he didn't dare face the bear yet, there was another enemy in the forest.

His forest.

Jack ran in the opposite direction. They couldn't have gone far. The trees zoomed past him, he ducked under branches and jumped over bushes like an Olympic athlete.

He wasn't going at full throttle now, just enough to stay fast. And he was being silent.

He flew into a forest path, and through a patch of bushes, he spotted them. The hobgoblins were huddled in a circle, discussing something, possibly him. He shot right at them like a barbaric missile.

He'd struggled against one hobgoblin when he was level 5, but he'd now reached level 10, plus the increased bonuses from the ice pond. He was massively stronger than before, and most importantly, he was fully warmed-up. So what if they had shortswords? They couldn't touch him.

The hobgoblins turned to look, and one of them caught a punch in the face, sending it flying into a tree and cracking the bark. A trembling groan escaped the hobgoblin's lips before it stumbled, still upright but barely. Its fuzzy eyes met Jack, and it drew its sword.

Jack didn't go after it. As soon as he landed the first punch, he stepped into the ground with enough force to extinguish his momentum. The dirt exploded. His entire body creaked, but he didn't mind. Before the hobgoblins could escape their surprise, he elbowed a second one in the chest, cracking ribs and sending it kneeling on the ground.

He then punched ahead, but the third hobgoblin jumped back in time and drew its sword. It adopted a well-trained stance, and despite Jack's overwhelming ambush, the hobgoblin's eyes didn't falter.

The first hobgoblin, the one he'd punched in the face, stepped behind him. It still hadn't recovered from the strike—it might even have suffered a minor concussion—but it was ready to fight.

Hobgoblins were nothing like goblins. They were disciplined, trained warriors. They were hardened veterans. Tricks and ambushes wouldn't be enough to take them down.

And Jack knew that. He wasn't counting on an ambush. He wanted to fight them head-on, test himself against their blades. He was flooded with battle lust, eager to try out his skills at the edge of danger.

He banged his fists together, eyeing the two hobgoblins that were trying to surround him. "Come!" he shouted.

The two of them looked at each other and nodded.

Jack, still in their encirclement, watched them intently. Besides the two standing hobgoblins, the one that had been elbowed before still struggled to stand due to its broken ribcage, but Jack didn't discard it entirely. It could still throw out its shortsword, trip him, or do other nasty things if he wasn't careful.

But he would be.

The two goblins rushed him at the same time, one in front and the other from behind. Their movements were sharp, their stances solid. Jack didn't see an easy way to attack or dodge.

Despite that... they were slow.

Jack's stats had already jumped beyond theirs. Training and expertise could only achieve so much in the face of absolute power.

As they fell on him, blades swinging, Jack's body came alive. He twisted, dodging attacks at the last moment even when they seemed unavoidable. His speed was such that their weapons couldn't follow, and their carefully devised stances weren't designed against overwhelming opponents. Hobgoblins were used to fighting other hobgoblins, not superheroes.

Jack was like a dancer. His reflexes were so fast he moved at the same time they did, and his speed was such that he'd dodged before they even finished their attack. Two shortswords fell from different directions, and Jack weaved between them masterfully, passing through gaps the naked eye could only barely catch.

This wasn't just his stats, of course. His Fistfighting skill was running at full throttle, and as he dodged and weaved, he grew more and more familiar with his body at a stunning rate.

Dodging like this wasn't easy. Jack was dancing on the razor's edge, and yet, he kept going. When he had the opportunity to counter-attack, he didn't. This feeling of harmony was beyond wondrous, and he felt if he stopped now, this opportunity wouldn't reappear easily. He had to grasp at straws to survive this dungeon, to dig out even the last dregs of his potential. A little danger was nothing.

His movements sharpened. His thoughts accelerated. He leaned from one movement to the next, using skill to dodge instead of pure speed. His body became one with his will, and he felt in complete control of his every limb and muscle.

The hobgoblins didn't know he was holding back, of course, so they remained careful, not daring to attack too wildly in case he struck back. Unbeknownst to them, they were spelling the doom of their tribe.

Finally, in one movement, everything came together in Jack's mind. He, his body, and his enemies became one.

Ding!

> **Skill upgraded. Fistfighting (I) → Fistfighting (II)**

Through the battle haze, he grinned.

Chapter 12
The Jack-Goblin War

Everything suddenly became so much easier. The trajectories of the shortswords were clearly telegraphed before his eyes, and he could tell where the next attack would come from before the hobs even moved to enact it.

These weren't veteran fighters, they were merely familiar with fighting. Their stances weren't refined, just decent. They had holes he could see and punch through.

And he did.

Through the maelstrom of attacks, a fist jumped out and fell on a hobgoblin's face like a meteor from the side. It stumbled, and Jack rounded on the other hobgoblin, dodged an attack to get into its guard, and stared it down.

Its face was hideous, but in its eyes, there bloomed fear. He was a head taller to begin with. Right now, he felt incomparably grander.

The hobgoblin froze in fear as a fist shot into its gut, then the same fist slammed its falling face into an uppercut. The impact was so strong that the hobgoblin's feet left the ground, and it flew a couple of feet before it landed on its back, unmoving and very dead. This was the same hobgoblin he'd punched at the start—the amount of punishment it could take was limited.

Jack then turned to face the other hobgoblin, dodged the strike heading for his head, grabbed it hard by the throat, and pummeled its face into mush with his other hand.

A second later, the hobgoblin was dead.

He turned to the third goblin, the one that couldn't stand due to its broken ribcage. He frowned as he looked it over. Its eyes were still fearless and full of fire, but he couldn't just execute a fallen enemy.

"What should I do with you?" he asked.

"Kill me," the hobgoblin spat out in a rough, calloused, yet slightly high-pitched voice, "or I will kill you."

Jack shook his head. "No. I think I'll—"

Whatever he was going to say, it disappeared. A stick snapping behind him was the only warning Jack got. He jumped aside and barely dodged the earth bear's charge, which barreled through his previous position and into the kneeling hobgoblin.

It hadn't been more than two minutes since it stopped chasing Jack, so it was still nearby. Hearing the sounds of combat, it'd come to investigate.

Jack rolled upright and eyed the beast, already moving backward. "You can't catch me," he said. "Just get the fuck out."

The bear met his steady gaze, and this time, it didn't chase. It was still exhausted from the previous run. So was

Jack, actually, but the bear didn't know that. It only knew it'd lost once.

Jack had already retreated a couple dozen feet, more than enough to escape any surprise attack and run away.

The bear growled once, clearly dissatisfied, then turned to the hobgoblin, which lay by its feet. It tried to grin heroically. "I—" A claw easily snapped its neck. The bear threw a last glance at Jack before leaning in for its meal, and he only grimaced before turning away.

Despite his skill upgrade, he still didn't feel confident against an earth bear—not without an ambush.

That was fine with Jack. He was confident in his strength, having finally graduated from prey to hunter.

He even had choices on what to hunt. The bears were doable. He'd be in huge trouble if he failed the ambush, but he liked his chances. He'd succeeded twice, after all. However, the risk of death was still there, even if not high.

The only problem was that Jack was reluctant to kill too many bears. There had to be bigger, meaner variants deeper in their territory, along with a group boss, and that mystery filled him with a sense of dread he'd rather not provoke.

The other option was the goblins, who also had the promising High Speed Bush. They'd holed up in their tribe, leaving Jack helpless before, but now, he was forced to reconsider. His current power was enough to steamroll hobgoblins, of which there were only two left. There were dozens of regular goblins, but he could face those in his sleep.

They could only be a problem if they utilized ranged weapons, large numbers, as well as...

The shaman.

The goblin shaman was at level 9, close to Jack. Plus, his powers remained a mystery.

Finally, there were the monkeys, but Jack still felt somewhat apprehensive. Not only were they dangerous, with the only group he'd seen sporting the equivalent of five hobgoblins, but they were also monkeys, which implied a level of intelligence that could doom him if he wasn't careful. The System could have installed a Monkey Sage as their leader, or something equally ridiculous, and he didn't want a bunch of gorilla bouncers scouring the forest for him.

Plus, they hadn't tried to kill him. That was a major concern for Jack.

In the end, the High Speed Bush of the goblins won him over.

Alright. I'll take one more bear to level up, then try the ice pond again, and then... I will destroy the goblins once and for all.

Night had fallen in the Greenway Natural Reserve. The moon was hidden, but the stars shone bright, lending their light to the night like fireflies stuck on ceiling glue.

For the first time, Jack was out and about in the dark. He'd only used the night to cook before, but now, he was using it to skulk. To prowl through the undergrowth unseen and hunt his enemies.

The goblin tribe was arrayed before him, an amalgamation of little green things, rough huts, and random squealing from said huts. There were more than thirty huts, each housing two goblins, indicating their original number to be around sixty or seventy. Jack estimated there were around forty left, including the goblin shaman and the two hobgoblins—as well as any hobgoblins he'd missed the first time.

It wasn't a fight he could take. The shaman was an unknown variant, the hobs needed time to neutralize, and the goblins were so many they could swarm him.

Fortunately, he didn't need to fight them head-on. Hence the night.

Killing the leader would despawn the entire monster group, according to the System. All Jack had to do was infiltrate, reach the shaman's hut—the largest one, obviously—and slit its throat. Then, goodbye, goblins.

Despawning them would lose him some experience, but at this point, goblins just weren't worth it. They were too low-level. Even if he manually took out the entire tribe, he'd only get two levels at most, and half of that would come from the leader himself.

Risking himself for a smidgeon of extra EXP—to speak in game terms—just wasn't worth it. He would assassinate the leader, benefit from their High Speed Bush, then go fight bears and monkeys to level up.

> **High Speed Bush (F-Grade)**
> *A resource guarded by the goblins of the Forest of the Strong. Commonly found in the wet jungles of planet Peruvian, the leaves of this bush can enhance a person's reflexes, speed, dexterity, and agility. They can also make you high as a kite.*
> *The stat increase is a one-time bonus.*

According to Jack's estimate, this bush was exactly what he needed. The bonuses could help him consistently outrun the earth bears, at least the low-level ones, significantly decreasing the risk of his ambushes. It could also help him escape the monkeys, when he decided to head that way.

Plan determined, Jack inspected himself a final time before jumping into action.

> **Name: Jack Rust**
> **Species: Human, Earth-387**
> **Faction: -**
> **Grade: F**
> **Level: 11**
> **Physical: 30**
> **Mental: 9**
> **Will: 7**
> **Skills: Fistfighting (II)**

He'd killed an extra bear for a level up, and also managed to take an extra step into the ice pond—the seventh one—almost reaching its halfway point. Thanks to his Physical stat, he overflowed with power.

He also checked out his upgraded skill.

> **Fistfighting (II): Grants expert knowledge of fistfighting. While fistfighting, enhances the user's physical attributes, reflexes, and kinetic vision.**

It wasn't a large change from the previous version, just a few of the adjectives had changed.

Still, Jack wasn't going to complain. The difference between basic and expert was massive, as he'd experienced when fighting the hobgoblins. He clenched his fists, and was filled with the confidence that comes from skill.

He prepared himself for the coming action against the goblin tribe. His eyes sharpened. His bare feet—given his high Physical, shoes slowed him down tremendously—were tickled by the moist grass below. The night breeze swept around his bare chest, hugging it, and his nape-length hair fluttered.

He smelled blood in the air. There wasn't any yet, but there would be.

Jack slid into the bush and down the hill. He was quiet. His bare feet made no sound on the grass and soil, while his breath was deep and steady. He was used to high adrenaline now.

He darted from bush to bush like a rabbit, easily hiding from the sentries' sights. Though their leader had devised an excellent patrol pattern, the goblins were too dumb to understand it, and they ended up looking the wrong way. Jack snuck through the gaps, a human-shaped wolf entering the sheep pen.

There were many guards tonight, but that was expected. The three hobgoblins hadn't returned. The goblins were undoubtedly on high alert.

The tribe was situated in a large clearing—System-made, as Jack didn't remember it being here before—and he reached its edge without being noticed. Then, things got tough.

There was a thirty-foot gap between the last bush and the first tent, a gap he couldn't easily cross. The goblins had no torches—they could see in the dark—but the starlight was enough for Jack. The problem was that the lack of torches meant a lack of shadows for him to sneak through.

But, well, Jack was Jack. If there weren't holes in their defense, he'd make one.

The moon swung overhead as time passed. The ten goblin guards were split into groups of two, patrolling in and around the tribe. There weren't walls or palisades, only these ten little goblins.

As a duo of goblins circled the clearing, arguing about something in low voices, two hands sneaked out of a bush, grabbed their mouths, and pulled them in. Then, silence.

The other goblins didn't realize a patrol had gone missing. The gap was enough for Jack to go through.

He slithered across the clearing as quickly as he could manage while remaining stealthy. He reached the first hut and dove in its base, making himself one with what little shadow it cast. Low squeals came from inside, but he didn't pay any mind. These goblins had been at it for a while.

He circled around the hut to avoid a passing patrol, then headed deeper inside. Stalking in the dark, Jack felt like a primal, nocturnal beast seeking prey. The feeling was wildly exciting, and his body adapted to the hunt.

He followed the hut walls deeper into enemy territory. There were patrols even inside the tribe, so he had to be careful, not to mention the entire camp was so small he could be seen by pretty much anywhere.

As Jack skulked by a wall, a door opened right in front of him.

Chapter 13
Punching a Boss

Jack froze for a fraction of a second before darting behind the wall he'd been skulking by and held his breath. Inwardly, he cursed. He didn't just have to watch out for patrols, but also random goblins that needed to pee!

The door sandwiched him against the wall, and he was forced to put out a hand and gently stop it. He cursed again. In the silence of the night, and with his senses heightened from all the stalking, the door's creaks came to his ears as loud as lovemaking pigs. Admittedly, they *were* pretty loud—goblins weren't the best of builders, even though these huts had obviously been spawned by the System.

Through a crack in the door, Jack could see a naked goblin on the other side. It rubbed its eyes to send the drowsiness away, then, with a, "Hmm?" it gazed at the door, which didn't make the normal *bang* of hitting the wall.

Jack prepared to attack.

The goblin then shrugged and went about its business. Taking two steps to reach the corner of its hut, it started pissing at it. Jack's brows spasmed. He stifled a groan.

Ugh. Disgusting...

When the goblin was done, it went back to the door, grabbed it from Jack's gentle hands, and shut it. Jack was left plastered on the wall, not knowing whether to be relieved or irritated that he had to hide from such beings.

He settled on resolve.

His feet slid across the dirt, carrying him across another gap and next to the wall of the largest hut. He looked around; nobody had spotted him. Good.

Jack put his ear against the wall, and hearing nothing, raised his head a bit. There was a window here, like most huts, and he peeked through.

Before him lay a despondently empty space. There was a rough table and chair, the pinnacle of goblin furnishings, as well as a shamanic staff leaning against the wall. A large pile of stones waited behind the closed door—an alarm system that Jack would bypass—while the fur of some unknown animal served as bedding on the ground—unprocessed, of course.

On the beddings, covered with another fur, lay the sleeping form of a goblin. Jack grinned. He stuck his head a bit deeper inside, inspecting all corners where a guard might lay in wait, then raised himself through the window. Now inside the goblin master hut, he got a better view.

He wasn't an idiot. Something was fishy here. This was too easy.

Yet, there was nothing besides the alarm stones by the door. He even wondered if this was another goblin serving as bait, but the shamanic staff was here—a crooked piece of wood adorned with colorful feathers and animalistic tokens—and the sleeping goblin wore the same face paint as the last time he'd seen it.

Either the goblin shaman was incredibly smart, or it wasn't. Given its goblin nature, Jack was inclined to believe the latter.

He paced to the sleeping goblin and snapped its neck. Then, he waited. Nothing happened. No notifications, no warning bells, no fuss. Jack frowned. He looked outside the window and saw a goblin patrol at the edge of the clearing. He looked back at the dead goblin. He frowned deeper.

Well, shit.

And *then* came the warning bells. Shouts rose from the edge of the tribe, rousing all goblins within earshot—that is, every single goblin.

"Fuck!" Jack cursed. He didn't know how they'd discovered him, but they clearly had. And worst of all... he'd been outsmarted by a goblin.

That left a sour taste in his mouth. Thankfully, he was determined to kill said goblin, and killing washed all sour tastes away.

As the tribe burst into activity, Jack jumped outside the window and landed on an unfortunate goblin passerby. He turned its head to mush before looking around, only to find at least a dozen pairs of eyes on him. Both hobgoblins stared him down, surrounding a goblin thinner than most, with creepy painted lines on its body and sparks dancing on its fingers.

"Kekeke," it chuckled. "Stupid intruder. We will eat your fingers one by one as punishment, and I'll wear your hair as mine."

"Oh, yeah? Give it a shot, little man."

Jack wasn't going to play around. As forty goblins screamed and pounced at him, he clenched his fists. His body caught on fire. His eyes sharpened, and his breath deepened. He became a fighter—an expert fistfighter.

It was time to crack some skulls. Jack roared.

Screams came from all sides as the goblins swarmed him.

Jack became a force of nature. A storm made of fists.

One punch took a goblin's head clean off. Another landed on a chest and broke it apart, while a third uppercut a goblin hard enough to send it flying. His hands turned into blurs, but there was a limit to his power.

A swarm could not be stopped by single-target attacks.

Though some goblins died, many more landed on him. They were fearless, ignoring the death of their comrades to attack him frenziedly, and they succeeded in harming him. Claws ripped into his skin, teeth tried to dig his eyes out. Jack grabbed goblins and tossed them off his body like cats, but they were too many.

No matter how many he killed, more arrived to take their place. The wounds were shallow—his body was extremely durable—and his critical places were well-protected, but the sheer weight and violence of the goblins dragged him down. Something had to be done, or he would fall.

Through the bodies that covered him, Jack could see the two pale forms of the hobgoblins approaching. Their swords glinted in the moonlight, and their yellow eyes shone like embers.

His every instinct kicked in at once, inciting the familiar state of all-encompassing resolve. His muscles pulsed and groaned as they pulled beyond their limit, and his primal urges took to the forefront. Gone was the man, leaving only the warrior. Cold heart and burning body.

It was intoxicating.

Jack roared again. He dug his heels into the ground, stuck to the wall behind him, and spun around, smashing all goblins into the wood. The large hut creaked. The goblins' claws drew bloody lines on his skin as they were torn away. He succeeded; he was free, if only for a moment.

Jack didn't waste any time pummeling them. Already, goblins watched him from the nearby rooftops, and they jumped down like little green suicidal bombers—but when they landed, Jack wasn't there.

His soles smashed into the ground, raising hell under a dark sky as he darted through the village at speeds the goblins couldn't follow. He danced between walls and huts. He jumped on roofs and broke through them. Goblins flew around him, some attacking and some tossed away by brutal punches.

Jack was a hurricane that tore the goblin tribe apart, huts, bodies, everything, and only the rock that made up the huts' foundations could withstand his fury. The goblins shrieked, only seeing a blur before getting punched to oblivion.

Jack was a moving storm, and the tribe could not take him.

But the shaman could.

His body suddenly slowed. Red ethereal snakes wrapped around his limbs, dragging him down, impervious to his touch. They were ghosts. At the same time, frigid cold assaulted his soul. Fear and despair threatened to overtake him, and his heart was shackled, trapped in cold iron.

Jack lost his footing and fell from the rooftops, landing on the soil a few feet below. A hobgoblin was there. A shortsword stabbed unerringly at his throat while his eyes were cloudy.

The shortsword missed its mark, and a punch landed on the hobgoblin's sternum so hard it spat blood and flew back amidst the sound of breaking bones. Jack was there, squatting and panting, his eyes redder than the snakes binding him.

The chill to his soul had been tremendous, but Jack had withstood the ice pond. How could a mere goblin shaman stop him?

The goblins reached him as he struggled. The little fuckers still didn't care for their lives, and they fell on him in waves.

Jack was a menace.

He grabbed one by the head and crashed it into another. He punched a goblin so hard that three flew back, like pins in a bowling court. He ducked under a goblin's assault, grabbed its leg, and used it as a weapon to send more of them flying.

Yet, there were many, and he could not face them all. He was bleeding from a hundred little wounds, and the losses were beginning to accumulate. He had to do something.

His gaze cut through the swarm of goblins, through the remaining hobgoblin, and into the eyes of the goblin shaman. It grinned as it met his stare, and Jack grinned back.

He flew backward. Some goblins missed him and fell to the ground, only to be stomped by their companions as they chased him. Jack ran around the village, letting the mindless goblins gnaw at his heels as he changed directions. The red snakes still bound him, but his soul could handle them, for now.

A moment later, he emerged at the center of the tribe, where the huts formed a small opening, and where the goblin shaman waited. A hobgoblin stepped in Jack's path, shrouded in pure resolve. Its entire body shone black as phantasmal lines covered it, and Jack thought he saw a ghost.

He didn't care.

He fell onto the hobgoblin without slowing in the slightest. It backpedaled to keep him within range, its shortsword weaving clean lines through the air. Jack struggled to dodge. With the red snakes around his limbs, moving was difficult, but he was still faster and better than a mere hobgoblin.

His face morphed into a mask of utter focus. His fists dove through the gaps, smashing into the hobgoblin. The shortsword cut him deep, but he didn't stop—because if he did, the goblin swarm would catch up.

One punch broke the hobgoblin's jaw, another cracked its ribs, a third tossed the shortsword away. Jack caught a swing with his shoulder, letting the sword carve his outer arm as he punched the hobgoblin right in the face, sending it reeling and barely missing the shaman, who only cackled devilishly.

"Foolish human!" it shrieked. "You're almost dead!"

Jack barely heard it. Not only was he bleeding profusely, the hobgoblin had also scraped the surface of his arm so deep that the bone showed. He was in terrible pain, surrounded, and with an army at his heels. Moreover, the red snakes still tried to infiltrate his soul, and the more exhausted he got, the weaker his resistance.

He no longer had the strength to escape the tribe. All he could do now was kill the shaman.

Everything else disappeared. Only that hateful little creature was left, with its evil laughter and gloating eyes.

It was within range. Jack pounced. His punches dug into the goblin's body and tore it apart, destroying it so hard it turned into smoke. Jack roared in triumph.

But goblins didn't turn into smoke.

"Kekeke, silly human."

He turned around, and the shaman was there, on the large hut's rooftop. This time, it held its staff, too. Jack was sure this was the real body—but through his pain and haze, he looked deeper.

As soon as he did, the goblin shaman turned transparent, and a new body appeared, watching him from behind a flood of goblins that poured right at Jack. "Not so silly," the shaman gloated. "But tasty, anyway. I will eat your brain. Kekeke!"

Jack grunted. The sound was barely human, more like a bull's, and so he acted. Bringing both arms before his face, he ducked deep and ran at the horde, aiming to blast right through it. The shaman laughed. "You're crazy!"

And maybe he was—but it worked.

Faced with Jack's unstoppable charge and their own momentum, the goblin army was broken. Some flew away, others were stomped, and yet more were simply pushed aside as Jack plowed through.

Some goblins grabbed on to him, trying to carve his skin even further. He paid them no mind. Only one thought remained: the goblin shaman had to die.

"Fool!" it shouted. Its staff shone red, and a wall of flames rose from nothing to block Jack's path. He faced an open oven, a wildfire in the middle of the forest. Whether he turned left or right, more goblins awaited to tear him apart.

Jack didn't turn left or right. He didn't break pace, either. He just kept running.

He dove into the flames. The goblins on him screamed as they were scorched, and Jack screamed too. These weren't normal flames. Every spark was like molten iron on his skin, every ember striving to burn through his bones. Even the red snakes were extinguished.

But Jack was strong, too. He screamed through the pain and kept running, channeling the resolve he'd built in the ice pond.

It was only a second, but it felt like eternity.

Everything was worth it when he burst out of the flames and met the goblin's shocked, fearful gaze. He stood before it, bleeding, injured, burned—*triumphant*.

"What?" it muttered, stepping back. "That's impossible!"

"Nothing is impossible."

Jack reared his right fist, gathering as much strength as he could. The goblin waved its staff, trying to cast something, but it was far too late. His fist dug deep into its face, smashing the goblin against the ground so hard it bounced off higher than his head. It was dead before it landed.

At the same time, a wave of euphoria flooded Jack. He'd won.

The flames disappeared, but behind them, the remaining goblins jumped at him once again. His eyes snapped back to reality. *What! But I—*

> **Level Up! You have reached Level 12.**
> **Level Up! You have reached Level 13.**
> **Level Up! You have reached Level 14.**
> **Level Up! You have reached Level 15.**
> **Goblin Boss defeated! Would you like to despawn the group? Y/N**

Wh—Yes! Yes! Fucking yes!

The blue screens disappeared, revealing a claw heading right for his face. Jack closed his eyes.

And the claw never arrived. When he opened his eyes again, the goblins had disappeared, soundlessly dissolving into thin air. Despite his pain, he looked around incredulously. Not the slightest hint of their presence was left. Their weapons, their bodies, their clothes, even their huts were gone. Jack was left alone and bleeding in an empty forest clearing, where only the High Speed Bush remained.

He invested all eight stat points from the level-ups into Physical, and his skin squirmed as mortal wounds shut themselves. The bleeding slowed down, then stopped. He still felt dizzy and weak, but at least he was alive and would continue being so.

Those four levels saved his life. For once, the System had been kind to him.

Jack fell to his knees. His strength left him. So did the battle haze, and the pain of all his wounds shone through, but it was welcome. It only showed he was still alive.

That he'd won.

And, at the end of it all, a new blue screen shone before his eyes.

> **Level 15 reached. Congratulations! Cl ass System unlocked.
> Please choose your Class:**

Chapter 14
Class Time

After the goblin tribe was defeated, Jack lay on the grass, struggling to take in his rewards. He couldn't sleep here. He needed to move.

Four levels at once was a massive bonus, and it indicated there was something else at play besides the experience from individual monsters. Maybe the monster group counted as a big monster itself?

He'd also gotten the High Speed Bush, the resource guarded by the goblin tribe. Finally, the System had informed him he could now choose a class—and, knowing video games, this should be a bonus even greater than those levels.

Jack lay on the grass for a while, letting his tension die down before he dragged himself up and made his way to the High Speed Bush.

From up-close, the bush looked pretty natural. It was short, wide, with a multitude of branches extending from a barely-visible trunk in its center. The leaves were laid on thick, and were long, thin, and appeared soft. When he reached to touch one, it bent easily under his fingers and graced them with a thin, slippery coating.

This coating was the bush's excrement, which apparently made the goblins high. Jack looked at his finger, then licked it.

It didn't taste like much, similar to thin oil. He waited, but nothing happened. This quantity obviously wasn't enough for someone of his size—and stats.

Sighing in resignation, Jack plucked a few leaves off the bush and licked them one by one. It was a weird thing to do, but he couldn't just sit around. His battle against the tribe hadn't been discreet, and there was no telling what manner of creature was already galloping this way.

Just as Jack considered that maybe he'd misunderstood something, a blue screen appeared with a ding.

> **High Speed Bush bonus acquired!**

Well, what is it?

He opened his status screen but saw no changes besides those he already knew.

His Physical was still climbing to the heavens, but that was just the points from the four level-ups. Where did the bush's bonus go?

He considered it, chewing on a leaf.

Maybe the bonus was too small to count as a full point? Like, 0.4 Physical or something? But that's so little... It can't be right. All this for a quarter of a level's worth? The ice pond has given me seven points already, and it can provide at least double overall. I know it's E-Grade, while the bush is F-Grade, but I refuse to believe the difference is that large.*

Maybe it compounds as I consume more leaves? I'm not the slightest bit high yet.

He licked a couple more leaves, then sucked on a few more. No more status screens came, but he didn't mind that much. Points were just numbers; he had a fist, and the fist was always stronger than math. The professor might disagree, but if so, she should go fight a goblin tribe.

Jack giggled at the thought of the elderly lady lecturing the goblins.

Right. It's okay, my bushy friend. You can keep your extra points. Maybe you need them more than I do. I mean, licking any more leaves would be inappropriate, right?

Giggling again, Jack decided to explore his class choices. He'd planned to retreat and do this at the cave, but why? If there was a reason, he couldn't remember it, so it didn't matter.

Jack took in the wall of text and giggled. He liked reading. He squinted as he approached the screens, his nose almost touching them, and he tried to make out the letters.

He struggled to focus for some reason, but it didn't matter. Why hurry?

> **Goblin Fighter:** Goblins are genetically engineered lifeforms that make for great first enemies. They are usually slain by the native species during a planet's Integration, but when they aren't, they proliferate rapidly. If left unattended, goblins can span planet-wide empires, with peak specimens even reaching the D-Grade in power.

> Goblin fighters rove the cosmos while destroying goblin infestations, as well as any of the many variants. They are perfectly equipped to locate, investigate, and exterminate them, and they are rewarded handsomely for their services.

Goblin fighter sounded cool! But also dumb. He didn't want to spend his life hunting stupid, annoying goblins.

> **Survivor (Elite):** Survivors specialize in withstanding extreme environments. They usually act by themselves, exploring desolate planets, infiltrating monster-infested biomes, and expertly treading the razor-sharp edge between life and death.
> Survivors don't always succeed in their endeavors, but they almost always escape with their lives. Adapting is their second nature.
> *"Where there is life, there is opportunity."*

Elite. That was a new word. Well, not quite—it's new for the System. In video games, which the System was proving similar, elite meant strong. One plus one equals two.

The first paragraph excited Jack tremendously. He almost chose it on the spot before reading the next one, too. He scowled.

I don't want to be a turtle. I want to fight!

He remembered the burning of his body as steel flooded his veins, the razor-sharp awareness that came with life-or-death battles, the sweet release of violence when he was at the good end of it. The exuberance of being completely one with himself, in his element, vibing.

He giggled. Just thinking about it got him fired up again.

Escaping from the bear had been fun too, just not as fun as punching the shit out of things.

Then again, Jack didn't want to die, either. His entire reason for trying so hard was to survive—and, taking things one step further, did he want to become a punching monster? Or was he, at heart, a survivor? Maybe most survivors were weak and failed often, but he could be strong!

> **Pugilist (Elite): Pugilists are one of the few F-Grade combat Classes ranked as Elite. This adjustment was made to reflect their tiny proportion compared to other Classes, as well as the difficulty of reaching Level 15 as an unarmed, non-magical combatant. Pugilists are devastating in close combat, an advantage counterweighted by their lacking survivability. Their battles are simple, straightforward, and barbaric. When a Pugilist enters the fray, there are no half-measures; it is victory or death.**
> ***"Fist means power."***

This was exciting. The Pugilist's description sounded underwhelming compared to the others, but Jack's blood boiled as he read it. He needed no fanfare, no flowery words; simple meant strong. The straightforwardness drew him in, the hidden resolve behind these seemingly simple words.

Fist means power. He savored the phrase. He liked it.

A corner of his mind whispered that the Pugilist was suicidal, and Jack's main drive was survival. Punching was fun, but it wasn't the main goal.

Everything else in his mind resisted that thought. Punching *was* the goal. In a moment of clarity, he realized that survival had been the starting point and a handy excuse, but at the core of his being, he just loved to fight.

Jack Rust willed himself into a Pugilist.

> **Congratulations! You are now a Pugilist (Elite).**

Yay!

> **Physical subcategories unlocked: Strength, Dexterity, Constitution. Stats distributed. Class Skill unlocked: Drill (I). More Class Skills will be unlocked at regular Level intervals.**
> **Drill (I): Passive Skill. Your punches now carry a hint of drilling power, letting them penetrate hard defenses.**

Woo! New stats! New skills! Armored magic bears, here I come!

If the System still followed video games, Strength represented his muscle mass, Dexterity his fine control over said muscle mass, and Constitution his ability to withstand damage.

However, just as Jack willed the blue screens away, his world changed.

He was no longer in a forest. He wasn't on Earth, either. An endless expanse stretched before him, a desert of tremendous proportions. Purple sand reached the horizon, and the sun burned so hot he questioned how he wasn't on fire yet.

Looking down, Jack understood the answer. He had no body.

A loud growl drew his attention, a sound loud enough to burst his eardrums, if he still had any. His gaze met a colossal serpent, a form resembling a bipedal, spiked crocodile. His eyes widened.

Godzilla!

> **Lizard Titan, Level ??? (C-Grade)**

C-Grade!

Jack couldn't even see its level, but C-Grade now felt so far beyond him. Just how wide were the gulfs between grades?

The massive beast was tall like a mountain, and—why was it growling? Jack squinted, and there, before its feet, stood a human. He was tiny—normal-sized, but tiny compared to the beast.

Jack quickly scanned him as well.

> **Human (Earth-4), Level ??? (C-Grade)**
> **Faction: Exploding Sun**
> **Title: Eighth Ring Conqueror**

Exploding Sun? Eighth Ring Conqueror?

Jack didn't understand anything.

This man was bald with plain features, donned elegant yellow clothes, and wore a red cape. However, his simple face was practically chiseled from stone. Facing the full brunt of the beast's fury, he only clenched his fist. He opened his mouth, and his words fell on Jack's ears like thunder.

"Fist means power."

He jumped hundreds of feet into the air. Sand and rock crumbled below his feet, and from the distance, Jack could only stare.

The man reached the height of the beast's chest and punched. It was just a simple punch. Yet, the moment his arm completed its motion, a storm of violence erupted. The sky shook and the earth rumbled from the momentum of this one punch, and as it met the beast's colossal, scaly chest, both exploded.

One punch drilled through the beast, mincing scales, flesh, and bones alike. It wasn't merely a fist, but an irresistible force of nature.

This is a real punch.

The scene replayed itself in Jack's mind, ten times, a hundred times. This ideal punch stabbed through the air and drilled into the beast's body, and he soaked in how everything worked. It wasn't just a punch. There was something more, something so much more.

At some indeterminate point, it clicked.

Jack had a sudden realization. Understanding dawned on him, and the next moment, it receded, as if he wasn't able to utilize it yet. It retreated into the depths of his mind and locked itself there, waiting, slumbering.

The essence of what a fist was and what it could be. An insight greater than anything he'd ever comprehended. An understanding so gigantic and world-breaking it should have been impossible. He couldn't fathom it yet, but when he could, it would already be inside him, shining like a beacon.

When he exited his own mind and returned to the purple desert, time seemed frozen still.

A large hole had been punched clean through the beast's chest, wide enough to fit a house, perfectly round, and completely empty. As the large body began to collapse, the man looked at his fist and shook his head.

"Still not enough," he muttered.

The vision disappeared. Jack was back in the forest, but all vestiges of highness had evaporated from his system. He was covered in cold sweat, shivering, and his eyes were wide as saucers.

"What the fuck was that..." he whispered.

C-Grade... Holy hell, those guys are gods.

It was nothing like the movies. He'd felt the man's power in his *soul*, comprehended the seeming invincibility of the giant beast. Seeing superheroes on-screen was completely different than experiencing their power first-hand.

Jack sat on his butt, then looked at his own fist. He managed to clench it.

"Is that... a Pugilist?" The shock in his voice turned to awe. "Such power... If I can have it too, how amazing would that be?"

His feelings wavered. He was overtaken by childish excitement and equally childish fear. He had no doubt that the vision he'd seen was real. Those things existed. The monsters in the dark were part of his world now, and he had the strength to fight them—no, he didn't have it yet, but he could earn it.

The class hadn't given him extra muscles but something so much better.

Now shivering from excitement, Jack regained his bearings. He stared at the bush accusingly.

I must be careful... Even with 38 Physical, I still lost my mind a bit. Oh, right! My Physical was broken into Strength, Dexterity, and Constitution. I wonder how much I have.

He opened his status screen and immediately gasped.

What? That high? This is impossible!

Chapter 15
Beary Strong

> Name: Jack Rust
> Species: Human, Earth-387
> Faction: -
> Grade: F
> Class: Pugilist (Elite)
> Level: 15
> Strength: 38
> Dexterity: 48
> Constitution: 38
> Mental: 9
> Will: 7
> Skills: Fistfighting (II), Drill (I)

There were so many high numbers. When his Physical broke into three sub-stats, he expected his 38 points to be divided, not tripled.

What does this mean? Did I become three times stronger? And this Dexterity...

He didn't feel three times stronger than before. A bit, sure, but not to such a degree. *What does this mean?*

Thankfully, Jack was a scientist—he did almost have a PhD.

Maybe a point in Physical always meant a point in each of the stats. It's the same thing. Nothing changed. I just saw a simplified version so far.

This hypothesis was based on little, but it made sense. The System wouldn't just triple his power for no reason.

Still, why is Dexterity so much higher? Is it because of the High Speed Bush?

Unlike his other stats, he *did* feel faster than before, more flexible, more in command of his body. It had to have been the bush, unless the ice pond's bonuses were skewed toward Dexterity, which shouldn't be the case. He hadn't noticed an imbalance before, but he could feel it now.

Huh. Then why did my Physical remain at 38 after the bush bonus? Maybe it's not the average, but the minimum? Or some other, more complicated function?

In any case, he could see the utility of breaking down the stats. Keeping things simple at first was nice, but a stat imbalance would be hard to depict in a single number. Plus, if Jack's suspicions were correct, this would allow for greater customization of himself.

There was a question mark on how exactly his points would be distributed from here on. Would he still get two per level, or six? And if it was six, did that mean he could put six into Mental, for example?

I probably still get two points as I did before, but if I want to put one point into the Physical sub-stats, it becomes three subpoints to allocate however I want.

Only that made sense, so it had to be true.

In the end, he didn't intend to scrutinize the System's choices. It was seemingly omniscient and omnipotent. It should have its reasons for everything. Still, he wouldn't be surprised if the professor had already released a peer-reviewed publication criticizing the System's procedures by the time he returned to civilization.

He chuckled.

She can handle herself... probably.

It was a grim thought. Not all people were as equipped as him to handle a global overhaul... Then again, neither was he. The professor was a genius. She'd pull through.

Jack snapped out of his thoughts. The clearing was as quiet and empty as ever. That was lucky. He'd overstayed his welcome while high. He didn't know how long the vision took in real time, but he must have been idling here for at least twenty minutes.

Minutes...

Another sobering realization. He hadn't considered time in minutes for... a while. The sun's position had been enough.

Done reminiscing, Jack decided it was time to get going. He'd already taken everything he could from the bush, and there was nothing else in the clearing.

His feet took him into the bushes and up a hill, heading in the familiar direction of his cave. He still had to go into the pond again to see if he could take any extra steps—or rather, how many.

Midway to the cave, he stopped. Yes, he had to try the ice pond... but he really wanted to see the effects of Drill. He was far enough from the clearing now. Nothing was following him.

Clenching his fist, he shot it at a random tree trunk.

The moment it made impact, he sensed the change. His punch was so straight and controlled that no energy escaped the point of impact. Instead, its entire momentum bypassed the tree's surface and exploded deeper, not mitigated at all by the hard bark.

The entire tree shook—leaves fell from its branches, and the trunk itself groaned and cracked from the inside.

Jack stared at his fist in surprise, then grinned. Its next target would be an earth bear and its stupidly hard magic fur.

There were a few more things to settle, but they all went by quickly.

The ice pond was the first. After submerging his entire body into it for the first time and withstanding the ensuing agony, the cold closed his wounds, healing him completely in the span of a few minutes. For the zillionth time, Jack thanked his lucky stars for spawning this gift of the gods beside him.

Due to his increased stats, he also managed to take another two steps into the ice pond. It was great progress! He was now at two thirds of the way to the waterfall. As he'd approached, he could now better estimate it would take him thirteen steps, and he'd made nine.

One last thing was left, and that was to test his strength.

I hope all that pain bears fruit... he thought, walking outside his cave and surveying the poor rocks and trees.

He had earned four levels for beating the goblins. He'd also taken two steps into the ice pond, each giving him a point in Physical—well, to be more precise, in each of his new physical stats—so his stats had risen by the equivalent of five levels. Moreover, he hadn't really measured himself in a human scale in... a long time.

He itched to know how strong he was.

With a stupid grin, he stood before a boulder that reached up to his waist. There was no way a pre-System human could lift this thing. Jack bent his knees, grabbed it by the edges, and lifted.

"Heave-ho!"

The boulder shot up.

"Wha—"

He let it fall, and it did with a massive thud that shook the night forest. "What the..." he repeated, looking at his own two hands. "Did I do that?"

Knowing he was strong was one thing. Actually comparing himself to the pre-System him was a different matter altogether. More real.

He flexed his fists, sensing the raw power that lay within, just waiting for him to direct it. Without thinking, he turned and punched a tree. Its entire trunk shook, leaves fell from above, and a few birds that perched on its branches hurried to fly away.

Jack's hand was unhurt.

He jumped on the tree. Each leap could easily reach the lower branches, and his agility was such that he was certain he would never fall, even if he didn't have the terrible gripping power that he currently possessed.

Letting himself drop, he somersaulted once midair before landing on his feet. It was easy.

"Wow..." he exclaimed breathlessly.

He thought back to the pain, the panic, the anguish he forced himself through to survive. Every fight brought him close to death, starting from that very first goblin, but he always survived. The goblin shaman had almost destroyed him, but he'd prevailed.

It had been hell, and still was—but not for nothing. With danger came power.

Now, he was no longer weak, no longer helpless. He wasn't a pest that had to hide from little goblins. He was a strong player in this dungeon. He'd earned it.

Jack clenched his fist tight, and the relief that flooded him was enough to almost bring tears to his eyes. He tightened his lips and nodded.

This wouldn't be the end. There were the bears to fight, and the monkeys, and the damn wolf that saw him as a bug. Outside this dungeon, there was a wide world, too. Gone were the days of endlessly toiling away at a lab table.

Jack always yearned to feel alive. His wish had been granted. An entire planet waited for him after he conquered this dungeon, an entire galaxy, even, full of mystery and power for him to grasp, and he had a head start. He was so excited he got goosebumps.

The bald man had been at the C-Grade. The Animal Kingdom, the power that now apparently controlled Earth, was B-Grade. Jack didn't know what those meant exactly, but he would reach that level of power, and then, even higher. There was so much to learn, so much to discover, so much to experience. He would go all-out in a world that finally fit him. He would thrive. He would *live*.

He could see the path. F, E, D, C, B... and A. Sleep with the lights on, world. Jack Rust is coming.

However, long dreams would have to wait. First came the bears, the dungeon, and then the world.

Jack chuckled and shook his head as he walked back to his cave.

How far I've come, and how far there is to go.

Satisfied from a day and night full of rewards, and filled with dreams for the future, Jack went to sleep. The night was still young, and he deserved to rest well for once. A few hours after the sun rose, Jack was already crossing the forest toward the bear territory. They would have the honor of being his next opponents—or prey.

His fists itched to face a bear head-on, but he kept himself in check. Even the weakest earth bear was at level 13, and though he could probably take it, every close battle carried a substantial risk of death. There was no need to throw his life away.

Stronger, faster, and harder than ever, Jack fell into a routine he knew well. He crafted a trusty stone hammer—heavier than the previous one—and snuck around the edges of bear territory, aiming for weaker specimens.

The worst part about traveling this area of the forest were the carcasses. Not the eaten ones—bears left little behind—but the ones that had been broken for sport. Earth bears were quite sadistic, apparently. That was bad for the nearby wildlife and good for Jack, because it meant he could keep killing them without moral remorse.

He averted his sight and kept going. Unfortunately, the bears had a slim population, so it took him a long time to finally find one. When he did, it was level 15.

Normally, he would have let this go and looked for another bear. However, he'd already spent a good chunk of time looking.

Jack was a biologist that focused on evolution. He knew about bears. The normal kind—the non-magical ones—weren't territorial, unlike what the System suggested. However, he could adapt his knowledge.

Since these bears were territorial, and given the places at which he'd located them, he assumed they'd split their wider territory into chunks, and each bear got one chunk. That was why he'd spent so long looking for one; he'd been searching the chunks where he'd already killed a bear.

Due to his job, Jack had visited this reserve many times, enough to know its general layout by heart. He understood the size of the bear area. Assuming all chunks were similar in size, he estimated there were thirteen to sixteen earth bears. That wasn't much. It also meant he'd probably run out of low-level bears and have to dive deeper soon.

He still hadn't seen the bear boss or any stronger variant than the earth bear—all in due time. Jack was finally ahead of the curve, and he'd take full advantage of it.

The clock was still running. He wasn't going to search the entire area for a slightly weaker bear. Level 15 would do.

He climbed a tree and held his stone hammer at the ready. The bear didn't come by, and Jack scowled as he rushed to another branch, keeping tabs on the bear's location by its growls and other sounds.

Two hours later, after failing yet another branch ambush, his patience was growing thin.

Why wait for hours when I can just kick its ass?

Because I might lose, he replied, regaining himself. He wasn't rash or stupid. Even if on the clock, rushing things would bring ugly consequences. He was nowhere near the king of the forest.

Another hour later, as the sun reached its peak, Jack heard the bear approach. He tensed up in joy. *It's happening!*

A brown shape with yellow splotches came under his branch, its wide ass swerving from side to side as it walked. Jack descended.

Bonk!

He stood over its headless corpse, frowning. This was quite anticlimactic...

Not even a level up... Fine. I'll find a level 14 or less and try to fight it.

Since he now understood how their territories worked, he could start from the ones at the edge of the bear area, which, according to game logic, would have the weakest bears.

And it worked! Only half an hour later, Jack parted the leaves of a bush to spy on a level 14 behemoth. It was busy stomping a bunny's corpse to death.

At least eat it, you fat prick.

Coincidentally, this was the same bear that chased him down before—he would recognize it everywhere. Jack's spirit burned at the thought of finally taking revenge.

He set the stone hammer aside and cracked his neck, then his knuckles as he prepared himself for a good fight. Ambushes were easy but time-consuming, and he didn't want to waste hours on each bear. With some luck, he could take one down without major injuries—and, if not, he was confident in escaping. He'd done it with half the stats.

Now ready, Jack bumped his fists together one more time, then calmly walked toward the bear. When he stepped on dry wood, it turned to look, yellow eyes easily spotting him. It growled. Jack held its gaze and grinned.

The bear was confused now. It recognized this creature, but last time, it had run away. Everything tried to escape when it growled. What was this?

Jack stepped between the trees and approached the bear. They weren't in any sort of clearing, so the terrain would only help him.

The bear growled again and charged. Jack charged right back, releasing a roar of his own.

An enraged behemoth was charging right at him, fangs wide and claws racing to tear him apart. For a moment, he reconsidered all his life choices; then, he realized the bear was slow. Too slow.

It lunged, but he jumped to its side. The bear rose on two feet to rip him apart.

He ducked under a hairy arm, then another. Jaws snapped shut before his face but couldn't touch him. He swerved aside, dodging a blow before stabbing two quick jabs into the bear's fur. Like last time, a yellow patch rose to meet him.

This time, however, the yellow patch was ineffective. Jack felt the difference. His fist slammed into protected fur and sent the impact through it, directly onto the bear's skin. He couldn't go deeper yet, unfortunately, but this was already a massive improvement.

The bear growled as it stepped back, falling on all fours. It eyed him warily. The impact had clearly hurt it.

Jack didn't eye anything warily—he only attacked harder.

He was on the offensive. Blow after blow rained on the bear. Each of his attacks couldn't hurt it too much, but when they stockpiled, the weight became unbearable.

The bear frothed at the mouth. Claws, jaws, even the back of paws and body slams came his way, but Jack dodged it all. After consuming the High Speed Bush, speed was his specialty, and it was also this bear's weakness.

He grinned at what was happening.

In game terminology, this bear was a slow tank, and he had both the speed to dodge everything and the skills to gradually decimate it. Thanks to Drill and the High Speed Bush, he countered the bear completely.

That's not to say it was easy. Each of the bear's strikes were cataclysmic, and though they were slow to Jack's eyes, a pre-System human couldn't even see them coming. For Jack, dodging one attack was easy, but the more the bear attacked, the higher his chances were of making a mistake.

He kept his cool. Danced around the bear, gracefully weaving between attacks as he landed his own. His brain was honed and at maximum capacity the entire time.

The fight took place at great speed but still lasted more than three minutes. Jack didn't make a single mistake.

Eventually, the bear slowed down. Jack's punches increased in strength and volume, and the large beast was taken down. Its head slammed against the ground, leaving Jack panting, sweaty, and victorious.

He raised a fist into the air and roared his triumph.

"Fuck yeah!"

He'd finally defeated an earth bear, these devils, for the first time!

No level up yet, but they would come. Now that he knew he could handle it, Jack's hunting speed would increase by many times. The fight required his full focus, but it wasn't too difficult. He hadn't even come close to getting hit. He could easily be consistent for that long.

Grinning and leaving his stone hammer in that random bush, Jack went on with his hunting. The earth bears of the Greenway Natural Reserve were quickly whittled down, from the weakest to the strongest. Over the next twenty-four hours, eight more monster bears lost their lives to the forest's rising star.

Until, on the ninth bear, the rising star met the king.

Chapter 16
A Summit of Kings

It happened as Jack was stalking his ninth earth bear in a row, a prowling beast at level 18. In the past day, he'd already cut down their population by more than half, meaning only the high-level ones were left. He'd even seen one at level 20 but avoided it.

He'd also gotten two levels for his hunt, bringing him to 17. By willing the free points into his Physical, all stat points were distributed evenly between Strength, Dexterity, and Constitution. He could always choose a different ratio, such as putting all points into Strength, but the balanced approach had worked well so far, so he stuck with it.

Name: Jack Rust
Species: Human, Earth-387
Faction: –

> Rank: F
> Class: Pugilist (Elite)
> Level: 17
> Strength: 44
> Dexterity: 54
> Constitution: 44
> Mental: 9
> Will: 7
> Skills: Fistfighting (II), Drill (I)

As Jack stalked this bear, debating whether to attack it or not, a low growl hummed through the trees.

Jack knew this growl. He instantly froze. He didn't dare to even look around.

The earth bear also recognized the growl. It looked around in sudden agitation, the fear clear in its yellow gaze. A dark shadow shot out of the bushes straight for it. So fast, even Jack's enhanced kinetic vision only saw a blur.

The bear panicked. The sound it made wasn't a growl, closer to whining. Jack didn't know bears could make that sound. Yet, the dark blur showed no signs of stopping, and the bear could only try to fight back.

Its claws sliced, but the blur ducked under them and smashed hard into brown fur. The bear flew back—Jack could at most make it stumble—and made a desperate attempt to bite down on its assailant. It missed, and at the same moment, another set of jaws found its way around its neck. With a deep crack, the earth bear was dead.

Jack was still frozen.

A dark wolf now stood atop the bear's corpse, holding it by the throat. The two bodies were similar in size, but the wolf's power was far, far higher. The bear Jack would need several minutes to dismantle, if he didn't die first, had fallen in two attacks.

> **Black Wolf, Level 49 (Elite) (Dungeon Boss)**

It was the second time he'd met this king of the forest. He had grown a lot since that first crossing, but the difference between them hadn't closed by much... and Jack's only way to escape this dungeon was to defeat it.

He did, however, notice a scar on its snout. It wasn't there last time, he was sure. Was there something that could rival the king in this forest, or did an earth bear get lucky before its death?

The wolf glanced at Jack, and he quickly looked at the ground, all thoughts forgotten. He didn't dare challenge it—not yet. However, before averting his sight, he'd managed to catch a glimpse of its eyes.

One would expect the Dungeon Boss to be a regal, proud, sage-like existence. It wasn't. In its eyes, Jack only saw a fierce animal, a killer. Cold sweat drenched his back, and his legs began to shake a bit. His fight or flight instincts didn't even activate. What level 17? If this wolf wanted to kill him, he could do nothing to resist.

Still feeling its gaze on him, as if deliberating its next move, Jack repeated his trick from last time. He fell on his knees and bowed to the wolf, acknowledging its strength and status as the king.

The wolf still didn't look away. Jack stayed like that, perfectly still, trying to calm his breathing. Time slowed. Was it a second, a minute, or an hour?

Finally, the sound of fur dragging on dirt came. The wolf darted away, easily carrying the massive earth bear in its mouth and disappearing between the trees, headed toward the center of the reserve.

Jack remained kneeling. Only after another minute did he dare stand. He looked at the ground ahead of him, where the bear's blood had dyed the dirt red.

"Fuck me..." he whispered.

He'd thought himself ahead of the curve, and in a way, he was. He could finally choose his prey instead of settling for what was not prohibitively difficult. However, strength brought a price.

Last time, the wolf hadn't even glanced at him. He'd been an ant to its eyes. This time he had clearly received its interest. Had it recognized his increase in strength and considered him a future threat? Or was his current power a source of worry anyway?

In any case, Jack could clearly see the pattern. The wolf would spare an ant, but not an elephant.

The next time it met Jack, it wouldn't let him go. He had to hurry and get the strength to protect himself... or hide in his cave until someone rescued him. But Jack hadn't come all this way to cower. He clenched his fists as sparks jumped in his eyes.

I must get stronger, and fast.

He was still very much on the clock—a clock he'd helped accelerate.

Thanks to Jack's hunting, the wolf's prey was dwindling. Both of them hunted the same big game. The fewer the bears became, the higher the chances of Jack and the wolf meeting, and it would eventually realize the implications. It might even come directly after him.

This threw a wrench into Jack's plans. He'd been an idiot. He could no longer hunt bears, as they were needed to satiate the big wolf's appetite. He had to start hunting monkeys, level up fast, then defeat both the monkey and bear boss. Then, maybe he'd be strong enough to match the wolf if he used his human intelligence to its maximum extent.

The moment he'd had that thought, Jack's face went hard as a rock. His chances were grim, but he had to try.

A second growl cut through the forest. Jack became rigid, thinking the wolf had returned, but this growl was different. He dove back inside his bush.

From deeper inside the bear area, a massive form slowly made its way through the trees. A giant of a bear, a walking tank. Its body was at least nine feet in length, probably more, and it was taller than Jack while on all fours. Its fur wasn't just covered in yellow splashes, it was riddled with yellow, rock-like surfaces that served as shields, and its claws were so long and sharp, they cut grooves through the dirt.

Jack raised his brows.

> **Rock Bear, Level 30**
> *When Earth Bears mate, they have a small chance of producing Rock Bear offspring. This variant is bigger, stronger, and more closely attuned to earth than a normal Earth Bear. Rock Bears command the innate respect of Earth Bears, allowing them to form and control packs that share a single, large territory.*
>
> *In the Ursus Forests of planet Ursi, Rock Bears are regional overlords, only under the Tyrant Bears in strength. Their power usually reaches the E-Grade.*
>
> *This particular Rock Bear is the group boss of the bear monsters of the Forest of the Strong.*

That was an extensive description that did Jack little good besides providing context. From the earth bear description, there was a planet called Ursi that probably had a lot of bears—ursus meant bear in latin, and ursi was the plural of that, though what did latin have to do with the System? Now, he also knew earth bears were weaker than rock bears, which were, in turn, weaker than the so-called tyrant bears.

He could even understand how their ecosystem worked, and how they formed pack hierarchies that stretched through a large number of smaller sub-packs. Unfortunately, all that interesting knowledge couldn't help Jack in the slightest.

The rock bear approached the spot where the previous bear's blood still smeared the ground. It hadn't noticed Jack yet—thankfully he'd been hiding somewhat farther away.

It sniffed the ground, then raised its large head in the direction the wolf had taken. Jack could see its eyes from where he was hidden. The bear was angry, bloodthirsty, but also hesitant. There was a grudge in the way it looked toward the center of the reserve, one it could not fulfill.

Jack held his breath. Would the bear boss fight the wolf? That would be such a waste of levels for him...

In the end, the bear didn't give chase. After staring, it stood on its hind legs—God, was it tall—and smashed a paw into a nearby tree, easily breaking it into pieces. Jack blinked in surprise.

The bear then released a massive, earth-shaking roar, the likes of which Jack had never heard. It would obviously reach the wolf's ears—though it wasn't a challenge. It was just a venting of the rock bear's impotent rage.

There was just nothing it could do.

But the wolf is proud, thought Jack. *Will it come after the bear boss next?*

It was a worthy consideration, unless there was some rule that forbade bosses from fighting each other, but that just sounded stupid. There had to be some eco balance. A bear boss without its pack wouldn't be much of a boss, and Jack assumed the System had the ability to craft circumstances that would favor the creation of a balanced monster ecosystem.

Maybe it did, and I was the one who broke the balance, somehow. Maybe the goblins served as a food source for the other monsters, including the wolf, and me killing them forces everything to fight each other.

Is the dungeon going to implode on itself? Am I the pest here?

It was an amusing thought. Then again, if the System cared about its delicate ecosystem, it shouldn't have placed him in the fucking middle of everything.

These were Jack's thoughts as he watched the rock bear steam in rage. However, when it turned around to leave with heavy steps, new ideas sprung in his mind.

If the wolf hunts down this bear, as it probably will, I will lose a bunch of levels. I need those levels. Unless... I kill the bear first.

This sent his mind spinning in a wholly new direction. *Can I take it right now?* he asked himself, not believing his own thoughts.

It's just a bigger bear. It's stronger and more durable, but not much faster than the earth bears. I can ambush it just like the others, and if worse comes to worst, I can probably run away. Plus, its increased defense can do nothing against my Drill punches.

A plan was taking form in Jack's mind, and as more and more ideas sprung up to support it, he was overtaken by equal parts anticipation and disbelief.

Our level difference is large, but each individual level matters less and less the more I climb. It's not about the raw number, it's about percentages. This bear is a bit over one and a half times my level. When I killed a level 13 bear at level 7, wasn't the difference even greater? And it still died to a single, well-timed strike from my stone hammer.

I no longer have the hammer, and making a new one would take too long, but my punches shouldn't be that far off. Its head can't be made of rock. If I can pull off an ambush, I can probably kill this bear and shower in levels.

Oh, God... I can't believe I'm considering this.

But he *was* considering it. And the more he thought, the more reasons he found to reaffirm this crazy course of action.

If I delay until I'm certain of victory, the wolf might kill the bear first, and I'll lose all those levels I desperately need. No. I can't let this opportunity go to waste. It's already near impossible to kill the wolf and escape this dungeon. If I don't take some risks, I'll never make it.

Slowly, everything came to a point. Jack's body moved by itself, stealthily following the level 30 titan of a bear. His eyes sharpened.

I must hunt this bear. Right now.

CHAPTER 17
JACK RUST VS. BEAR KING

The rock bear's steps were slow and heavy as it trudged through the forest, heading for the depths of its territory. This entire bear area belonged to it; the earth bears were only renting small parts.

As they dove deeper into the forest, bear first and Jack second, the scenery didn't change much. The trees remained normal, pre-System varieties, the chirping of birds filled the air, and uneaten corpses still littered the ground, proof of these bears' monstrosity.

Their path crossed another bear, a stunning level 20, but it reverently made way for the rock bear, which didn't even look at it. An hour later, the rock bear reached a small lake in the middle of a clearing, where a stream branched off to head for the northwestern end of the reserve.

This lake hadn't been here before the System, Jack was certain.

A rock outcropping stretched over the lake, and the bear stopped there. Its enormous body—it must have weighed at least a ton—splayed fully on the rock, which held without a problem. It rested, but Jack could still see the clouds in its mind. It was clearly distraught. The black wolf was killing its kin, and there was nothing the rock bear could do about it besides assisted suicide.

Of course, the fact they'd walked an hour to get here sent chills down Jack's spine. The rock bear arrived at the site of battle less than a minute after it was over. It had clearly been in the area already, looking for whomever was killing its kind like flies. This beast had been on his trail.

If the wolf hadn't shown up, and Jack had been the one to attack the level 18 bear, it was very probable the rock bear would have caught up before the battle was over. Jack would be pincer-attacked, and there was no way he was getting out of that alive.

The black wolf accidentally saved him. Jack, unfortunately, would have to do the exact opposite.

For now, he stayed hidden in a distant bush, observing the rock bear's lair. The small lake—more a pond than a lake—was spawned in a clearing where the only notable feature was the rock outcropping that stretched over one quarter of the pond's area like a pier.

This area was beautiful. Jack could see why the bear had taken it as a lair.

Fortunately, it was also pretty handy for an ambush. The bear was currently resting on its rock outcropping, so, when it left, it would probably head for the nearby edge where the first trees stood. One of those trees had thick enough foliage for Jack to hide in. There, he would have a good shot at success.

Without leaving himself more time to consider his actions, he made a big circle around the clearing to arrive at its back side. He then moved slowly to his chosen tree, less than fifty feet away from the bear. It wasn't a short distance, but Jack knew better than to underestimate an animal's senses—especially a magical one's.

His high stats made it easy to quietly climb the tree, and before long, Jack lay on a branch ten feet off the ground, completely still and with his ears stretched. A bug climbed on his back, and he let it. Another paraded before his nose, and he gently blew it away.

The ridiculousness of it all was blatant. He, Jack Rust, was trying to ambush a van-sized magical bear and kill it with his bare hands. He'd been in a laboratory only a week ago, doing boring things for boring people, and he was excited to catch a rare caterpillar six days ago, when the System descended.

No, not descended—integrated. That was the proper terminology, according to the blue screens.

What was the world like right now? How did people react when they weren't trapped by themselves in a deadly dungeon? What happened to society and politics? Was there resistance? People had guns and nuclear weapons, there was bound to be resistance. Then again, the System seemed quite omnipotent so far. Nuclear weapons might only be a tickle to an alien starcraft.

He remembered the announcement from the B-Grade Animal Kingdom, whatever that was. B-Grade sounded strong.

And the announcement warning them about an Integration Tournament in fifteen days, which sounded extremely important. Jack didn't know what it was, but if it included punching stuff, could he maybe join? This dungeon was bound to put him way ahead of the curve if he could survive.

Of course, killing the wolf came first, and he doubted his chances of success...

Jack let his mind travel to forget his tension. He envisioned scenarios of revolutions around the world, of white-collar tyranny and uprisings of battle-hardy nations. He pictured some people like the orcs in movies, ready to go to war and give everything for strength and honor. He saw dozens getting classes as he had, probably in a streamlined way of human ingenuity, and new, strength-based hierarchies springing up from the ground.

What level would it take to catch a bullet? How strong were wizards?

All these beautiful thoughts dispersed like smoke when a tired growl echoed from the clearing. Jack dared peek through the leaves—the rock bear was standing. It made its way from the pond with slow steps befitting its stature, approaching Jack's hiding spot.

His ambush just might work! He panicked. He'd started hoping the bear would choose another way.

What am I doing? Maybe I should just stay hidden. The strongest creature I've killed so far was level 17, and this bear is 30. Who knows what hidden weapons it has? What hidden abilities and magic? I don't even have my stone hammer. This is suicide.

The bear inched closer, mockingly slow.

No, this is the right way. The chances are with me, and I must risk to survive. I can and will kill this bear.

The bear's form kept growing in his eyes.

I'll stay hidden. There's no way I can take it.

It disappeared, too close to his branch to see through the leaves.

I will fight.

A muzzle entered his field of vision, parading below him as if daring him to attack. It was a large muzzle on a long body. Like watching a train go by.

I will stay.

The bear fully entered his sight. It hadn't noticed him, and its head came right below his branch, completely exposed from above. He could even see the individual hairs on its fur. It was the perfect opportunity. Jack steeled his heart.

I will fight.

He let himself fall, using everything he had to strike the bear's head with enough strength to pulverize it. The bear, like all of its kind, looked up just in time to meet his punch with its nose.

The moment Jack crossed eyes with the rock bear, from only a couple feet away, he suspected he'd fucked up.

His punch met the bear's nose so hard, so violently, that a bell-like sound echoed alongside the crack of bones—the inside of its head was rock-hard. Jack's body almost stopped in midair from the recoil.

The bear's eyes flickered, almost passing out. Blood dripped from its ears, and its nose was nearly entirely broken. Its brain threatened to turn into mush, or it partially did. The bear wobbled and almost fell—but *almost* was the key word here.

It was the perfect ambush, but it wasn't enough. And so began Jack's punching marathon against the rock bear. On one side stood a tall, bare-chested man with finely chiseled muscles. On the other, the king of bears.

The rock bear was a tremendous creature. Seeing it from up-close, with nothing between you and a gruesome death, was quite the experience. When Jack rolled on the ground and stood across from it, he gulped. He'd gotten used to earth bears, but this was no earth bear. It was far bigger, stronger, and nastier.

The bear's face was the size of his torso. Stone plates slid on its brown fur as bulging muscles swam underneath, and its sharp jaws released a stench so visceral, he struggled not to gag.

This was a majestic, fearsome beast—and one that was currently injured. Blood dripped from its orifices, and its furious gaze hid clear pain. Its movements were slow, not much faster than an earth bear's.

I can take it, Jack thought and raised his fists. The very next moment, he felt like an idiot. He was tiny.

The bear roared and attacked. Clawed paws whooshed through the air, each strong enough to uproot a tree. Jaws snapped shut before him, and they could easily crush his entire skeleton to paste. The bear's humongous body lumbered after Jack, and getting caught by that thing, even in the slightest, would spell his doom.

Fight or flight? asked his mind.

Fight, Jack responded, and his entire being complied.

All thoughts left his mind. There was no hesitation, no fear. His body was fire and his mind ice. The world slowed as his mind raced at incredible speeds, calculating and telegraphing everything. Facing the primordial fear of a bear, his mind was faster than at any other time, so fast he could glimpse at the million little calculations and adjustments that always happened in the background.

He could feel how his muscles contracted to step back, sense the trajectories his fingers followed to form a fist. When his eyes took in the bear's incoming paw, Jack saw the options his mind instinctively discarded before dodging to the right.

It was a unique sensation, and one that could not be understood until one has felt it.

The bear's attacks came like an avalanche, and its body plowed across the ground like a truck. Jack weaved between them. At this moment, he wasn't a human, but a fly, and he dodged all attacks heading his way. No matter how fast the bear struck, or how many times, it couldn't catch him.

A fist met the bear's hind leg, buckling it. Jack's power could penetrate its defenses but not quite harm it. The damage was minimal. Jack wasn't a fly, but a wasp, darting around the bear and pelting it with annoying stings.

So what if his strikes were weak? They were getting through. The damage was there, just not immediately visible. And, since the bear couldn't catch him, he refused to believe he'd fall from exhaustion before it.

Roar came after roar, strike after strike. As Jack and the bear danced around each other. Their battle moved through the clearing's edges, tearing trees and bushes apart. Jack had to dodge these obstacles too, making things a bit harder, but the bear also took some time to uproot or break them.

Jack bobbed, and weaved, a veritable leaf in a storm, that wasp stubbornly facing an enemy much larger than itself. Yet, he persisted.

One minute turned into many, and the moments dragged on. Jack's body was growing heavier, his mind imperceptibly slower, but his strikes were accumulating. After the first five minutes, he'd struck the bear at least a hundred times, if not more.

His knuckles were flayed from striking stone and hard fur. There was no skin there anymore, only bone that held strong. The pain was great, but his adrenaline-filled brain shut it out.

Sensing the damage, and with its fury continuously mounting, the bear redoubled its efforts. It roared and hit harder, abandoning all defense to catch this vicious little creature. Jack accelerated in response. His body turned into a blur, his punches faster than a blink.

Jack and the rock bear were a maelstrom of violence ripping the forest apart. Where they passed, only destruction followed. Animals scattered in all directions, the birds having long left the area. In the back of his mind, Jack worried that more bears might arrive, but there was nothing he could do about that.

He ducked under a flying bush and took a branch to the chest, ignoring it. It could only scratch his skin. Another bush flew into the bear's face, blinding it. It raised a claw to rip it away, and as it did, Jack found the opportunity to nail a hard straight into its belly, shaking its insides. Something within that stone body gave way.

The bear growled deeply and pounced again. Jack dodged around it, moving to the back and punching again. A leg flew back to meet him, but he was no longer there. The bear jumped to the side, and he barely avoided it, darting back.

Jack was undoubtedly much weaker than the bear. He shouldn't be able to take it in a straight fight, regardless of the ice pond bonuses or his class.

However, he countered it perfectly. His speed was enough to evade everything so long as he made no mistakes. His skills perfectly countered the bear's hard defenses—all that enormous strength was useless if it couldn't catch him.

Plus, the ambush he'd landed at the start had clearly been effective. Even now, the bear still bled from its muzzle, its eyes were bleary, and it occasionally stumbled for no reason. It had internal injuries, not just dizziness. Jack was glad for that.

The only question was, could he last long enough without making a single mistake?

Chapter 18
King of the Ring

Jack and the rock bear kept dancing through the forest, tearing it apart. Trees, bushes, and rocks flew. So did a fox.

After ten minutes, Jack's arms were heavy. The ecstasy violence brought was dying down. His dodges were sloppy, his strikes missed. More than once, he only escaped a swiped claw by a hair's breadth. He was dizzy, exhausted, and the world swam in his eyes.

The bear was equally troubled. It had slowed down considerably, forcing strikes with clear intervals between them. It was also panting, and one time, it even lost footing and collapsed, rising back up that much more whittled down. Its rage hadn't abated, but there was a limit to how much its body could endure, especially after being pummeled by a man with 44 Strength for ten minutes straight.

Jack, too, had his limits.

The human body placed many limiters on itself. The muscles could only operate at 30 percent efficiency, and the brain kept its processes low. Under extraordinary circumstances, these limiters were removed. That was how women lifted cars to save their babies, or how grown men could fight wolves.

If pushed to its limit, the human body was strong, even before the System's arrival. Humans were one of the strongest animals in their weight category, even stronger than most monkey species, and they could only decisively lose to gorillas or big wolves.

When push came to shove, they could release incredible strength and feel no exhaustion. Humans could punch fast, hard, and inexhaustibly.

However, these limiters existed for a reason. To unleash such power, the human body destroyed itself, and it could only last for a small amount of time. Ten minutes was already beyond such capacity.

Jack's entire body burned, and not in the good way. His muscles were in pain, ready to snap. His mind was muddled, overheated, and overworked. He could sense his conscious control over himself slipping away, diving into slumber, and he only acted on instinct now.

Punch, dodge, weave, punch. Duck, slide, punch. Punch. Duck.

The bear was in pain with every step it took. Jack had felt many of its bones breaking under his fists, and many of its organs faltering, but it still stood, refusing to stay down. It was slow but relentless.

Jack, too, kept going, but he was running dry. He'd thrown everything he had at the bear, and his soul was bleeding as he forced himself to draw even more energy.

Retreat was impossible. One of them would kill the other.

Over the next five minutes, Jack wasn't sure what was happening. The bear still stood, that much he knew. It swiped at him occasionally, threw its body over. He dodged by the skin of his teeth, mustered all his energy to throw himself aside. He could only keep going because the bear had slowed down tremendously.

He even fell down thrice, tripping in his attempt to dodge. Every time, the sweet release of sleep almost took him, and every time, he forced his eyes open, forced his body to stand through the pain and keep going. Jack refused to die. He refused to lose.

Injuries peppered his body. Scratches ran over his bare chest and back, and three long gashes covered the right side of his ribs. He didn't remember if he'd been hit. His gums were bleeding from all the gritting, and he'd lost all feeling in his hands. He didn't even know how they remained clenched; they were probably stuck.

There was no pain in Jack's mind, only limitless exhaustion, and it was worse than any pain he'd felt throughout his life. Only the goblin shaman's fire came close to this, but that only lasted for a moment, while Jack's present torment stretched to infinity.

They weren't even moving anymore. Both enemies were stationary, striking each other whenever they found the strength.

The bear growled low, bleeding internally, from many places, and its bones were cracked. Now it no longer stood. Only its arms moved, and it threw them out like stones to hit the human before it, its greatest enemy. It tried its best.

In a flash of lucidity, Jack's eyes met the bear's. There was anger there, hatred, exhaustion. The bear wanted to lay down and sleep, and so did he, but neither did. In the bear's eyes, Jack found understanding and recognition, and so did the bear in his. They acknowledged each other's pain and resolve.

They silently agreed to give it their all until one died, not knowing who would win.

Jack's mind became a haze. His movements were so slight they weren't proper dodges, but the bear missed by itself. It could no longer aim, and after another punch in its face, it couldn't see either.

Move. Duck. Punch. Dodge. Punch. Punch.

Jack couldn't see either. His vision was muddled. When he dodged, he followed the patterns engraved in his body, not reacting to any of the bear's attacks.

Punch. Punch. Punch. Move. Duck. Mo—

Jack slipped, fell, and stayed there. He no longer had the strength to stand. He didn't have the will, either. Every part of his being had bled dry already.

He could only wait there, laying face-down on the ground, for death to come. As his consciousness dissipated, Jack didn't blame himself, nor did he regret anything. He'd tried his best. It simply wasn't enough.

Jack woke up to an oink in his ear.

"Ohh..." he groaned. The little boar next to him, scared, ran away.

With strained, pained movements, Jack forced himself to roll over. He opened his eyes and found the rock bear's muzzle over him, staring, debating which part of him to eat first.

"Cra—" He tried to roll away, but his body refused to obey. He belatedly realized he was in massive pain and released another groan, this one louder. He balled up on the ground and hoped for this to end fast. A whisper from the back of his head said that bears started with the legs or entrails—a gruesome death, in any case. Jack hoped magic bears were more efficient.

However, though he waited, no jaws closed around his body. He looked back again.

The bear was there, but it wasn't moving. It was dead, sprawled on the ground and bleeding from many places. The stones on its fur had been broken, though its menacing yellow eyes were still open.

Did I... kill it?

Jack heaved a massive sigh of relief, then grimaced as his chest rose in pain. When he'd fallen, the bear had already been dead. Maybe it had died a long time ago. Who knows how long he'd spent fighting alone?

A blue exclamation mark blinked in the corner of his vision, and Jack willed it open.

> Level Up! You have reached Level 18.
> Level Up! You have reached Level 19.
> Level Up! You have reached Level 20.
> Level Up! You have reached Level 21.
> Level Up! You have reached Level 22.
> Earth Bear Boss defeated!
> Would you like to despawn the group? Y/N

There was one more screen, but Jack willed it away for now. He sighed again. This was a lot to take in.

First, he split all extra points—there were *a lot* of them—equally among his Physical stats, as he'd been doing so far. For the first time in a while, the increase was noticeable. He could feel his muscles repairing themselves and growing tougher like iron strings. His limbs became lighter, bending easily to his will. His entire body hardened, his skin tightening—a quite chilling sensation.

Finally, he noticed the skin regrowing on his rubbed-off knuckles, and this time, they felt as if made of metal. Despite the pain, he grinned. This was nice.

Without thinking, he turned and punched a nearby tree. The bark exploded at the point of impact, and the softer tissue behind it erupted out by the power of Drill.

Jack's grin widened even further, then he winced. That foolhardy move aggravated his injuries. He was just too excited to *not* try out his power. It was amazing how he kept growing beyond what his mind indicated was the limit.

Now, he was *strong*.

The extra points hadn't healed him magically, they'd helped recover his energy a bit. With energy came thought, and with thought, Jack realized he needed to get the hell out of here. Bears were attracted to the smell of blood. Given his luck, so were Dungeon Bosses who liked to snack on Jacks.

Actually, that was rather unfair on his part. Jack had many things to complain about, but luck wasn't one of them.

He forced his body to stand before inspecting the status screen.

> **Earth Bear Boss defeated! Would you like to despawn the group? Y/N**

He almost replied yes on reflex. Then, almost replied no on reflex, before finally willing the screen away again.

He didn't want to despawn the bears, as the wolf boss needed something to feed on while he got stronger. However, saying no right now wasn't good, either. What if he met a bear on the way back? He couldn't possibly fight in his current condition. He needed to get to the ice pond as soon as possible.

Since the System gave him no time limit, he simply ignored the screen. If a bear came after him, he'd have to despawn them.

However, why weren't any bears here already?

The sun was falling toward the horizon, meaning Jack had slept for an hour at most. Maybe the bears hadn't dared approach the leader's den yet, but they would. He needed to get out of here.

There was one last blue screen to check. It was the greatest reward he received from the fight, probably, but Jack decided it could wait. He had already delayed long enough.

Amidst groans and panting, Jack dragged himself away. His left hand held his right ribs, where the bear had grazed him with its claws. Every step was painful. There was probably something cracked in there, if not broken.

The trip back wasn't quite agony, as the fight itself had been, but painful nonetheless. He had to stop several times to rest, always fearing a wolf, bear, or even monkey would assault him out of nowhere. His battle with the rock bear hadn't been discreet. Who knew what was heading his way.

Eventually, he made it to his cave without incident. He forced himself through the narrow passage, gritting his teeth to avoid screaming, then dove into the ice pond.

The pond offered healing, but everything had its price. In this case, the price was excruciating pain. Jack's ribs went so cold he thought his soul would freeze over. It felt like needles were sewing his bones together, as if his skin was burnt away and a new one grew in its place.

Ten minutes later, Jack crawled out of the pond and lay on the hard rock, more grateful than ever for its even temperature. He almost drifted asleep before remembering he had one last thing to do—for good measure.

He opened the last status screen, the one he'd put away for later. His greatest reward from the battle.

> **Congratulations! Level 20 reached.**
> **New Class Skill acquired.**

Chapter 19
Crossing the Pond

> Congratulations! Level 20 reached.
> New Class Skill acquired.
> Pugilist Body (I): Your body is a vessel of your fighting style. You gain extra flexibility, reflexes, and durability, as well as increased hardness on your knuckles.

Ohh! Jack's eyes flashed as he read through the skill. *A harder body... and finally, hard knuckles.*

While he'd gotten the skill right after defeating the rock bear, it seemed that reading about it acted as the activation trigger. As soon as Jack finished reading, his body squirmed.

It was a disturbing, unnatural feeling. His skin tightened, then somehow stayed there and felt normal. His insides were clenched, but more like he'd been way too lax until now, and this was his normal state. Moreover, his knuckles momentarily burned, and when he tapped them, the skin felt hard like iron.

He grinned. *Finally.*

With all changes completed, Jack reviewed his status screen before falling asleep.

> **Name: Jack Rust**
> **Species: Human, Earth-387**
> **Faction: -**
> **Grade: F**
> **Class: Pugilist (Elite)**
> **Level: 22**
> **Strength: 54**
> **Dexterity: 64**
> **Constitution: 54**
> **Mental: 9**
> **Will: 7**
> **Skills: Fistfighting (II), Drill (I), Pugilist Body (I)**

Come morning, Jack awoke to the glowing darkness he was used to. The sunlight didn't reach his cave, meaning it was always illuminated by the ice pond's white glow. Nothing changed here. An entirely isolated world.

Jack rubbed his eyes and stood, noting the ease with which he pulled up his body. He felt light as a feather and strong as an ox.

After taking a moment to go over yesterday's events, making sure he wasn't forgetting anything, he directed his gaze to the ice pond. He calculated.

With his five new levels—seven, actually, because he hadn't attempted the pond in a while—he could probably go fairly deeper than he used to. When he last entered, he'd reached the ninth out of thirteen steps. If his predictions were correct... he could now touch the waterfall.

He looked over. A stream of ice-cold, glowing water fell from a crack in the cave wall, dropping three meters to the pond's surface. Despite the pond's small size, the waterfall was substantial. As it fell, it fanned out and came crashing down into the waters.

This ice pond had saved Jack's life many times, both with its healing and the extra stats it provided. It was his lucky star.

However, he feared it. Its freezing cold could reach the soul, and he'd almost died inside it once. Moreover, it was full of mysteries. Where did the water come from? Where did it go? There had to be a tunnel feeding the waterfall's output into an underwater current, but how exactly did this work?

And, finally, what would happen when Jack reached the waterfall? His instinct told him it hid great rewards, along with great danger. The moment he touched it, the cold could skyrocket, and if he was already at his limit, he'd be frozen solid.

He'd still go for it, of course. Jack didn't have the luxury of waiting. Except it required him being at his best, and that made Jack turn away from the pond for now.

"In a few hours," he declared behind his back, "I'll return to defeat you."

He then left his cave.

As he went over yesterday's events, he realized something, and he even brought up the dungeon description to be sure.

> **Forest of the Strong (F-Grade)**
> *A forest where only the strong survive. There are three monster groups, each holding a unique resource and representing a unique challenge. Slay the leader of a group to despawn them.*
>
> *This dungeon is in conquer-or-die mode. Defeat the Dungeon Boss to exit or die trying. We applaud your bravery for entering and wish you the best of luck.*

Three monster groups, each holding a unique resource. Then, where was the bear's resource?

The goblins had the High Speed Bush. Meaning the bears had to have something similar, he'd just missed it due to the heated battle. Now, he would search.

Jack crossed the forest at a brisk pace. He didn't care much about stealth anymore. He didn't need to. With his all-around upgrades, he was confident the only creatures that could threaten him now were the black wolf, which was stealthier than him anyway, and the monkey boss, which shouldn't leave its area.

Even the level 20 earth bear would barely be a serious opponent.

It was a touching thought. The Greenway Natural Reserve—the Forest of the Strong—once held terrifying monsters at every turn, and even the weakest link could eat Jack alive. Now, he was almost the apex predator, and only the strongest were his opponents. How far he'd come.

Less than an hour later, he stood by the rock bear's corpse. It had been eaten in places, probably by other bears, and it looked like shit, but Jack still paused.

This bear had been his greatest opponent so far, the one who'd brought him closest to death. They'd fought with their lives on the line. There was a camaraderie born of that, an acknowledgment—even if it was a man-eating monster.

Jack nodded deeply at the bear, then carried on.

The clearing opened before him soon after. This was his destination, the rock bear's den. Any secret resource had the highest chance of hiding here.

This clearing had a clean pond in its midst, larger than Jack's and without the frigid cold, with a rock outcropping over it. An earth bear currently sat on that rock outcropping, having already assumed the pack's leadership.

> **Earth Bear, Level 20**

Jack didn't give a flying fuck. He walked out of the bushes and met the bear's surprised stare with his own calm one. This earth bear was the largest he'd seen, but so what? He could take it if need be.

The bear stared him down and growled, revealing its teeth. Jack smashed his fists together, producing an almost metallic sound from his knuckles. "Fuck off," he commanded. His intention was clear: he wanted this clearing.

Surprisingly, the bear hesitated. It could have been his confidence, or they may have had a way to sense when they were facing higher-leveled beings. Maybe the bear even smelled the rock bear on him or had spied on the battle from afar and knew he'd been the one to kill it.

Whatever the case, facing Jack's steely stare, the earth bear retreated. Under warning growls, it became one with the overgrowth, then disappeared.

Jack, meanwhile, raised a brow. He hadn't expected that to work.

Huh. Well, better for me.

A single bear wouldn't give him a level now. It was more useful as a wolf meal.

He turned his gaze to the clearing and the pond in its center. This scenery was too striking to be coincidental. He suspected the resource had something to do with the pond, maybe a plant at its bottom or even a cave under the rock outcropping.

As he thought that, and his gaze lingered on the pond inquisitively, Jack barked out a laugh. *I should have known!*

> **Clear Pond (F-Grade)**
> *Clear Ponds are naturally-occurring formations spread around the universe and often used as parts of resorts. Anyone who relaxes in these waters will find serenity, their body will loosen completely, and their potential will emerge, making the entire body sturdier.*
> *The stat increase is a one-time bonus*

Jack grinned at the screen, then at the pond. Some relaxation was exactly what he needed. Without removing his clothes—he only wore pants—he dipped his toes into the pond and was floored.

The temperature was ideal, the water so soft it hugged his pores. This was completely unlike the ice pond's brutal test. This was heaven.

Jack quickly entered the waters, submerging his entire body. The pond was shaped like a shallow bowl with a diameter of twenty feet. At its center, the water was barely over Jack's head, and its shore was smooth and easy to rest on.

It was this shore that Jack leaned against, letting his head fall back and closing his eyes. A week of incessant fighting poured off his body like grime, dissolving in the waters. He was as free as a baby. The next moment, he slipped deeper into the pond, relaxed to the point his body might just dissipate entirely, or maybe his limbs would float away without him noticing.

The feeling was beyond euphoric. It was the single best thing Jack had experienced in his life, and he unconsciously released a long, drawn-out, heartfelt groan of ultimate serenity.

Everything was worth it for this moment.

Despite its extraordinary effects, the pond had no addictive properties, not a hint of mind control. It was just damn good.

Jack couldn't help himself, he deserved it, and stayed in the pond for an hour before finally pulling himself away, rising as a new man. His mind was calm, his spirit steady, and his body elastic without losing any of its hardness.

Clear Pond bonus acquired!
Strength: 54
Dexterity: 64
Constitution: 64

He smiled. His Constitution had increased by ten.

Going by this pattern, the monkeys should have a strength-boosting resource... That would explain why they're so buff.

Jack's path was clear. He would go to the monkeys, gather a few levels off them, defeat their boss, then use the strength-boosting resource. Then... he'd find a way to deal with the wolf.

What could go wrong?

Before that, there was something else he ought to do. After serenity came endless torment. He'd enjoyed the clear pond. Now, it was time to see the end of the ice pond.

Jack faced the ice pond, staring it down like a warrior. The pond ignored him, as ponds ought to do.

He took a deep breath, then stepped in. The first step was refreshing now. The next few were only somewhat chilling.

Jack recalled the times when just dipping his toes into this pond was harrowing. He shook his head and kept going. The fifth step, the sixth. The familiar cold bit into his body but found no purchase. The seventh, the eight. His legs were shivering now, reminding him of swimming in March.

The ninth. This was his previous limit. The pond was deepening too. By this point, it reached his waist, and the cold held his lower body like a vice. It was hard, yes, but he could go on. This was nowhere near his limit.

The tenth step. His legs went numb.

CROSSING THE POND

> **Ice Pond bonus: +1 Physical**

The eleventh step. The temperature dropped exponentially as he approached the waterfall. There was no way this was anywhere close to the freezing point—far below it—but the water here didn't seem to care.

> **Ice Pond bonus: +1 Physical**

The twelfth step. The cold raced through his body and into his head, trying to freeze his thoughts. The waterfall was close now, and drops of liquid ice splashed him occasionally, speaking of temperatures far below the current one. Moving was difficult, but Jack could still go on.

> **Ice Pond bonus: +1 Physical**

The thirteenth step was the hardest. Jack sensed himself turning into ice. His legs were cranky, his body hard to move. The waterfall splashed right before him, showering him in icy droplets. Even breathing was difficult, but Jack persisted.

> **Ice Pond bonus: +1 Physical**

Finally! Jack had crossed the entire ice pond! Only the waterfall was left, but he was already very close to his limit. If he went any farther and the difficulty spiked, as he imagined, he might be in danger...

Except he'd already come this far. He couldn't retreat now. He put a hand through the waterfall and gasped. It was so terrifyingly cold... but he could stand it, for a bit. Probably.

Jack took a deep breath and plunged into the waterfall.

Chapter 20
World of the Waterfall

Jack's arms were outstretched as he dove into the waterfall.

He instantly lost his vision and all his senses. The world disappeared. There was only him and endless cold, so piercing and biting it encompassed everything. He couldn't even feel pain, regret, or fear. All he felt was cold.

Jack's body froze. Not metaphorically—it literally froze into an ice statue. His blood barely kept circulating, and his heart and brain slowed to such a degree, he might as well have been dead.

In his own little world, Jack was alone. Everything had been lost, even his own thoughts were solid ice. He could only stand there, in a blue, empty world.

However, even though his body and part of his mind had frozen, a vestige of his consciousness remained. In that moment, as everything else faded away, Jack experienced absolute clarity. He felt like a god. His mental reserves were limitless, and he had no needs. He could devote everything to any path he desired, and could travel endless miles in a second.

His mind was unfettered, lost in endless tranquility. He was acting on instinct. A scene appeared before him, the scene of a man punching through a mountain-sized beast. The vision he'd only glimpsed before was magnified, analyzed, slowed down, and replayed from multiple angles.

Jack barely had any awareness of himself. He was an empty shell, and that shell was freely flooded with the essence of that fist. He became the fist and the bald man who wielded it. He became the punch that tore through the beast. Became the beast itself, sensing everything as his body was torn apart.

He felt everything. There were so many things that didn't make sense, so many things to learn.

That scene had been carved in his soul with all its details, but his mind hadn't been capable of comprehending them. Now, it was, and though he only understood the tiniest part, his world was growing. Jack was on the cusp of a realization so massive it dwarfed every thought he'd ever had.

It was the same realization that came to him with the original vision, the one that had slipped out of his grasp.

However, just as he was on the verge of understanding, something tugged at him. An annoying feeling rose from his legs, slowly spreading to the rest of his body, as if he were losing control. He frowned in annoyance, unwilling to lose focus over something so small, but the feeling persisted.

A voice in his mind whispered that he should leave. That he was in danger.

Danger? he finally wondered. *Why?*

And the moment he did, the whisper turned into a thundering shout. The vision dispersed as his own voice thundered across the little realm he stood in.

"LEAVE!"

Jack opened his eyes and fell back. He could barely feel his body. The cold had invaded his every nook and cranny, from the wrinkles of his brain to the marrow of his bones. Only the System's magic—his Constitution—saved him. Terror blanketed him.

I almost died, he thought.

Everything was fast. When he fell back, his body practically teleported to the lake's bottom. His lungs were swiftly losing their oxygen, and the water danced over him like crazy.

No, it wasn't that the world was fast. He was slow. Frozen. The only reason his lungs still held was that his bodily functions underperformed so greatly they didn't draw much oxygen.

I will die.

He'd had nightmares like this before. He was slow, much slower than everything. In those dreams, he'd try to rise from his bed, only to fall on the floor, unable to coordinate his body at such painfully slow motion. He'd try to speak, to call for help, but he could only make deep, unintelligible sounds.

His current situation was similar, but it wasn't a dream. He couldn't control his body. He could barely sense his thoughts. And the more he waited, the greater the pain became—everywhere.

Jack was drowning in more than one way. He struggled to stand, it was simply impossible. In the end, he turned around on the pond floor and crawled forward, his arms uncoordinated but enough for such a simple task.

The pain kept growing. His head was about to burst. His eyes were frozen. His lungs burned. His focus narrowed on the simple motions of reaching out, dragging himself forward, and repeating.

Jack was sure he'd die, but for some reason, he pressed forth. He didn't want to go quietly into the night. He would charge ahead, break through everything with overwhelming power, or die trying.

He was a fist.

Time passed. Jack didn't know how he found himself on the shore, but he did. Next thing he knew, he was heaving and panting, his body surrounded by a little pond of his own. Time had returned to normal—*he'd* returned to normal.

He was shivering, and not just because of the cold.

What the hell was that? he thought, still shaken to the core. What had happened? Just how freezing was that damn waterfall? And how had he survived?

He didn't know. His memory was a jumbled mess. All he remembered was the empty blue world, the crawling through ice water, as well as a giant, world-encompassing fist...

What the hell just happened? he repeated the question, then turned to the one entity that might know. The System.

> **Ice Pond bonus: +5 Physical**
> **Ice Pond bonus acquired!**

That was all. Jack was left staring at the first screen. *+5!*

An insane amount! He'd finally gotten all stat benefits of the ice pond, according to the second screen, and they were a total of 18 points in Physical—or 18 in each of his physical stats. That was the equivalent of nine levels!

However, he'd paid dearly for such a boon. He didn't even know how close he'd come to death, but it couldn't have been more than a hair away. If he hadn't retreated at that final moment...

He spared a glance for the waterfall, which still poured down calmly, as if harmless. Only Jack knew the incredible danger that hid below its surface, and he gulped. He swore not to approach it again unless he got significantly stronger. No matter how dire his situation, that was a risk he couldn't afford.

But how dire was his situation, really? With all the ice pond bonuses and the other resources, Jack secured a gain of over ten levels worth of points. Given that he was level 22, his current fighting prowess should be in the mid-thirties. In this forest, besides the wolf boss, who could stand up to him?

Only the monkey boss held a chance, but not for long.

Jack saw a glimmer of hope. If the monkey monsters gave him enough of a boost... maybe fighting the wolf wasn't that far-fetched of an idea.

Jack lay there for a long time, putting his thoughts in order and letting his body readapt to the environment. He shivered, and water kept rolling off him, escaping his body from wherever it had entered.

Eventually, he felt ready. There was a battle to fight. No more distractions, no more bonuses, no more side-quests. Monkeys, then wolf. That was all.

Jack stood, testing his body and finding it in perfect condition. He clenched his fists and prepared himself for battle.

Before he left the cave, Jack spared a final look for the waterfall.

That blue world wasn't a dream... What did it mean? What was it? What secrets does the ice pond hide? And that fist...

He clenched his own. He hadn't forgotten his insights while in the blue world. The fist was a weapon, a path forward. It was relentless, brutal, visceral, and primal. It represented strictness and discipline, the law of the strong, and how everything came down to killing and harming each other.

The fist was *not* a pretty thing. it was necessary and natural, representing the conviction that, in life, there was only the path. Ever forward.

Fist meant power.

These were pretty thoughts, if useless. And yet, he was on the cusp of... something. These ideas and concepts, if properly understood, hid special meaning. The bald man's fist in his vision wasn't merely a fist. It was a world of its own. A way of life. A path.

If only he could comprehend it, he had the feeling his entire existence would ascend to a completely new level.

Jack shook his head. There was something there, he was sure, something vital and fundamental. Something titanic. His instinct screamed it was there, only a paper's width out of his grasp.

Yet, as great as fist magic sounded, he still lacked something, a focus to complete his understanding, fill in the holes and turn thoughts into reality—into magic. And the thing he missed wasn't something he'd discover through thinking. He'd find it through punching.

As it should be.

Jack's eyes shone as he exited his cave with steady steps. The steps of a warrior. His bare feet crunched leaves and snapped sticks. He arrived in the monkey area and stared deep into it.

Red eyes gazed back from its depths. They didn't attack, only waited. And then, Jack hesitated.

The truth was, Jack wasn't a murderer. A killer, maybe, but not a cold-blooded one. The goblins had made it easy by trying to kill him first and being disgusting little fuckers. The bears had eased his doubts by being bloodthirsty, aggressive, and sadistic enough to torture the little animals in their territory even without eating them.

But these monkeys had done nothing wrong. If he massacred them, it would be cold-blooded, undeserved genocide.

Jack followed the law of the jungle. He would do it if he had to... maybe. But he didn't want to become that person. If there could be another way, he wanted to at least give it a shot.

When he'd invaded the monkey territory, they'd only thrown poop at him and chased him out despite having the strength to kill him. They'd let him go. Couldn't he do the same?

Such mercy might doom him.

These were Jack's thoughts as he hesitated, debating what to do. The monkeys still stared from their trees. In fact, they'd approached enough that he could make out their brown, beefy forms.

> **Gymonkey, Level 9**
> *A monkey variant from planet Green. Gymonkeys inhabit all forest biomes and move in packs, defending their territory with flying poop and great muscles. Their unique name comes from their habit of lifting heavy things to increase their strength.*
> *While not particularly aggressive, they are highly territorial.*

The one he scanned was of medium beefiness. The pack that approached contained seven monkeys ranging from levels 5 to 12, from normal monkeys to bodybuilders-turned-primate. He wasn't afraid of them, of course.

They stared at him, and he stared back. *What should I do?*

A deep growl came from deeper in the monkey area. Jack supposed it belonged to a gorilla—though, with how stupid the name gymonkeys was, he assumed the gorilla would have an equally silly one.

A thought struck Jack. They were watching him, and they were magical monkeys. Could they be... intelligent?

The moment he thought that, he sighed. He knew where this would lead, and he felt stupid for even thinking about it. Yet, what choice did he have? Between suicidal, psychotic, and stupid, he'd always choose the latter.

"Hello," he said, surprised at the sound of his own voice. He hadn't spoken to anyone in days, barring crude battle taunts. "I'm Jack."

The monkeys glanced to each other. One of them exclaimed what sounded like *ooh-ah-ah* to him, which he obviously couldn't understand. They made sounds at each other, seemingly conversing about something.

Jack's suspicions were further reinforced. These monkeys clearly understood him, or at least understood he was trying to communicate. They had some degree of intelligence. Moreover, they weren't hostile.

The biologist inside him was intrigued. The survivalist, annoyed—but fuck that guy.

One of the monkeys turned around and motioned for him to follow. Jack, grinning, complied.

He had no idea where this would go, but he really wanted to find out.

Chapter 21
The Strongest Monkeys

Jack followed the gymonkeys into their territory.
They jumped from branch to branch, and trunk to trunk. They didn't have the patience to walk, apparently, and Jack jogged to keep up. The branches above creaked from the weight of those beefy bodies.

As they dove deeper, more monkeys appeared. Some stared at Jack warily, dry poop ready to throw. Others made faces at him or approached to inspect him. One lifted his arm and sniffed his armpit.

Jack laughed. He wasn't afraid of these little guys, of course.

A gorilla appeared from behind a tree. Its entire body was covered in dark fur, unlike the monkeys' brown, and its yellow eyes stared Jack down from below a wide, wrinkled forehead.

Of course, the gorilla was full of muscle. Even its fingers had biceps. Jack was certain that below its fur hid a perfect six-pack.

The monkeys guiding Jack stopped, beginning a series of *uu-uu-aah*. The gorilla ignored them. Walking on its knuckles, it approached Jack. From this close, it reminded him of a grumpy old man. It could have been funny if it wasn't vaguely threatening.

> **Brorilla, Level 16**
> *A gorilla variant from planet Green. Brorillas live with Gymonkeys and train them in the ways of working out. It is due to the Brorillas' unmatched pecks that Gymonkeys use poop to fight—they consider themselves too weak for anything else.*
>
> *Brorillas are usually calm, measured animals. However, if anyone harms their little cousins or invades their territory, they go bananas.*

Hmm... Not the boss, then.

"Hello, I'm Jack," he said.

The gorilla looked him in the eye, then turned to the rest of the monkeys. Their conversation comprised of various monkey sounds Jack couldn't bother to decode, as well as very expressive jumps and body language. One monkey mimed that Jack was strong by flexing its biceps, and another smashed its fists together, conveying a message Jack didn't understand.

The rest of them got it, though. After a series of wondrous exclamations, they began walking again, heading deeper into the forest. The gorilla led, Jack followed, and about ten monkeys trailed behind.

Jack began to suspect this was not a good idea.

However, he was a biologist at heart. As they walked, his previous questions about the gymonkey evolutionary traits resurfaced. Why did they work out? Natural predators? Mating preferences?

Looking around, he spotted something alarming. All the gymonkeys around him were female. The brorilla was—of course—male.

Oh, hell no.

His brows spasmed. If all brorillas were male, as he suspected from their name, and all gymonkeys female, that was ridiculous from an evolutionary standpoint. They seemed too different to mate. Sure, cows and bulls had their differences, but they were the same species. Were these ones, too?

Is that why the System called them cousins in the brorilla description? Oh, come on. This is just ridiculous.

Jack began to suspect their habit of working out was based on mating competition, but he wasn't in the mood to care anymore.

At least their antics were cute. It wasn't every day he saw flexing monkeys and gorillas. His non-scientist self was having fun.

The forest became sparser. More monkeys arrived to take in their weird visitor—all female—making the thick trees groan under their collective weight. One more brorilla showed up, joining its bro after a few questioning growls. When the two brorillas met, they flexed their muscles at each other in greeting, while the surrounding gymonkeys stared in awe.

Jack held back a chuckle. The more ridiculous these monkeys became, the less danger he felt, and the smaller his desire to harm them was.

Eventually, the forest gave way to a clearing, and Jack could only stare.

A massive gap in the trees was occupied by a series of equipment. There were sticks with heavy rocks on both their ends, inclined wooden surfaces, benches with rows of weights above them, as well as a primitive machine that allowed one to pull weights with their legs.

You have got to be kidding me.

It was a forest gym, and a dozen monkeys were currently working out on the various equipment. Sweat dripped down their bodies, and their muscles shivered as they completed one repetition after another. A brorilla was also working out, raising multiple stone dumbbells with one arm, and a few gymonkeys surrounded him, possibly admiring his gains.

Another brorilla stood in the middle of everything, watching the gymonkeys with a sharp eye and barking out corrections when they messed up their stance. Occasionally, its gaze would flick to its bro, and it would nod in manly acknowledgment.

When Jack entered the clearing, everything went silent. The brorillas both struck him with stony gazes, and the various gymonkeys all rushed to equip themselves with poop—there was a reserve pile at a side, as many were already pretty clenched from working out.

The brorillas leading Jack initiated the greeting ritual with the other brorillas. Each of them nodded at every other brorilla individually. Then, all together, they assumed various bodybuilder poses and flexed their muscles, while the armed gymonkeys forgot all about Jack, now blinded by this demonstration of gains.

Done with their greeting, Jack's brorillas explained to their bros what the situation was—unfortunately, Jack

THE STRONGEST MONKEYS

couldn't understand them, but he was fine enjoying the show.

A brorilla motioned at Jack and indicated his lack of muscle. Another shrugged, while Jack's brorillas looked at him questioningly. One threw him a dumbbell, which he caught easily—or tried to, as the blasted thing must have weighed more than the average man. He settled for gritting his teeth and raising it above his head a couple of times.

The brorillas nodded approvingly. To be precise, they all nodded at him, and he returned a nod to each individually. When in gorilla-land, do as gorillas do.

A low, commanding growl cut through the clamor. Jack turned toward the edge of the clearing. A banana tree stood there, looking completely out of place in the forest, but he hadn't noticed it behind the monkeys' homemade forest gym.

From behind that tree, munching on two bananas at once, came the largest gorilla Jack had ever seen.

Big Brorilla, Level 25
A gorilla variant from planet Green. Brorillas usually live with Gymonkeys and train them in the ways of working out. It is due to the Brorillas' unmatched pecs that Gymonkeys use poop to fight—they consider themselves too weak for anything else.

Brorillas are usually calm, measured animals. However, if anyone harms their little cousins or invades their territory, they go bananas. This particular Brorilla is larger and stronger than most, righteously becoming their Big Bro. It is the group boss of the ape monsters of the Forest of the Strong.

Big bro stood a head taller than Jack even on its knuckles. All over its body, muscles bulged underneath its fur, and it walked with the confidence of a multiple-times Mr. Olympia winner. Its large hands, easily able to squeeze a human head dry, now held a banana in each, and it chomped down on them alternatively while its yellow eyes took in Jack.

Through all the chaos, Jack's mind insisted that banana trees had no place in this forest. Moreover, these bananas bulged oddly, as if they were flexed biceps instead of fruit.

> **Bananarm Plant (F-Grade)**
> *A resource guarded by the apes of the Forest of the Strong. Commonly found in the plains of planet Green, the bananas produced by this plant are so rich in nutrients they can instantly develop one's muscles. They are also said to be a rare delicacy.*
> *The stat increase is a one-time bonus.*

Of course it would be bananas. Why the hell not? We already have a gym forest and gorilla bros.

The big brorilla casually made its way to the center of the clearing and stopped. The four brorillas nodded in respect, and the big brorilla only returned a single nod at all of them. It was clearly the big bro, eyes solemn. He didn't look very friendly.

Jack nodded, then tried to be polite.

"Hello, big bro. I'm Jack. Wanna team up against the wolf? I'm sure it will start eating you guys soon, if it hasn't already."

The brorilla stared, not moving a muscle—of which it had many. Jack wondered if it could understand him. The monkeys could—why not their big bro?

The brorilla finally replied. It let out a series of noises that Jack couldn't make heads or tails of. It flexed its gigantic pecs, pointed its thumb at itself, followed by a thumbs-up.

"Are you saying you'll handle it yourself?"

The brorilla shook its head, then spread its arms to indicate the entire pack.

"All of you are going to handle it?"

A nod.

"Oh. Is that why you're training so hard?"

A brief pause, a shrug, then another nod.

"Okay. Can I help, too? I'm strong."

The big brorilla clearly had its doubts. Jack lifted the dumbbell above his head again, but the big brorilla wasn't impressed. It picked an entire benchpress off the ground and tossed it at him.

"What the—"

Jack barely jumped aside as the massive gym instrument crashed into the ground. He rolled back up.

"Bro! That wasn't nice! I can't catch a fucking benchpress!"

Every single gymonkey and brorilla gasped. The big brorilla frowned in dissatisfaction.

"What?" asked Jack, looking around. "Was it something I said?"

He grew worried. He was strong, sure, but he wasn't confident in taking on every monkey in this clearing and their big bro, especially when said big bro threw gym instruments around for breakfast. Maybe coming here was unwise.

The big brorilla stood on its hind legs, reaching nine feet in height. It pointed a finger at itself and another at Jack. The two fingers then came together, and when they did, one was clearly higher than the other.

"Ohh, it's because I called you bro before. You're the big bro and I'm the little one, right? That's what you're saying," he tried. The big brorilla stared. "I don't mind. Still, though, can I help against the wolf? I don't know if you guys can see levels, but it's pretty strong... I don't think you can handle it just by yourselves."

The big brorilla's frown deepened. When it didn't reply, Jack continued, "Okay, maybe you can do it, but it will be easier if you let me help. I'm about as strong as you. With me here, imagine how many of your little bros will be saved."

A second collective gasp. The big brorilla's body shivered, flexing every muscle it had at once. It stared Jack deep in the eyes, then beat its chest and unleashed a loud, deep roar.

The monkeys went bananas. They started throwing poop into the air, pushing each other, and jumping in place. Jack was lost. He had no idea what was happening, but he didn't like it.

Calming down slightly, the gymonkeys and brorillas ran around and formed a large circle around an empty part of the clearing, then kept hollering at the top of their lungs like monkeys often did. The big brorilla jumped over them to land in the circle. It pointed a finger at Jack, then himself, then smashed its two large fists together.

"Oh, no, I didn't mean to challenge you. I'm just saying—"

The brorillas behind Jack pushed him, sending him stumbling into the circle, which then closed behind him. "Hey!"

The big brorilla growled, then assumed a boxing stance and hopped in place. Its large fists rotated around each other like a mill.

"Will you guys *listen* to me? I'm not a monkey!"

They did not listen. He snorted.

"Fine. Fine! You think I'm afraid? If you guys don't want to play nice, I'll show you who's the boss around here."

More frenzied hollering and wild cheers. The big brorilla leveled its stare at Jack, who also adopted a boxing stance.

Jack could take this gorilla. It was at level 25, while he'd calculated his current battle prowess to be in the mid-thirties thanks to all the stat bonuses. If this big bro wanted to be taught a lesson, he would oblige. Becoming the monkey leader would make things easier in the long run, anyway.

Can I become a group boss? he mused, eyeing the gorilla from between his fists.

For a moment, he wondered what they saw. His muscles had developed as he got stronger, eventually covering his entire body in fine, symmetrical lines. He was like a perfect barbarian facing down a massive gorilla. He was a warrior.

The image lit a fire in his heart. Something drew him in. Maybe it was the incessant hollering that filled his ears; maybe it was the battle lust around him, or the allure of winning a public fight; maybe it was the excitement of boxing a fucking gorilla.

Whichever the case, Jack dropped into a state of mind he didn't often reach. All his battles so far had been desperate life-or-death struggles. There was no room for anything else.

Here, where he was called to prove his might against a worthy opponent, things were different. Honestly, even if he lost, he felt that the monkeys wouldn't kill him. His primal instincts didn't completely take over, as they always did. There was room for other things.

He felt the stress of the coming battle. The anticipation. The fear. The anxiety. He was more aware of himself, and thanks to that, he saw a side of battle that normally stayed hidden.

For the first time, he wasn't fighting for his life, but for himself. To prove his worth. To achieve things. To become great.

And, as Jack explored this aspect of battle, a wall in his mind cracked a little. He'd experienced the bald man's world-ending fist in the waterfall world. He'd seen it from many angles, pondered on its secrets, and from the sight of a single punch, he'd drawn so much inspiration about what it truly meant to fight.

He was on the cusp of something great, something titanic, but there was still a thin barrier stopping him—something was missing. Now, that barrier was cracking, and the big brorilla would help him open it up completely.

The gorilla attacked. So did Jack, and they began to box.

Chapter 22
Boxing a Gorilla

The monkey hollering was intoxicating. The rush, the haze, the spike of adrenaline as Jack faced a gorilla with his bare hands. He grinned. He didn't burst into action. Action burst out of him.

Jack and the big brorilla crashed into each another like trains and began boxing. Despite his small physique, Jack was strong. Very strong. He wasn't instantly annihilated like a pre-System human—he stood his ground and met the gorilla's big fists with his own small but hard ones.

Jack had adopted a boxing stance as dictated by his Fistfighting skill, which was completely in its element. He weaved and bobbed, dodged and jabbed where he found an opening. Jack's punches flew straight and true, impacting the big brorilla's body with strong thuds, making it grimace.

The brorilla's punches were like homing missiles. Its muscular arms carried such power, a single punch could

BOXING A GORILLA

undoubtedly rip a normal human's head clean off. But Jack was no normal human, not anymore. He couldn't just dodge, he could block, too!

The gorilla was stronger, as it was a strength-oriented creature, but Jack was much faster and, surprisingly, more durable. He could take those massive fists, while the gorilla buckled every time Jack sneaked in a strike. His little punches fell like hammers, bypassing the gorilla's thick fur to strike the skin underneath.

The big brorilla's eyes widened. Its mouth opened, revealing a pair of sharp teeth. It couldn't use the System to inspect Jack, but it could vaguely sense the level difference between itself and another creature. Most animals and monsters could.

That was why the monkeys invited Jack in. That was why the brorillas and even the big brorilla spoke with him. That was why, when Jack was disrespectful, the big brorilla challenged him. It could sense they were roughly on the same level, but it should have been slightly stronger.

However, that didn't appear to be the case. Its little mind was puzzled. Here it was, boxing with all its tremendous strength, driving punch after punch into the body of this small creature, but it took everything like a champ. Instead, when the little creature's punches struck the gorilla, they felt like swinging logs!

The big brorilla growled and struck faster, harder. He howled and became a flurry of blows on Jack, who still fought skillfully. He dodged one strike, blocked another, parried a third, and dug his fist into the gorilla's belly. The gorilla bent, and it spat saliva on Jack's head from above. Its eyes shook.

How could this little creature be so strong!

All around them, the monkeys were going bananas. They jumped up and down, climbed on branches to see better, and generally raised a ruckus that would make any sports fan go green with envy. The smart ones even snacked on bananarms. Some were even smarter, and distributed bananarms to other monkeys in return for favors or kisses.

The gymonkeys had invented stadium snacks.

More monkeys appeared from the trees as the battle raged on. Even three brorillas rushed over, bringing the total up to seven. All the brorillas then spent a minute greeting each other like proper bros.

Jack didn't miss all this. Though the fight was hectic, he was in control. It wasn't that difficult. He hadn't lost himself like usual.

He could sense the crowd's burning gazes. They landed on his body as intensely as the big brorilla's punches. Their excitement, surprise, fervent joy at such a spectacle was palpable. Even their respect for his strength was obvious to him, a creature who could match their big bro.

He felt like a champion.

It wasn't only good. There was undeniable pressure, a great amount, and there was hostility from some of the monkeys. He was under scrutiny, like his every movement was judged. He felt a veil stretching over his fists and dampening their blows.

The big brorilla sensed his weakness. It smacked him harder, abandoning defense except for its most vulnerable parts. Its punches rained down like meteors, and its monkey cries filled Jack's ears. He was forced on the defensive. The monkeys cheered, watching their big bro recover the upper hand, and some even booed Jack.

Jack grew frustrated. Why was this happening? He didn't understand. He had the higher stats, the finer skills...

Why was he losing? Why were his movements weak and his reactions slow? Why did he make bad calls and expose his weaknesses?

This was the reverse of his vision. The bald man had exhibited strength that his body couldn't possibly contain. Jack was failing to use the strength that his body definitely possessed.

Why?

He knew why.

The tension was getting to him. He could fight with his life on the line, except now, he hesitated. The booing drew him away. The myriad movements at the edges of his vision sapped his attention. The pressure fell on his punches like fabric, making him slow and clumsy.

The big brorilla, on the other hand, was used to fighting like this. It kept the upper hand and pushed.

Jack was back to the basics. Facing elementary weaknesses he never had to deal with against the goblins or bears. His body knew the way, but his mind and soul couldn't follow.

He was incomplete. His foundation was lacking—and then an epiphany washed over him. He'd been trying to grasp the bald man's secrets, but those were so high up the ladder he didn't even deserve to reach for them. He didn't even have the first step.

Slow and steady. Wait a moment. This is like academic research!

A punch to his jaw made him spin in midair and snapped him out of irrelevant thoughts. Jack landed on his feet and ducked under another punch, then delivered a devastating uppercut on the gorilla's chest—height difference. The poor animal almost left the ground but quickly replied with a deft jab that Jack dodged.

Basics, he repeated to himself, trying not to lose focus. *I must work my way up. To become a good fighter, I must first become a fighter. I must be able to stand on stage and fight. I must develop the mental resilience to perform under any circumstances. I must not allow myself stupid, gaping flaws.*

He looked at the big brorilla with gratitude. This was such a great opportunity. He'd found his missing piece. He needed the heart of a fighter—the eye of the tiger.

A punch whistled by his ear, and another smashed into the gorilla's belly.

Jack returned to the fray with renewed resolve. He opened his mind to the surrounding tension, letting it flow over him without affecting him. He'd spoken on stage before, had even given lectures. He could handle it.

Only, this wasn't the same. The eyes of dozens of monkeys and a few brorillas were all on him, and the pressure wasn't something his razor-sharp battle brain could handle. Resolve alone wasn't enough.

With growing terror, Jack realized he couldn't ignore them. He couldn't tune it off. It worked great in theory, but not in practice.

Crap!

This was bad. He was lost and confused. His brain refused to act at normal speed. On the other hand, the big brorilla had gathered so much momentum and confidence it was about to steamroll Jack. This was now a fight he could lose, and he would, if he didn't find a way to recover his footing.

This must be how athletes feel... But I don't know how to handle the pressure! How do they do it?

Wait. I don't need to handle it, he realized. *I have fists. I can simply break it.*

BOXING A GORILLA

He grinned. That's right. So far, he remained a scientist at heart. The fighter only emerged automatically while fighting. Jack now had to summon him at will.

A scientist would ignore the pressure. A fighter would muster his stubbornness and smash right through it.

His fists clenched harder. These monkeys wanted to boo him? Their burning gazes would make him cower? Hah!

He stood straighter. His gaze, that had been trapped at the gorilla's chest-level, reached its eyes and stared defiantly. The big brorilla noticed the change. So did the brorillas and gymonkeys. Their sounds changed. Their boos hesitant.

The big brorilla tried to smash a fist into those defiant eyes, but Jack was no longer there. So far, he'd been pummeling the gorilla's torso, whittling its endurance down. He couldn't reach any higher due to the height difference—the big brorilla was nine feet tall.

However, Jack now realized he shouldn't care. If he dared, his Fistfighting skill knew the way.

The crowd's pressure was still wrapped around Jack's fists, obstructing them, but so what? He ignored it, pushed harder, and ripped right through it. He was the king of the ring, and he fucking loved it.

The brorilla's fist met empty air. In the next moment, Jack rose from the ground, jumping up and reaching the brorilla's head. Its eyes widened. Jack pulled his hand back. The brorilla tried to recover, to dodge, but there was no time. It saw death.

Jack's punch drilled straight into the big brorilla's face, stopping a few centimeters before its nose and turning it into mush.

The gorilla flew back and collapsed to the ground. Jack landed on his feet, a wild grin on his face. He hadn't lost himself. He was still in complete control. He simply enjoyed this fight enough to smile, and he didn't see a reason to hide it. He would do whatever he wanted. Fuck them all.

The brorilla growled as it stood. It faced Jack, and he stared deep into its eyes. There was anger there, shame... and helplessness. Resignation.

The big brorilla gave a sad growl as it fell to both knees and bowed toward him.

In that last strike, Jack had stopped his punch before it struck the gorilla's face. Otherwise, his Drill skill would have sent the momentum deep enough to break several delicate bones, and he might have even killed the gorilla on the spot.

He wasn't sure if his actions had been noticed, but apparently, they had. These apes were smart animals.

As soon as the big brorilla bowed, the rest of the monkeys followed suit. Seven brorillas and around thirty gymonkeys bowed to Jack, who accepted his victory.

Due to his science, he knew how monkey society worked. As ridiculous as it seemed, he'd challenged the alpha male and won. He was their leader now.

Jack looked at the various monkeys, all of them buff as fuck. He had a monkey pack under his command, valuable allies against the black wolf. Moreover, the fight with the big brorilla helped him discover a major flaw and fix it. He now had the heart of a fighter—or at least the beginnings of one.

This difference might sound small, but Jack could feel it resonating with the vision inside him. The bald man approved. Now that Jack had the heart, he understood that the bald man was similar. He was a fighter through and through, pushing forward until nothing remained.

Maybe that's what made his punch so magically unstoppable.

Jack was on to something. A light bulb shone in his mind as all his insights started to come together. A vague form began taking shape—

—and then a ding came out of nowhere, breaking his concentration. The idea retreated back to the very edge of his mind, right outside his reach.

Motherfu—He stopped himself. No meaning in insulting an omnipotent entity that could read your thoughts.

Stifling his frustration as best as he could, he turned to look at the status screen that interrupted him.

> **Primate Boss subjugated! Would you like to despawn the group? Y/N**
> **Level Up! You have reached Level 23.**
> **Level Up! You have reached Level 24.**
> **Level Up! You have reached Level 25.**

Forcing a boss to surrender clearly counted as a victory. It didn't matter much to Jack. *No*, he replied. He wasn't going to despawn his new allies.

However, it seemed his assumption of each monster group counting as a killable entity was true. By defeating the group, he'd gotten the respective experience, even though he didn't kill a single monkey.

And these levels mattered. He allocated all bonus points equally among his physical stats, of course. The difference between him and the black wolf was closing by the day. His battle prowess now had to be around level 40.

Not too far away... Unless that Elite tag means what I think it does. Dammit.

In video games, Elite enemies were stronger than their levels would indicate. Jack really hoped that wasn't the case... Even if it was, he had an Elite class of his own, plus a monkey army that would help him pull through, especially if he trained it a little.

Finally, there was one extra benefit from all these level-ups. Jack grinned as he looked at the last status screen. It was almost enough to make him forgive the System for distracting him—almost.

> **Congratulations! Level 25 reached.
> New Class Skill acquired: Calamitous Punch (1).**

Chapter 23
Calamitous Punch

> Congratulations! Level 25 reached.
> New Class Skill acquired.
> Calamitous Punch (I): All warriors have a finishing strike. At the cost of exhaustion, overdraw your body's potential to unleash a devastating attack.

Unlike his previous skills, this one was active, not passive. Suddenly, something appeared inside him. Like a switch or a big red button.

There wasn't an actual red button in his head, obviously, but that's what it resembled. Jack got the sense that, just by willing it, this skill would tug at all his muscles and unleash every scrap of strength in his body at once. The result would undoubtedly be catastrophic—both for the enemy and himself.

But not so catastrophic that he couldn't test it.

He turned to the monkeys, whose reverent eyes watched him. He raised a clenched fist.

"My friends!" he began, hoping they could understand him. "Don't call me big brother—your big bro is right there. Call me Jack. I am not here to conquer you, but to help you and be helped in turn. We share a common enemy. The hateful black wolf that wants to snack on your brothers and sisters, rip your muscles apart, and feast on your bananarms."

Jack was gambling a bit here, but it worked. The gymonkeys and brorillas were riled up, unable to believe the size of this wolf's audacity. Not their bananarms!

"But don't be afraid!" his voice thundered, cutting through the clamor. The monkeys shut up. "I am like you! We will fight *together*! We will put our lives on the line and kill that arrogant canine. We will be *free*!"

They cheered, even the big brorilla. Jack ramped up for his finale.

"For victory! For alliance! Apes together"—he clenched his fist and drove it toward the ground, activating Calamitous Punch—"STRONG!"

It was a nice finale. Simple, direct, and targeted. Perfect for riling up a monkey pack. The only problem was that Jack had no idea how strong his new skill was. The effects of Drill and Pugilist Body had been useful, but nothing too pronounced.

He wanted a simple bang. That's all.

When he activated Calamitous Punch, his clenched fist already heading for the soil, the world went dark. His punch accelerated so hard it pulled him completely off-balance. Yet, his movement remained perfect, as if his body knew what to do.

CALAMITOUS PUNCH

Every unnecessary muscle went lax as all strength left him. It gathered on his torquing waist, his turning shoulder, his clenched fist. Jack sensed the power of this one fist and was overcome with terror, and he couldn't stop it. It reached the ground almost instantly.

Color returned to the world with an explosion. Jack flew back. The ground erupted under his feet, showering the nearby gymonkeys with gravel, and the impact's booming sound echoed over the entire forest.

"Fuck..." Jack gritted his teeth. His right hand lay limp at his side, many bones broken—only his 79 Constitution saved it from shattering completely. The monkeys alternated their incredulous stares between him and the point of impact, unable to believe their eyes.

Where Jack used to stand, there was now a half-foot-deep crater as if a meteorite had fallen. The soil was upturned in its perimeter, the center scorched black, and Jack could even see an underground rock that his fist had torn through like paper.

Calamitous Punch sure packed a punch. Only a full-power strike from the rock bear could come close to this level of destruction. It was a real calamity.

Of course, the price was heavy. Jack's entire body was sore and exhausted as if he'd just run a marathon. He was starving, and his hand was broken. He'd underestimated the strength of his new skill, but that was okay. Now, he knew its strength. It was a last resort, a hidden ace in his sleeve.

It was the weapon that would kill the black wolf.

His new friends recovered from their stupor. The monkeys gathered around the crater to inspect it, while the big brorilla and two of its gorilla bros approached Jack to make sure he was okay. He assured them he was fine and thanked them for caring.

Another brorilla approached a minute later. It had apparently gone behind the bananarm plant, where they kept some of their gym equipment, and fetched a roll of processed leaves that could serve as bandages. Jack thanked this brorilla, too, wrapping the leaves around his broken hand, grimacing in pain—or rather, in expectation of the pain.

The broken hand itself was nothing compared to the ice pond and the agony it would demand while fixing it.

Somehow, the gymonkeys had come to the conclusion that they should fill the hole with poop. The big brorilla sent the brorillas to enforce order and awaited by Jack's side.

Jack looked at the gorilla. Just a few minutes ago, they'd been fighting frenziedly, and now they were bros. He chuckled and shook his head.

This world keeps getting crazier and crazier...

The gorilla extended a hand to help Jack up—he'd been sitting against a tree till now. It pointed one finger at Jack and one at itself, then brought the two fingers close together, and again, one finger was clearly higher than the other.

Jack laughed. "Nah, bro." He grabbed the lower finger and raised it. "Both of us are big brothers. In fact, you know what? There's no big brother between us. I'm just Jack, and you are..." He considered it for a moment. "Harambe. Yes, I think that's suitable. It's from another gorilla, an honorable one. Do you like this name?"

The big brorilla thought for a moment, then nodded. Suddenly, its eyes were filled with manly tears. It extended a hand and gave Jack a firm, earnest handshake that would make any father proud.

"The honor's mine, Harambe. Now, let's go kick some wolf ass, shall we?"

The gorilla cheered. The monkeys and brorillas, not knowing what was happening, cheered too, and the clearing was filled with hollering that quickly turned into war cries.

Jack raised his voice again. "But before that, follow me." An evil grin appeared on his face. "I will make you guys even stronger."

The monkeys cheered again. They had no idea what was waiting for them.

They were on the clock. He'd despawned the goblins, killed the bear boss and most of the bears, and took over the entire monkey pack. He had basically turned the dungeon on its head, and the boss was sure to know.

In fact, it *could* already be after him. They had to hurry.

Under Jack's instructions, the monkey pack abandoned their gym equipment for now, took some bananarms for the way, and headed for the bear area. This all took them ten minutes, and most of those were spent trying to make the monkeys understand what he was saying. Thankfully, they were fairly intelligent. He was glad he didn't treat them as monsters.

While the big brorilla was organizing things, Jack had also tried a few bananarms. He was stunned. They were delicious!

Flavor overflowed from inside them. Their juices were thick enough to fill his mouth and thin enough that they weren't sticky. Jack had eaten at many good restaurants in his time traveling the world for conferences, but nothing came close to the taste of these forest bananarms.

In fact, the bananarms were so thick in nutrients, that the taste resembled meat a little, but in such a way that it meshed perfectly with their natural fruity flavor. There was sugar, too, along with a bit of spice, though Jack had no idea how it had gotten there.

This heavenly taste was like the love product of bananas and the finest beef.

Which was a tiny bit suspicious, too, given that earth's bananas had been selectively bred to reach their current state, but Jack didn't want to be too paranoid.

The first bananarm also gave him ten points in Strength. Along with his recent level-ups, Jack's status screen was quickly becoming a sight that would entrench any proper number junkie.

> **Name: Jack Rust**
> **Species: Human, Earth-387**
> **Faction: -**
> **Grade: F**
> **Class: Pugilist (Elite)**
> **Level: 25**
> **Strength: 79**
> **Dexterity: 79**
> **Constitution: 79**
> **Mental: 9**
> **Will: 7**
> **Skills: Fistfighting (II), Drill (I), Pugilist Body (I), Calamitous Punch (I)**

Things were looking up. He was now a real superman.

The big brorilla growled something to get Jack's attention, and turning, he saw everyone ready to go. Thirty gymonkeys and seven brorillas, led by their big bro, all awaited Jack's commands. It brought a tear to his eyes.

"Let's go," he said, closing his status screen. "A battle's waiting."

Their first stop would be the former bear territory. As the monkeys left their area of the forest, they looked around in wonder and behind in hesitation. They briefly warred with some instinct that told them to stay put—the System's mind control, probably—before following Jack out.

Their eyes were instantly filled with new life, and their enthusiasm rocked the world before Jack shushed them. They had to be stealthy, or the black wolf might come and slaughter them. They weren't ready yet.

Stealthy like that, they crossed into the bear territory and headed deep inside. Jack wasn't worried about the remaining earth bears. Even if they spotted his group, he and the big brorilla could make quick work of any bear unlucky enough to cross their path.

They reached the clear pond without any accidents, and Jack sent all monkeys and gorillas to relax in its waters. It was a bit crampy, but they fit. He stood guard outside.

> **Clear Pond (F-Grade)**
> *Clear Ponds are naturally-occurring formations spread around the universe. They are often used as parts of resorts. Anyone who relaxes in these waters will find tranquility, their body will loosen completely, and their potential will emerge, making the entire body sturdier.*
> *The stat increase is a one-time bonus*

The monkeys' reaction was priceless. They first tested the water with their toes, afraid of entering it, but soon, they lounged inside, full of euphoria. Their sighs and moans of relaxation were so pronounced, Jack grew uncomfortable.

He let them relax for ten minutes before pulling them back out—literally. All monkeys and brorillas now had eyes full of serenity, and their gazes at him were filled with gratitude. Clearly, they loved the clear pond. Jack grinned. Each one of them, from the weakest gymonkey to the big brorilla, had increased by a level.

Jack then turned sharply to the left and led them south, to the goblin area. Thanks to the clear pond, they were even quieter than before, and no wolf crossed their path. In fact, the pond's relaxation powers were so intense, that some monkeys even fell asleep and had to be carried by others.

Eventually, they reached the large clearing where the goblin tribe used to be located. It remained empty; almost. A lone boar walked in circles around the High Speed Bush. Its eyes were red like traffic lights and it could barely stand. Jack grabbed it and unceremoniously placed it back into the forest.

"Be careful," he instructed the monkeys. "This stuff is strong. As soon as you feel yourselves getting stronger, stop *immediately*."

They nodded.

> **High Speed Bush (F-Grade)**
> *A resource formerly guarded by the goblins of the Forest of the Strong. Commonly found in the wet jungles of planet Peruvian, the leaves of this bush can enhance a person's reflexes, dexterity, and agility. They can also make you high as a kite.*
> The stat increase is a one-time bonus.

Ten minutes later, Jack cursed loudly. How could the monkeys know about the delay between licking a leaf and its effect kicking in?

The brorillas were fine, thanks to their high stats, but most of the monkeys were rolling on the ground and laughing like crazy. A few had even formed a gang and tossed poop at the big brorilla from across the clearing, heedless of its growls, and giggling like human children that had rang a doorbell and ran away.

True to its description, the bush made them high as a kite.

It took a few minutes for Jack to round them all up and make sure they'd gotten the Dexterity bonus. This time, their power had increased by two levels, not one—Jack assumed this was a rounding error from before.

By now, gymonkeys ranged between levels 8 and 16, brorillas between 17 and 20, and the big brorilla stood proudly at level 28. They were a force to be reckoned—or they would be, when the bush's effect wore off.

Monkeys weren't the most disciplined creatures. High monkeys, of course, were completely uncontrollable. It took massive effort from Jack and the gorillas to guide them, and any concepts of stealth were thrown out the window.

It didn't matter. From the goblin clearing to Jack's cave was a short way.

Laugh while you can, thought Jack, staring at the high monkeys. An evil grin reappeared on his face. *Soon, you'll get your lesson.*

Jack had visited the clear pond first, hoping the increased Constitution would help the monkeys resist the High Speed Bush better. Maybe it worked, maybe it didn't. They reached his cave, and he ushered them through the narrow opening. The big brorilla couldn't fit, but they broke some sharp rocks at the sides, and then it barely managed to get through.

The cave was crampy with so many creatures inside. Jack held his nose, too. However, as soon as the monkeys laid eyes on the ice pond, they froze, and their eyes became filled with wonder.

Jack's evil grin widened. The pond was extraordinarily beautiful, but the pain it hid was equally extraordinary. At least it was the good kind of pain.

For the first time, someone else would have to suffer this too. The monkeys had to get stronger—he couldn't wait to see their reactions.

Chapter 24
Monkey See, Monkey Do

Jack stepped into the ice pond first. He wanted to act like a proper leader. Unfortunately, the moment his broken hand touched the water, he screamed like a little girl.

The pain was the worst he'd felt so far. Someone may as well have been using pliers to readjust his bones, except these pliers were ice-cold and everywhere at the same time.

The monkeys watched from outside the lake, torn between trying to help and watching the water with fear. A moment ago, it had looked beautiful. Now, they no longer felt like swimming.

"It's fine!" Jack gritted his teeth and spoke through the pain. "This is only because I'm injured. Fuck! Just come in."

They looked at each other. They did not want to go in.

The big brorilla, Harambe, stepped forth. With a snort at his fellow monkeys, he stepped into the water and frowned. The cold had reached him, and though it couldn't harm him, it was a unique sensation.

The monkeys watched with bated breath as their big bro took a step forward, then another. Soon, the gorilla was halfway across the lake and still going, but now, his steps were slow. Measured. Careful.

The pauses between each step got longer. Harambe was shivering now. Ice glinted on his fur, shining like little stars. The monkeys cheered him on, ignoring Jack, whose screams of pain had died down.

The gorilla took another step, then stopped. Jack had needed thirteen steps to reach the waterfall, but Harambe, being larger, had only taken nine. The pond was thirteen feet long, anyway, and Jack resolved to measure it as such from now on. Confusion would help no one.

"Don't go any farther," said Jack. Harambe turned to look, and his face was pale below his fur. His eyes were shaking but still full of passion. "The waterfall is dangerous. Stay there for a while, get used to the cold, and I'll help you touch it safely."

He nodded. Jack turned back to the monkeys.

"All of you. In," he commanded.

The brorillas were first. They all frowned when they touched the water, but their brohood was too strong to fear a little bit of cold. Walking side-by-side in two rows—they could barely fit—they crossed the first half of the pond before slowing down. Eventually, each brorilla made it between the seventh and tenth foot, all of them pushed to their limits.

It was a brave attempt.

Finally came the gymonkeys, who weren't nearly as stoic as the gorillas. The moment they touched the water, they began screaming, jumping on top of each other and making faces. The fact that most were still high didn't help.

It took both Jack and Harambe to convince them to enter the pond. The monkeys weren't happy, but they complied, still letting out the intermittent cry. At least the cold washed away the High Speed Bush's effects.

In the end, the gymonkeys reached anywhere from the second to the fifth foot of the lake, with only one of them barely stopping at the sixth.

Their efforts weren't for naught. According to Jack's inspection, each gymonkey gained one to three levels, the brorillas got three to five, while the big brorilla, Harambe himself, increased in power by a whooping six levels, reaching level 34—and, if he could enter the waterfall, he'd get another few.

Everyone felt the change in themselves and were overjoyed. The monkeys hollered and did their best to advance farther, while the brorillas grinned and nodded at each other as they flexed their muscles. The big brorilla, intoxicated by power, stared at Jack, debating whether to challenge him again.

A moment later, he shelved the thought. He was smart enough to appreciate that this increase in his power was only thanks to Jack.

However, it remained that, while all the monkeys had ventured into the pond—whose power seemed inexhaustible—Jack himself was only at the shallows, nursing his wounds. The gymonkeys didn't care much, but all gorillas stared at him in question. Would he not surpass them? Was his mind too weak to traverse the pond?

Jack raised his eyes from the crystal-clear waters. He took in the gazes of the gorillas, the challenge in Harambe's stare. He grinned.

Watch and marvel. I'm healed already.

With slow, purposeful steps, he crossed the lake. He went past the gymonkeys. He reached the gorillas, whose eyes were transitioning from doubt to respect, and stepped past them without missing a beat. His speed was steady, his pace fluid.

The gorillas entered the ice pond for the first time, but Jack was a virtuoso.

He reached the big brorilla and stopped beside him. He met his stare with pride: *If you want to challenge me, I'm right here.*

Harambe growled but didn't act. Jack nodded.

"Come, Harambe. Since you could stay here this long, you're ready to touch the waterfall, but be prepared. The cold in there is incomparable to here. You might die. Are you ready to risk your life for power?"

Harambe didn't even consider it. He nodded.

"Good. Then go in. I'll spot you—to speak in gym terms. If you freeze, I'll try to pull you out... but I might fail."

Jack had grown stronger since last time, but not by too much. He had zero confidence against this waterfall.

Every single monkey watched with faith and curiosity. Harambe turned to stare at the falling water. On his grumpy face, yellow eyes shone with resolve. Despite the cold, he balled his fists, released a monkey cry, and dived right in.

Then, silence.

Through the hazy waters, everyone saw Harambe's body freeze before his voice was abruptly cut short.

The gymonkeys wreaked havoc with their howls, and even the brorillas growled. Jack ignored them. He kept his eyes glued on Harambe, watching him intently.

Freezing over wouldn't kill you—he'd tested that himself. The gamble was to pull Harambe out after he got the stat bonuses just before he froze to death.

Unfortunately, Jack didn't know how long he'd spent frozen himself, nor did he know when the bonuses would come. Therefore, he simply kept scanning Harambe over and over, hoping for his level to suddenly spike.

Nothing happened for a while. Harambe's fur took on a paler shade as time went by. The monkeys were going insane from worry. Jack remained still as a rock, ignoring the cold that slithered up his spine. He fired off one System inspection after another. Nothing changed.

Maybe I won't see it, he thought. Maybe the System won't let me cheat like this. Maybe it's already too late.

He steeled his resolve. Better a weaker Harambe than a dead one. He was a good gorilla and didn't deserve to die.

Jack took a deep breath. All of a sudden, he burst from immobility. His arms snaked into the waterfall to grab Harambe to pull him out. At that moment, he fired off an inspection.

> **Big Brorilla, Level 37**

The bonus was there.

Jack would have smiled if he could move his face. His arms in the waterfall were assaulted by relentless waves of soul-freezing cold. He couldn't feel them anymore. His mind was slowing down. His body was growing heavier. His fingers refused to close around Harambe's arm.

But he had to save his bro.

Jack gritted his teeth and screamed through the freeze. Veins popped in his forehead as if snapping through solid ice, and with a burst of will, he caught Harambe's ice-cold body and pulled.

The two fell backward into the pond. Jack struggled to recover and get back up—thankfully, he'd only barely entered the waterfall or he'd be frozen solid already. On the bright side, Harambe had frozen in an upright position—as upright as a gorilla on his knuckles could be—and he was big enough for his head to stay above the surface even when he fell back.

After Jack recovered, he pushed Harambe a bit toward the brorillas waiting close behind. They were fine. They grabbed Harambe and pulled him out, showering him with their worry. All the gymonkeys had already exited the pond, and were crowded over Harambe, pushing each other for the right to stand beside him.

Jack smiled. These monkeys really adored their big bro. Harambe would be fine—he was already defrosting.

Jack then turned back to the waterfall. It cascaded as calmly as ever, unconcerned with the mortal affairs around it. In its endless cold, a gorilla and a human were nothing.

But, in Jack's eyes, the waterfall was many things. It was a mystery, a challenge, and a blessing.

In that endless cold lay the hidden world he'd entered, a world in his own mind he could only unlock through this waterfall. Last time, he'd inspected the bald man's punch from all angles—the scene was carved in his mind with crystal-clear precision, but it was only in that frozen state that he could freely inspect it.

Jack had spent an unknown amount of time pondering on that vision, watching it again and again, trying to discern its secrets. How had that bald man unleashed such power? What did Jack lack?

Unknowingly, the vision had become an obsession. When he slept, he dreamed of the bald man's punch. When he rested, his mind kept jumping back there, analyzing every tiny movement.

There was something there. Something gargantuan hid just beyond his sight, he was certain. He could sense it, almost touch it, but every time he tried, epiphany escaped like a slippery fish. He wanted to know. He *needed* to know. It was extremely important.

Unfortunately, his progress was slow outside the waterfall. In there, he'd analyzed everything, and despite that, something was still missing. He was trying to solve a puzzle with a few important pieces still in the box, and no matter how he tried, whether in or out of the waterfall, he came up empty.

During his fight with Harambe, he'd discovered something, a clue in a direction he hadn't considered before. The bald man's punch was clearly magical, in some way. Why, then, would its origins be strictly physical?

This might have been the missing piece of the puzzle, and Jack yearned to enter the waterfall to find out. He needed that frozen state to progress fast.

The waterfall was dangerous, sure, but he'd survived it before when he was three levels weaker. Plus, he now had a bro to spot him. He would be fine. It was a risk worth taking.

But not hastily.

Jack turned around and followed the monkeys outside. Harambe woke up, and impressed everyone with his new power. He even considered challenging Jack again, but not only were the circumstances less than ideal, Jack was also busy.

He sat on a rock and stared at infinity, lost in thoughts so deep that even the monkeys' incessant howling didn't budge him. Harambe left him alone for now. Even stood beside him, making sure nobody disturbed his bro for any reason. Jack was clearly busy with something important.

An hour later, Jack stood. All cold had left his system, and his body was back in pristine condition. His eyes were sharp, his breathing steady, and he radiated an aura of no chill.

"Harambe," he said, making the gorilla turn around. "I will go in the waterfall. Spot me."

Harambe nodded. As the rest of the monkeys watched, the two of them headed deep into the pond—thanks to Harambe's stat bonuses from the waterfall, it was now easier.

They reached the waterfall at the back and stopped before it.

"Don't pull me out too early," said Jack. "I can probably get out by myself, so act only if you think I'm dying. I trust you, Harambe. Okay?"

The big brorilla met Jack's eyes and nodded. He wouldn't let his bro die, but he'd do his best to delay the saving.

"Good."

Jack dived into the waterfall and let the cold consume him. The next moment, he opened his eyes in the plain cyan world of tranquility, where his mind belonged entirely to him.

It was time to solve the riddle.

Chapter 25
Breaking Through

Jack stood alone in the empty blue world. There was nothing here, not even a chair to rest on. Only an endless cyan expanse, where the sky stretched from the horizon to beneath his feet.

He didn't remember many things. His mind had been frozen on entering, and only his innermost reality had carried through.

As he stood puzzled in this empty world, without any distractions whatsoever, a desire sprung forth from the deepest parts of his being. He wanted to be like that man.

A vision appeared. A bald man clad in yellow, punching through a beast taller than skyscrapers. He seemed tiny, and his movements inconsequential. However, the world shook the moment he moved, the air screamed, and the phantom of a fist crossed the air like a meteor to smash into and through the beast's scaly chest.

"Still not enough..." he muttered, looking at his fist, and the vision disappeared.

Jack made it replay. It was engraved deep in his soul—he could review it at will.

He didn't know how many times he saw the same vision. Setting, punch, destruction, finale. He reviewed it in slow motion and from multiple angles. He observed every tiny change in the man's body and the surrounding environment. He saw everything, but he was missing something.

How *infuriating*! All the information was there, right in front of him, letting him review it at will, and he still couldn't figure out the secret. The destruction wasn't caused simply by the man's bodily strength. Where had it come from? And why did it feel so... natural?

It was like watching someone else play a game they were good at. It seemed easy, but when you tried, you couldn't even take two steps without falling.

Jack was determined to succeed.

Think... a voice whispered in his head. It was his voice, coming from far away. *Remember...*

Jack frowned. The vision disappeared, replaced by other images.

He saw himself screaming as he mauled a goblin before the ice pond. That was the first real battle in his entire life. He'd discovered despair and the power it could give. He'd realized how much power humans kept in reserve, the part of themselves that never saw the light.

The images shifted to when he ambushed a goblin squad in the woods. He'd come to terms with violence, with survival of the strongest, with killing.

He ran away from an earth bear, barely escaping with his life. It was only proper. If he wasn't strong, he couldn't fight, and he had to run.

He ambushed three hobgoblins. He was unarmed, while they brandished shortswords but didn't know how to use them. Power mattered little without the skill to apply it.

He warred against the goblin tribe. He snuck through, then massacred. He faced great pain and despair but broke through everything with sheer stubbornness. And he won.

Jack stopped. He'd felt something in this last memory. A part of that battle, as he said, 'fuck it,' and ran through the burning flames, resonated with something deep inside him. At that moment, he'd felt complete, but was that all?

He sensed there was something more and followed the feeling to another scene.

Jack faced off against the rock bear. After his partially successful ambush, the two had fought fiercely for a long time. During that battle, and especially during the end, what drove him? How did he feel?

Despair. Fear. Rage. Bitterness. Frustration. The rock bear was forcing him to dance on a razor's edge. He had to dodge every single attack, hundreds of them, or he would die. He was on the weaker end. The world was suppressing him, trying to take him down, but he stubbornly refused. He stood his ground over and over, gritting his teeth and beating at the problem until he won or died.

There it was, again. The resonance inside him. This stubbornness, this undying will to make it, the headstrong approach to life that refused to take a single step back. It expressed him. Defined him.

Jack fought the big brorilla. His power was enough, and so were his skills. Yet, he'd almost lost. Why?

Because he was pressured, and he'd been trying to fight the problem as a scholar, like the pre-System Jack. Which didn't work. He couldn't let the problem wash over him without affecting him. That wasn't him. He wanted to face the obstacles head-on, set his jaw, and break through it. Punch through it.

Like a fist.

"Oh."

Jack blinked. Something inside him finally clicked, and then, he was whole. He saw it.

The Fist.

This was his path to life, the path he would walk to the end of time. He would face the world with strength, like a thrown punch, until either he or any obstacle broke. Never defeat. Only victory. Fist meant power and nothing else. This was his innermost truth, the way he was meant to be. This made him feel whole. This was him.

And not just him.

Riding the wave of realizations, Jack's mind expanded. That's what was missing before. This state, breaking through everything like a clenched fist, didn't just resonate inside him.

It reminded him of the bald man.

He'd seen the vision so many times that he felt intimate with him. He understood it. Suddenly, he realized he'd never once considered the bald man a person, only a punching machine. But that wasn't so.

He knew every tiny movement of the bald man's body as he threw the punch. Now, he understood that his state of mind mattered as well. If he could combine those, if he could reach the apex in both will and technique, if he could touch that absolute peak, even just once…

Only a faint gauze of mist separated Jack from something truly world-shaking. Only a last, tiny step remained.

Jack put himself in the shoes of the bald man and imagined what he might be feeling, facing down a titan by himself. Fear. Helplessness. Stubbornness. Resolve. When he punched out, he must have felt ridiculous, punching something so large with such a tiny fist. Yet, he persisted.

What drove him?

In the vision, the man's attack left no way out. He didn't hold anything back. He only punched, supremely confident that he could break through. It was a confidence fueled by his undeniable strength, and the more Jack considered it, the more he felt there was something deeper.

It wasn't just confidence. Even if the bald man hadn't been certain of success, he'd still punched out in the same unyielding way. There was a fire shimmering inside him that commanded him to act as such. He was a man that faced everything like a clenched fist. A man that could break but never bend. A man that went ever forward, laughing until he died. That was him.

And that was Jack.

Everything clicked. The thin gauze separating Jack from the truth wasn't lifted—it was broken through. He understood. For a moment, even the blue world disappeared, and Jack found himself facing a titanic fist, a Truth, a natural law. The majesty stunned him.

He only withstood its presence for a single moment, and it was enough to know with absolute certainty that this was his Path. The Path of the Fist. The massive fist saw him as well, not even an ant in its eyes, but acknowledged him.

Jack returned to the blue world, but he wasn't the same. He was a new man. Something shimmered inside him, burned like the bald man's heroic heart. The path of the fist was part of him, and he a part of it. He could borrow its strength. He could *understand.*

Jack closed his eyes. He found himself hovering over a purple desert, facing a titanic scaly beast. The heat caressed his skin, the fear and excitement, and the fast beating of his heart were all at the forefront. His resolve hardened so much it filled him completely. He could do this. He would never take a step back. He would break through this enemy. Absolutely.

Jack clenched his fist and shot it forward with the absolute belief that it would succeed. He'd seen the vision so many times that his movements unknowingly copied the bald man's to the last muscle. His soul did, too. They shared a vision.

The fist traveled forth, crossing the sky like a meteor, and smashed into and through the beast's chest. Of course it did.

He'd succeeded.

But he also realized just how far there was to go. His fist had pierced through a massive beast, but true meteors could destroy planets. The potential excited him. He sighed as he looked at his fist.

"Still not enough..."

Jack opened his eyes and found the blue world broken. He'd punched it. A large hole lay open before him, revealing stones and clean water tumbling over them. And he was so terribly cold.

Two large hands grabbed his shoulders and pulled him back. A wail entered his ears as, like a mirror, the blue world broke into tiny pieces that dissolved into nothingness. Jack could barely move, but he could sense Harambe pulling him through the ice pond. His body was almost failing. He must have stayed in the waterfall for far longer than last time... but he'd made it.

He grinned wildly. He was different. An aura shimmered around him like a clenched fist. He'd found his path in life. All was well.

Celebratory blue screens flooded his vision.

> **Congratulations!**
> **You have developed the Dao Root of the Fist.**
> *The world is endless, but your path is your own. Stride forth with vigor. Fist means power.*
> **Congratulations! For being one of the first ten people on your planet to develop a Dao Root, you are awarded the Title: Planetary Frontrunner (10).**

Jack was overwhelmed by cold and information. While he would need some time to put everything in order, for now, he knew one thing: He'd found his path. He would tread it to the very end.

And the first enemy to know his true strength would be the Dungeon Boss. The black wolf.

Harambe took Jack to the shore and collapsed beside him, while the gymonkeys and brorillas rushed to help. Not that they could do much. Time would take away the cold.

Jack managed to turn his head toward Harambe. "Thank you..." he muttered, barely able to move his lips. "You really waited... until the last moment..."

By his side, Harambe's monkey lips were drawn into a weak grin. He managed to form a thumbs-up.

Jack smiled. And then, he fell asleep.

It took some hours for Jack to wake up. The combined exhaustion from fighting Harambe, touring the forest, healing at the pond, and entering the waterfall had gotten to him.

Thankfully, the monkeys were good people, and they let him rest. They even stayed slightly quieter than usual.

It was morning, and Jack was finally putting things in order. He had a lot of information to go through, so he started with the easy ones.

Chapter 26
Exploring the Dao

System, Jack thought curiously, *what is a Planetary Frontrunner?*

> **Planetary Frontrunner (10):** A Title awarded to the first ten sapients to develop a Dao Root in an Integrated planet. A sign of great potential, marking the owner as a person worthy of the Immortal System's assistance.
> **Efficacy of all stats +10%**

System, what's a Title?

> **Titles:** A complementary system meant to award those who achieve extraordinary deeds. Titles are rare and can offer various benefits.

The System had an integrated FAQ. How handy. If only he knew earlier.

Two monkeys were bickering in front of Jack's flat stone, arguing about the ownership of a bananarm, but he didn't pay attention. Harambe appeared, grabbed the bananarm in his large hands, and broke it into two. He then gave each gymonkey one half and a glare.

Okay. So, I'm one of the first ten people on the entire planet to get a so-called Dao Root... That's so special. One-in-a-billion special. Can it be real?

Thinking back, there were a ton of coincidences that helped Jack. He'd been trapped in a dungeon and forced to go above and beyond to survive. That dug out his potential. He also had the ice pond spawn right next to him. Without it, he would have never survived this ordeal.

The ice pond also had the waterfall that granted him his epiphany, putting him in a frozen meditative state.

Moreover, everything he'd experienced up to now guided him toward the Dao of the Fist, where he was also personally inclined. This last reason wasn't necessarily a coincidence—after all, everyone saw things through their own eyes. Still, Jack had to admit that his experience so far seemed almost entirely optimized for getting a Dao Root.

Of course, none of this would have happened without his sweat, tears, and blood. Many people had opportunities, but very few could utilize them. This achievement belonged entirely to Jack.

So, if I make it out, I'll be super strong... Wow.

The vision blinded him for a moment. How would it feel? He'd be like a superman among mortals. People would form rows to watch his punches. He could guide them, lead them, protect them... and, most of all, he'd have freedom.

However, all of that would only happen if he defeated the black wolf. Jack snapped back to the present and focused on the more practical part of the Title.

+10% in the efficacy of all stats... God, that sounds huge.

Ten percent didn't sound like a large increase, except when it happened across the table, it compounded. Moreover, it scaled. If he previously had the stats of a normal level 40 person, he now had the stats of a level 44. This stat increase would stay with him forever, no matter how strong he got. He would always have a leg up over everyone else. And, if he could get more titles like this...

He almost salivated.

In a few words, it was an incredible bonus. Jack was a man of science. He knew how important even the tiniest of percentages were.

The black wolf thought it was the boss—Jack would show it.

Finally, he turned his attention to the most precious benefit: the Dao Root. He had no idea what that meant. Fortunately, he had someone willing to answer all his questions.

System, what's a Dao Root?

> **Dao: The Dao represents the world. It is the natural laws that govern everything, from the tiniest atoms to the largest stars. A deep enough understanding of the Dao can translate into real-world applications. For example, people who pursue the Dao of Fire can often breathe fire.**
> **The Immortal System has streamlined the Dao. It is recommended that cultivators progress simultaneously in Levels and the Dao for maximum benefits.**

Right. So, magic. Got it.

He was aware of the word "Dao." It was used in eastern philosophy, though he always found it too abstract to take seriously—it literally meant path. The System description had given some interesting tidbits of information, but it wasn't what he'd asked.

System. What's a DAO ROOT? He thought the words slow and intensely, hoping it would help.

> **Dao: The Dao represents the world.
> It is the natural laws...**

It was the same screen. The System obviously knew what a Dao Root was, so why wasn't it telling him?

Maybe it will only reveal the most basic stuff, and I have to discover the rest...

It was common practice in videogames, if annoying. Thankfully, Jack was smart enough to have his own hypotheses. He remembered the infinite vastness of that gigantic fist, having only touched its tiniest corner.

The Dao Root should be the first step toward mastering a Dao. The starting point, so to say. There are probably other classifications as one goes deeper... but it's suspicious. Everything else in the System is classified as numbers or letters. Even "Elite" is self-explanatory. So far, the Dao is the only thing with a more flowery hierarchy. Hmm...

It was an interesting mystery for later. Utilizing this Dao took priority.

He considered sparring with Harambe, who was also itching to test his power, but that wouldn't work. This cave was too cramped, and if they fought outside, the black wolf could jump on them at any time. They were the only creatures in the entire reserve, save for the natural animals and maybe a couple earth bears.

Thankfully, he didn't *need* to spar with anyone. The Dao of the Fist—as the System liked to call it—was a part of him. It was instinctive. He clenched his fist, and all sorts of notions began to unravel.

He was much more in tune with it than ever before. He even felt certain that this connection would help him in combat. His fists were decisively more absolute, be it in offense or defense, though it made no sense.

Had he finally attained magic?

Fist magic. He chuckled. Could be worse. I'm only an '-ing' away from getting censored.

He jabbed the air a few times. His fists shot true. He was aware of what they signified. Now, they weren't just powered by his body, but by his heart as well. He even thought he saw the air shimmer around them.

Nah. Must have been my imagination.

Lost in his musings, he didn't realize that the monkeys had quieted down. When he finally noticed, they were gathered around him, watching his practice intently like he was a piece of art. Even Harambe stared, and his eyes narrowed as if trying to comprehend something. There was reverence in those eyes.

Jack understood why. His Dao Root wasn't limited to his punches. It was a superior existence inside him, and it leaked into his every motion. When he walked, talked, or even turned to look at someone, he was very faintly exuding the aura of a clenched fist.

It wasn't noticeable unless someone paid close attention, or unless he was consciously channeling it into his fists. But it was there.

Facing the gazes of the monkeys, Jack raised his head higher. He sensed their desire for the power he bore. They were primal creatures of strength. Of course, they yearned for the power of the fist.

"The power I have," he said slowly, the monkeys maintaining absolute silence, "is called the Dao, and it is something you can all obtain. Work hard. Be true to your heart. And it will come."

They looked at him as if he'd given the greatest of sermons—which, in a way, he had. Harambe was the most touched of all. His eyes carried great admiration for Jack. He clenched his big fists and looked at them, still frowning.

"Don't stress, Harambe," Jack's voice floated over. The gorilla looked up. "There are many Daos. Maybe yours will be the fist, like mine, or maybe it will be something else. Don't try to copy me. Work hard, be true to *your* heart, and it will come."

Harambe looked deeply at Jack. Then, his eyes widened, and he nodded. He'd understood.

"Good." Jack clapped, snapping the monkeys out of their stupor. "We're going to hunt a wolf. It should be doable with our new powers, but many of us might die. However, for those who make it, danger hides opportunities. Be brave. Are you ready?"

It was a simple speech, yet the monkeys erupted in cheers and cries to the point where Jack suspected they'd gone to fetch some High Speed Bush leaves while he was asleep.

It wasn't that, though. They'd just gotten fired up by his demonstration of a Dao Root. It was a power that spoke to the hearts of all living beings, including Jack, which was why he'd been so obsessed with the bald man's vision.

Having given his rousing speech, Jack nodded with pride. These were brave monkeys.

There were thirty gymonkeys ranging between levels 9 and 19; seven brorillas, from level 20 to 25; and Harambe, who was at a whopping level 37.

The entire monkey army was vastly stronger than before, as was Jack, whose current battle prowess reached into the early forties—not including the Dao Root, whose precise strength was still unclear.

All in all, they were a brave group, and Jack was proud of them. In fact, he realized he'd neglected some things. He'd only treated them as allies so far, not as people, not as friends. Maybe he'd paid some extra attention to Harambe, but it wasn't enough.

Jack was all at once overcome with guilt, and he rushed to fix his wrongs.

"Brorillas," he said, stepping forth, and the seven of them hurried to do the same. "Do you have names?"

The brorillas glanced at each other and shook their heads. "Very well. From now on, you will be Oz, Herom, Amoh, Loha, Raza, Brodul, and Ehamba."

They were random names, but he felt they matched the brorillas' nature. He also named them in order of highest to lowest level.

"I am Jack. It is a pleasure to meet you all."

He shook hands with the seven brorillas, then joined them in flexing their muscles. Though his were admittedly smaller, nobody made fun of him or looked weird. His strength was all the proof they needed.

The monkeys cheered at this impromptu bodybuilding demonstration, and the brorillas nodded to each other with pride. They nodded deeply at Jack, then at Harambe, who'd also joined the flexing.

Jack then turned to the big brorilla. "Harambe, you will name the gymonkeys. Remember, as you are now people, you all need names!"

Harambe nodded. He then turned to the monkeys, pointed at them one by one, and uttered names that Jack's ears couldn't quite catch. Regardless, the gymonkeys seemed satisfied. Tears were in their eyes, proud to finally have proper names. Then, in an unspoken accord, they rushed toward Jack.

"Hey—"

They buried him in a big group hug that nailed him to the wall. Thankfully, he had high stats, or he might have been squashed.

"It's fine, it's fine." He laughed as he pushed them off. "We're friends now. We should help each other. Just a few names are nothing."

It was a touching moment. So touching, in fact, that Jack realized he'd made a mistake. Many of them might die against the wolf. Maybe he should have held back on the whole bonding thing…

What's done is done. Jack followed the Dao of the Fist. He was all or nothing, no half-measures.

"We've delayed enough," he spoke up, drawing everyone's attention. "Let's go. We have a wolf to kill."

They cheered again. Then, they streamed out of Jack's hidden cave like an army of ants, crossing the reserve and heading for its center, where Harambe knew the wolf had its den.

Jack was touched. He'd only been in the Forest of the Strong for a few days, but it felt like an entire lifetime. His time here was so full of tension, action, danger… and he'd grown so massively, too.

Now, things were coming to an end. He would escape and return to civilization. He would finally see what the world looked like, and he could live without fear for his life—hopefully.

Everything had converged to its final point: the black wolf. The Dungeon Boss.

Chapter 27
Wolf Hunting

Jack and the monkey army prowled through the morning forest. The pleasant chattering of birds, the last drops of moisture rolling off leaves, the vivid colors, these all formed a joyful mood that contrasted the soberness of the situation.

They'd chosen the morning because wolves enjoyed hunting at night. Also, because Jack was getting tired of all the monkey business in his cave.

A howl cut through the forest. Their bones rocked; their eyes narrowed. This howl hid fury and determination. The wolf was no longer playing around. It was out to get them.

Unless they got it first. It didn't sound like the wolf was sleeping, as they'd hoped, but maybe it was still in its cave—placing the howl's origin was difficult. With any luck, they could enact an ambush. If not, they would just wait for it to return.

The dungeon's final battle was arriving, swiftly and unavoidably.

Harambe led them through the trees until they reached a rocky hill in the middle of the forest. It stood only a few dozen feet tall and many dozen wide, and its back hid a shallow cave.

Fun fact: When the System arrived, Jack was on a tour to inspect two caves. If the coin had just flipped the other way, it wouldn't have been a level 2 goblin spawning beside him, but an Elite level 49 black wolf.

Jack and Harambe walked ahead. They found a hidden alcove in the rock and crouched to watch.

"Wait, Harambe," Jack whispered. "The wind is blowing toward the cave. It may smell us. Let's circle around the hill and approach the other way."

Harambe growled. They retreated with the monkeys and approached from the northeast, where the wind wouldn't betray their presence. Again, Jack and Harambe went ahead to scout. They hid behind a large rock.

The wolf's cave was a gaping maw in the side of the hill. It was pitch-black inside, as the towering rocks blocked the sun rays, giving the impression that the cave was endless. It could lead anywhere from two feet deep to China.

That they couldn't see inside was a bummer.

"It's probably empty," said Jack. "Why would the wolf howl from inside its cave? Let's see if this hill can hide forty monkeys, Harambe."

However, the big brorilla shook his head. His nose twitched, and he mimed jaws as he pointed in the cave.

"It's inside?" Jack raised a brow. Harambe nodded. "Very well. Then, we go with the original plan. We can't ambush it, but we can smother it. Let's fill the cave with gorillas."

They retreated to prepare. Two minutes later, the entire monkey army stood arrayed with the gorillas at the front, watching the cave's opening from just where they couldn't be seen.

"Get ready, everyone," Jack commanded. "We go quietly, and when I give the signal, we run. Got it?"

The monkeys nodded. He took a deep breath. Memories of his struggles passed through his mind: the goblins, the bears, the wolf that insta-killed anything it wanted...

"Let's go."

A gentle, rocky incline led up to the cave's mouth. The monkey army crawled over it, trying to stay silent so as not to spook the wolf. They wanted to reach the cave before it noticed them. In the open space outside, the advantage would belong to the wolf. In the narrow cave, to them.

Jack was first, with the big brorilla farther behind due to his large size. He leaned on a rock and peeked over it. He was only fifty feet away from the cave. Close enough to notice the two yellow eyes glaring at him from the darkness.

> **Black Wolf, Level 49 (Elite) (Dungeon Boss)**
> *Black wolves are mostly solitary creatures. They are also territorial, proud, aggressive, and infamous for being a scourge at the peak of F-Grade. If a Black Wolf is spotted, experienced hunter squads should be dispatched quickly, or all big game of the surrounding area will disappear.*

Jack froze for a single moment, then jumped forward like a spring. "Charge!" he shouted, initiating the battle, and waves of monkeys flooded the open ground behind him.

The wolf didn't expect the monkeys. It released a low growl and stepped outside its cave, making to escape.

Unfortunately for the wolf, the cave mouth was preceded by a short corridor of rock. Under normal circumstances, a few feet were nothing. But right now, Jack was bounding forth with long steps, jumping over the rock at speeds that would make any Olympic athlete jealous.

The wolf wouldn't make it in time. Its gaze landed deep inside Jack's eyes, who stared back. They'd met twice in the past—this was the third and last.

Yesterday, Jack might have been scared. He was charging at a superior opponent by himself. Today, however, he was a fist. This charge was his nature.

He slowed slightly, keeping himself close to the ground so he could react quickly. The wolf, realizing it couldn't escape, threw its head back and released a loud, drawn-out howl.

Hearing it from up-close was an experience. His ears rung and his vision swam. The sound penetrated his soul and shook it, but something fought back. The Dao Root of the Fist reacted as if it had met a worthy opponent, and it extinguished the wolf's attack.

Jack regained himself only to find the wolf's claws inches away from his face. He ducked on instinct, letting himself slide on the rock and gaining a long, bloody gash on the top of his head. He'd survived.

It has a Dao Root! he realized, paling. Shit!

He rolled upright and pivoted to face the wolf, which hadn't stopped running. It was charging the monkeys, who were still dazed, like a dark arrow.

"HARAMBE!" Jack roared.

A massive form stepped in the wolf's charge. A large fist shot at its face with the power of an elephant, forcing the wolf to slow and sidestep before lunging for Harambe's throat. A day ago, the big brorilla couldn't have dodged this, but the High Speed Bush and the ice pond had raised his speed tremendously.

He leaned back, barely dodging the wolf's jaws, then slammed a heavy uppercut into its lower jaw, sending it flying.

The wolf wasn't injured. It somersaulted in midair and fell claws-first right where Jack was waiting. He danced away and the rock under his feet was sliced into pieces. The wolf's claws weren't joking.

It landed on all fours and shot at Jack, chasing him down. Jack's eyes widened. It was too fast. He managed to dodge the claws, taking only a small graze on his forearm, but the wolf smashed bodily into him and sent him flying into a tall rock. He slammed into it, cracking the stone, then slid to the ground.

The wolf stared him down from ten feet away, its eyes colored by nothing except hatred, menace, fear, and animalistic fury. Jack stared straight back.

This wolf was stronger and faster than him. More durable, too, since Harambe's uppercut had seemingly dealt no damage. But Jack wasn't alone.

Monkey cries echoed over the hill. Thirty brown shapes surrounded the wolf from a distance, holding stones at the ready—Jack had convinced them that poop was mostly harmless. Jack faced the wolf from the front, Harambe from the back, and the seven brorillas had formed a loose circle around them, ready to intervene or slow down the wolf with their lives.

The wolf looked around—it was surrounded—and growled. Jack grinned and cracked his knuckles. "Come. I'll show you who's the boss around here."

It lunged sideways. Apparently, it still sought to escape, solidifying its relative weakness in Jack's mind.

The wolf charged between Jack and Harambe, trying to escape the encirclement from the side. However, there was a brorilla there. His name was Herom.

Herom opened his mouth and screamed at the approaching wolf. He stood on his legs and balled his fists, ready to box. His heavy eyes scowled under that wide forehead.

The wolf fell on him like a wrecking ball. Claws flashed and jaws snapped shut. Herom was sent flying in two pieces, but he'd achieved his goal. To kill him, the wolf had slowed down. And that was enough for a massive hand to wrap around its tail, jerking it still. The wolf looked back and shivered.

Harambe had arrived, and he was fucking pissed.

With a massive roar of rage, he swung the wolf from its tail and smashed it into the ground, showering the approaching Jack with gravel. He raised the wolf, then slammed it down again. And again. And again. Harambe had just seen one of his bros get killed. His rage could not be put into words.

He howled as he planted the wolf deep into the ground with each strike, making its bones groan. It couldn't do anything to keep from getting swung around by its tail. Finally, Harambe reached a boiling point. He smashed the wolf into the ground a final time and let go of its tail to beat it up with his bare hands.

A rain of punches and kicks landed on the wolf amidst gorilla growls. Harambe had turned into a beast. Jack didn't dare approach.

In the end, the wolf was stronger. Despite getting smashed like an octopus, it could still fight, claws glinting in the sunlight. It bared its fangs, and growled. Harambe was sliced by the right, then a pair of jaws wrapped around his left leg and broke it.

He screamed, letting the wolf squirm out of his grasp. It was bloodied, panting, injured, and with multiple broken or cracked bones, but it could still fight. In fact, being cornered and near death, this wolf was currently at its most dangerous.

However, it still tried to escape. It charged to the side, smashing head-first into Raza, a brorilla, and sending him flying, thankfully without other injuries. It then headed for the group of gymonkeys, who fearlessly showered it with stones.

Stones thrown by gymonkeys were nothing to scoff at. They were heavy, fast, and precisely aimed. The wolf received two in each of its eyes and many more all over its body, aggravating its wounds, but it didn't stop. It barreled into the monkey army and started ripping them apart, clawing blindly at all sides.

A few monkeys were bisected and many more were injured. The rest ran away with screams, letting the wolf claw away at nothing. Just as it was about to escape, a heavy fist slammed into its side. Its hard fur was useless against this fist. Its skin shook, and the broken ribs underneath sent burning pulses all over its body.

The wolf howled in pain as it flew sideways to land on a heap of rubble, and Jack was already upon it.

He'd seen what it did to Harambe, Herom, and the monkeys. His rage was boiling, but he wouldn't repeat Harambe's mistake. He wouldn't give the wolf a chance to fight back.

As it lay in pain and defenseless, Jack clenched his right fist. He reared it back, gritted his teeth, and as he was falling from the sky, smashed it into the wolf's face. It recovered from its pain just in time to see the fist landing.

"Calamitous Punch!"

There was an explosion. Rubble flew everywhere, along with blood and pieces of fur. The wolf's head was mangled, its body unmoving. It was dead.

Jack stood beside it, panting like he'd just run a marathon, and his fist was shivering. It wasn't broken like last time, when he'd Calamitous-Punched solid ground, just slightly injured.

But he'd done it. The wolf was dead. They'd won.

"We won!" he roared. Some monkeys cheered. Others, not so much. It was a pyrrhic victory. Harambe was out of commission, Herom had died, Raza was injured, many monkeys were killed or wounded, and the army was disorganized. Ironically, Jack was almost fine.

But they'd won.

> **Level Up! You have reached Level 26.**
> **Level Up! You have reached Level 27.**
> **Level Up! You have reached Level 28.**
> **Level Up! You have reached Level 29.**

Jack roared again.

A terrible, soul-stirring, wolf's howl answered him. His eyes widened as he looked down—the wolf's corpse was still unmoving. He looked up.

Beyond the injured gymonkeys, beyond the mourning brorillas and Harambe who was nursing his wounds, beyond the other half of the gymonkey army, stood another wolf. It looked identical to the first one, with two key differences: it was completely uninjured and absolutely furious. And its yellow eyes were trained only on Jack.

> **Black Wolf, Level 49 (Elite) (Dungeon Boss)**
> *Black wolves are mostly solitary creatures. They are also territorial, proud, aggressive, and infamous for being a scourge at the peak of F-Grade. If a Black Wolf is spotted, experienced hunter squads should be dispatched quickly, or all big game of the surrounding area will disappear.*

There wasn't one Dungeon Boss. There were two. And Jack's army wasn't ready to deal with the second one.

Oh, fuck me.

Chapter 28
Between Life and Death

J ack quickly allocated all his bonus points equally.

The wolf stared at him with boundless rage. Time seemed to freeze. Slowly, Jack understood what happened. He remembered the wolf's description.

Black wolves are mostly solitary creatures.

Mostly.

Well, these ones lived in pairs. They just looked the same. *Fuck you, System! Why do you do this to me?*

Unfortunately, the System didn't give favors. Sometimes, luck was on the table, and sometimes, there was misfortune.

Then it occurred to him—the last time he saw a black wolf in the forest, it had a scar above its snout. The one lying at his feet didn't. He stifled a dry croak. He should have known. This was so unfair.

Fuck you, System, he repeated, this time with heavy bile.

The wolf didn't give him time to think any further. It charged. The back half of the gymonkey army was only just noticing the wolf. It ripped into them with ease.

Monkeys were sent flying. Blood and body parts littered the ground. The wolf had seen Jack deal the final blow on its partner, but it understood that the monkeys were involved. It would give them no quarter.

Almost a dozen monkeys were slaughtered in the span of a few seconds. The rest were either injured or running away in fear. A growl came from the middle of everything as Harambe tried to stand and failed. His leg was thoroughly broken. After getting bitten like that, it was a miracle it was even still in place.

The wolf saw Harambe and pounced at him.

The five remaining brorillas saw blood. They formed a line before their big bro, determined to defend him with their lives. They flexed their muscles in unison to intimidate the enemy.

"No!" Jack screamed, already sprinting, but the wolf was faster. It fell on the brorillas like a piano from the fifth floor, ripping into them as easily as it had into the monkeys.

Amoh's leg went flying. His head followed soon after. The wolf ripped out a chunk of Brodul's shoulder as it broke through the brorillas, reaching Harambe. This was its goal.

Unfortunately, Harambe was in no shape to defend himself. He could only stare defiantly at the claw that came to behead him.

A hard fist smashed into the side of that claw, sending it off-course. A bare-chested human form stood between the wolf and the gorilla, tiny but full of resolve.

"Leave my bro alone," he commanded.

Seeing Jack, the wolf's eyes flashed with something between revenge and ridicule. He should have run, but he charged into death's maw instead. The wolf would oblige.

Claws slashed and jaws snapped shut. Jack dashed back, desperately dodging the blows. This wolf was as strong as the rock bear, but its speed was worlds apart. It deserved to be the Dungeon Boss. Jack could barely dodge, and not for long.

He danced left and right to distract the wolf, but those yellow eyes, full of rage and blood, followed him unerringly. He ducked under the jaws and tried to throw an uppercut, but a claw smashed into his side out of nowhere, sending him flying. He barely had time to defend. Three long gashes now adorned his forearm.

Jack smashed hard into a rock. All air shot out of his lungs.

The five remaining brorillas made gorilla noises as they threw themselves at the wolf. The gymonkeys joined the fray, throwing a hail of stones and hoping to hit something sensitive. However, the black wolf wasn't an opponent they could beat. It was simply on another level.

Its body became a maelstrom of sharpness. Claws were everywhere, jaws snapped beside their ears. The wolf's dark fur filled everyone's vision, infesting it with images of gruesome death. The world became dark—magically so.

The gymonkeys screamed and ran away. The brorillas clenched their fists, and their faces spasmed as they struggled to resist.

Jack rose from the rubble, darkness flooding his world. The sun was replaced by a bloody moon, and the stars winked out one by one. The breeze smelled of blood and iron as terror slithered down his spine.

Something inside him rebelled. The Dao Root shook in outrage. Jack roared and punched, and the illusion broke like a mirror.

The wolf stared at him, its gaze filled with bloodlust. It had lost its mind to rage and lived only to devour Jack, whose body was covered in the blood of its partner. Jack looked around. The gymonkeys were running away, and the brorillas had fallen on their butts. Harambe's wide forehead was wrinkled as he tried to shake off the illusion, but even if he succeeded, he was too injured to help.

Jack was left alone. He gritted his teeth and stared the wolf down. There was no retreat. He would live or die. His mind raced, his heart beat like a drum, blood shot through his veins and filled his body with power.

Primal instincts returned at full force, with Jack steady at the helm. He'd earned that right. His mind was ice and his body fire. Deep inside him, the Dao Root shimmered with the power to annihilate everything.

The wolf wasn't intimidated.

By using its Dao Root, Jack thought. It can create illusions. Can I do the same?

His instinct told him he couldn't. He could punch hard and that was it.

The wolves have different Dao Roots, he analyzed through this moment of slowed time. The first one was less developed, something to do with sound or fear. This is about illusions, maybe darkness, but I broke through. Can it be used again?

The wolf wasn't inclined to answer. It charged Jack, who stood his ground. Every single scrap of skill he'd accumulated was poured into this fight. This was the culmination of everything. He'd fought so hard to reach the end. He couldn't fall here.

Claws, jaws. Red lines on white skin, yellow eyes with black irises that never lost him. A body of darkness that fell on Jack like a freight train.

He resisted. The wolf's patterns weren't much different than the rock bear's, it was just incomparably faster. Jack understood these patterns well. He'd faced them for what seemed like eternity.

He dodged on instinct, knowing where to weave and where to duck, he predicted the next hit's trajectory. His Fistfighting skill, his greatest ally, shored up his weaknesses. For the first time since the skill reached the second tier, it became strained.

The wolf tried to bite him and missed. A claw came for his face. Jack had already turned, nailing a hard straight into the wolf's ribs. They creaked but held. The Dao of the Fist was making his strikes harder, and Drill helped him bypass the wolf's thick fur. Unfortunately, its skin was equally thick, and a large part of the damage dissipated before doing any harm.

Another claw. He weaved to the left, ducked, then spun to narrowly avoid a strike. He smashed a fist into the wolf's snout right as the top of its head slammed into his belly, sending him flying into the hill. He jumped back up just in time to dodge the wolf's claw, which buried itself into the rubble.

Jack and the wolf danced under the bloody morning sunlight, while the monkeys and gorillas could only watch. Harambe had escaped the illusion, but could only bite his lips. His eyes were filled with concern, hope... and faith in his bro.

Jack had no time to feel anything. The wolf's speed pushed him to the absolute limit. Surviving by the skin of his teeth was an achievement. Each strike he received bloodied him or cracked his bones, and each punch he dealt had little effect. He had no advantage. The battle was losing.

The Calamitous Punch was his only hope, but he could only use it once more, maybe twice. He had to time it perfectly.

The wolf pounced, a whirlwind of death, and Jack danced between its claws like a leaf in the wind. One punch after another flew out, but they could only push the wolf back. Jack was losing ground. His retreat sped up, but that only increased his disadvantage.

The wolf went in for a bite.

There! His eyes widened. Calamitous Punch!

His fist shot out like an arrow, faster and stronger than before, smashing hard into the wolf's snout. The impact was as calamitous as the name indicated, shaking Jack's entire body and the gravel he stood on. The wolf was sent flying, then rolled on the ground and recovered. Its nose was bloody, but not much else happened.

It had taken a Calamitous Punch in the face and easily survived.

Jack fell on his knees, panting. His secret weapon had failed. There was nothing else in him. Despair threatened to cloud his mind, and as the wolf pounced again, he almost stayed still and let himself die.

But at the last moment, his Dao Root pulsed like a second heart. The fear washed away, evaporating the despair. Jack jumped aside, dodging the strike. So what if he was going to die? So what if he couldn't win? He would just punch until the end and go out as a warrior.

He laughed in the face of the wolf, which looked at him like he was crazy. Its attacks intensified, menace growing, and Jack simply did his best. He'd abandoned all hope. Merely living to fight a little longer.

If anyone saw Jack right now, they would be terrified. They would see a bare-chested barbarian dancing chaotically between a black wolf's strikes. He survived on the edge of the razor. His eyes were red, as were the wolf's, and he was grinning. He looked like he was having fun, a madman with zero respect for his life. A terrifying man.

Jack's world was clear. He was going to die, that was certain. He couldn't beat this wolf. He barely had enough energy to fire off another Calamitous Punch, but even when timed perfectly, it couldn't harm the wolf. His normal punches didn't cut it. He could not escape. There were no tricks.

Therefore, he would simply fight and express himself in the purest way he could: by going down punching.

The monkeys disappeared from his mind, and so did the stakes. None of that mattered. Only the wolf's attacks remained, and though Jack was growing tired, things became slightly easier. In the nick of death, he'd unknowingly achieved a mental state perfect for battle, where he could act at his absolute peak. His world was this battle. Nothing else remained.

He entered the zone.

He read the wolf's moves before they happened. He bobbed, weaved, and punched—if ineffectively. He let some strikes land on him, perfectly aware of what he could handle and what he could not. He assumed complete control of his body, clenching muscles he didn't even know he had, to move better. His skin turned into a substance he controlled, and he willed it to become harder, stronger, more suitable for someone who used his fists. His Dao of the Fist told him how.

> **Congratulations!**
> Pugilist Body (I) → Pugilist Body (II)

He didn't see the screen. Only felt himself become sturdier and took full advantage of that. Jack accepted some strikes in order to retaliate. He let the wolf's momentum bleed into his own attacks. He became a menace. If the wolf was a beast, then Jack would be a warrior.

At some point, he abandoned defense. He let it run on autopilot. What did it matter?

Instead, he focused on offense. Amidst the howling and growling, and clawing and jaw-snapping, Jack swam like a fish, taking two light hits to land one. His fists smashed into the wolf's body with greater and greater force. Which proved useless. He could feel the skin's resistance nullifying his strength.

On instinct, his attacks turned sharper. His arm was straighter and steadier, almost longer. No energy escaped. The Dao of the Fist whispered how to punch, and Jack listened.

Punch after punch, he got stronger. His attacks hurt more. They were so direct that their energy didn't dissipate easily, penetrating both fur and skin to impact the soft tissue underneath. For the first time after the Calamitous Punch, the wolf growled in pain. Jack hammered another punch in the same spot and the wolf jumped back, wariness in its eyes.

> **Congratulations!**
> Drill (I) → Drill (II)

In the eve of death, Jack's full potential was unlocked. He'd only achieved such clear-headedness in the ice waterfall. His skills were advancing at a breakneck pace being forced to his limit. His Dao Root flooded him with meaning that he absorbed like a dry lake sucking in the rain.

Exhaustion didn't matter. Jack had shelved it away in some hidden part of his mind. He'd fight like mad and just collapse when he ran out of steam.

He was growing stronger by the minute, but would it be enough? The wolf attacked again—attacks flying in every direction.

Jack was a worthy opponent now. He wasn't winning, but he wasn't losing either. The wolf also accumulated injuries. Punch after punch, he was getting through, but his body was on the brink of collapse.

Suddenly, something changed. The wolf slashed, but Jack saw its entire leg get covered in darkness. He couldn't tell the claw's exact position. In such a high-speed, razor-sharp battle, one mistake could be fatal.

This wasn't normal. It was magic. A Dao Root at work.

The bloody bastard had been holding back. It'd been toying with him, humiliating and mocking him out of spite. It wanted to drive him to despair, give him hope, and take it away again.

Hot rage bubbled in Jack's gut.

Chapter 29
Meteor Punch

He didn't know where to dodge. Was it early or late? How far should he lean?

Jack would later swear that, at that moment, the wolf grinned. Its claw came at him, and there was nothing he could do except gamble. It possessed the Dao Root of Shadow but hadn't used it until now, except for that small illusion it activated at the very start.

The claw came for his head, its position vague. Jack had to make a decision. What was best?

His brain practically exploded. Every single synapse fired off at once. Time didn't slow, but he saw a thousand thoughts go through his mind at the same time, like he was watching a hundred bright minds work together inside his.

He had perfect awareness of his body. Could sense every muscle, every injury, the exact millimeter at which he could lean and how much time it would cost him to recover.

Even the wolf's stance. Every tiny thing was taken into account. He remembered all patterns he'd witnessed and contrasted them with the current one. His brain, trained by years of study as a biologist, was now fully devoted to battle.

A hundred simulations—the claw's most probable patterns on full display, three of them, and the different scenarios they would lead to. He included the inevitable feint. He considered every possible way to dodge and saw two moves into the future. He contrasted his options and the wolf's, pruning the scenarios with unbelievable speed.

For a single moment, he had perfect awareness.

> **Congratulations!**
> **Fistfighting (II) → Fistfighting (III)**

He dodged. His movement was accurate to the millimeter. He'd taken into account his momentum, his injuries, even the strain on his muscles. He knew how fast and where the wolf could move.

The claw sailed two fingers over his head. He leaned to the side with mathematical accuracy, letting the next strike pass just under him as he used his momentum to turn and jump back. The maneuver was perfect. Jack was safe.

In the next moment, his head squeezed with a terrible headache that assaulted him as if his brain were cramping. Under normal circumstances, he might have fainted on the spot. Except he didn't have that luxury.

But his reflexes dropped. The previous perfect awareness gave its place to lethargy, confusion, and dizziness. Everything was fuzzy. Jack's mind was spent, and so was his body.

That bastard... he thought, watching the wolf pounce with jaws wide open. He hid until the last moment... There was nothing I could do... I'd lost before the battle even began.

METEOR PUNCH

Jack was determined to fight until the very end. He scrounged up his last dregs of energy and prepared a Calamitous Punch. With the upgrade in Drill, perhaps it would work this time.

The wolf's head blurred in darkness. Jack chuckled. It didn't matter, anyway. His fist sailed forth unerringly. The two were about to meet. Jack would die, but at least, he'd go down with a bang.

At that final moment before his death, a tiny candle burned in his mind. Something called at him from deep within. He let it, curious where the thought would lead. He let himself become distracted because it really didn't matter.

Then, Jack saw the wolf's previous attack in replay. He saw how it'd fused its Dao Root into the attack.

He saw the bald man's punch. He felt the Dao of the Fist at work, operating at a level he couldn't fathom. And, for the first time, under the veil of death, he realized that Dao and fist didn't move separately. The bald man didn't envelop one in the other, as Jack assumed. They were one and the same. The Dao and the fist could become one—no, they always had been.

Jack snapped back to the present. His fist inches away from the wolf's open maw and felt himself activating Calamitous Punch.

Why stop there?

His Dao Root flowed into the fist as well, majestic and undeniable. Then, something magical happened. His Dao was absorbed by the System's skill, tamed, and released in a way far more effective than his own crude use.

Just before impact, the sun went dark. The world turned black and white. Every eye was drawn to Jack's fist as if the world were ending. In the colorless void, his arm left a meteor trail behind it. The fist shone purple. It sped up and attained such momentum that Jack couldn't control it anymore. Its power far belied his fist's size.

The punch exploded on the wolf's snout like a sun was born. Color returned to the world abruptly, along with a thunderous sound wave as an actual explosion enveloped the site of Jack and the wolf's clash.

> **Congratulations! Skill Calamitous Punch (I) upgraded into Dao Skill, Meteor Punch (I).**
> **Meteor Punch (I):** When meteors fall from space, they cause exponentially more damage than their size would indicate. Your punches can carry the same effect. Overdraw your body's potential and combine it with your Dao of the Fist to unleash a devastating attack.

Jack flew back and smashed into a rock, unable to move an inch. He moaned in pain. His hand wasn't just broken, it was completely disfigured.

But it was worth it.

Near the site of impact, the wolf lay still, bloodied, and headless. It was like a small meteor had fallen from orbit and smashed straight into its head.

Jack had won. *No*, he corrected himself, meeting Harambe's incredulous stare. *We won.*

> **Level Up! You have reached Level 30.**
> **Level Up! You have reached Level 31.**
> **Level Up! You have reached Level 32.**
> **Level Up! You have reached Level 33.**
> **Level Up! You have reached Level 34.**

He tried to shout in triumph but couldn't even move his mouth. Only the bonus points from the level-ups, which could be allocated by simply willing it, kept him conscious.

With a shallow sigh of relief, Jack quickly invested some points in Mental and Will, bringing them both to 10. The ensuing lucidity would help him stay awake, hopefully. It wasn't time to sleep yet.

His mind was expanding, his willpower doubling down over his body, the world unraveling in slightly clearer patterns than before. It was like a spiritual awakening—and, at the same time, Jack understood this wasn't his path. He'd grown, but the power of the fist inside him remained stagnant. He quickly invested the rest of the points into Physical, enhancing his body to limit the effect of his injuries, and shuddered as he sensed his muscles compacting further.

At least he'd brought both Mental and Will to a nice, round number, something he'd been itching to do for a long time. He used the mental enhancement to read the next few blue screens faster.

> **Congratulations! You have conquered the Forest of the Strong! If you belong to a Faction, you can choose to assimilate the Dungeon into your territory. Calculating rewards…**
> **1 F-Grade Faction-Forming Permit.**
> **1 Trial Planet Token.**
> **1 F-Grade Dao Fruit of the Fist.**

A few trinkets materialized before his feet.

...*What?* Jack was thoroughly exhausted and in tremendous pain. He was in no mood to deal the System's shenanigans. He also had no idea what any of those things were, but at least the screens confirmed this was the last black wolf. If there was a third one, Jack wouldn't know who to curse.

However, the screens still weren't over.

> Dungeon border lifting on hold. Total monster despawning on hold. Faction territory assignment on hold. Would you like to assimilate the Dungeon into your Faction's territory and assume control or proceed with the automated parameters? This decision has a time limit of 1 minute.

...What?

Jack still had no idea what was happening. He was at one of the most exhausted points of his life, and the System thought he was in the mood to play with interfaces. He almost willed the screen away before his addled mind caught up to one important piece of information.

Wait. Total monster despawning? Will it despawn the monkeys?

He gazed at Harambe. The big brorilla was giving him a thumbs-up, his grumpy face curved into a big smile. The gymonkeys were hesitantly celebrating from afar, while the brorillas were only now recovering from their shock. Four of them went to take care of their injured bros, while Oz, the strongest brorilla, rushed over to Jack and tried to mime something.

Jack ignored him. Moans and screams of pain littered the air—the cries of his allies, who'd risked themselves to grant him victory. There were also many others that would never make a sound again.

They will all be despawned? Jack's eyes widened. No!

He forced his mind to parse the information. Due to his exhaustion, he had to read through the screens thrice to understand.

No, he told the System. *Do not proceed with the automated parameters. Let me choose.*

It ignored him.

> **30 seconds left before automated dungeon recovery.**

Jack gritted his teeth. He couldn't take control of the dungeon himself—he needed a faction.

Unfortunately, he didn't have one.

> **20 seconds left before automated dungeon recovery.**

The reward! His eyes shone. The System had given him 1 F-Grade Faction-Forming Permit for conquering the dungeon. It was self-explanatory.

He gazed at the trinkets by his feet. One was a tablet made of blue crystal with a green F engraved on it. Going by instinct, he grabbed it.

Form faction! he shouted in his mind. *Form faction. Please!*

The tablet turned into dust.

> **F-Grade Faction founding activated.**
> **Please choose the name of your faction:**

I... uh...

> **10 seconds left before automated dungeon recovery.**

He looked at his fist. *Bare Fist Brotherhood!*

> **You have chosen the name 'Bare Fist Brotherhood.'**
> **Please confirm.**

Confirm, dammit, confirm.

> **5 seconds left before automated dungeon recovery.
> Faction registered. Please think 'Faction' to—**

He ignored the last screen.
Assimilate the dungeon into my faction, he thought.

> **2 seconds left before automated dungeon recovery.**

Come on! Please!

> **Forest of the Strong has been assimilated
> into the Bare Fist Brotherhood's territory.
> Automated dungeon recovery canceled.
> Please handle everything manually.**

Jack felt more relief than when his first date said yes.
Oh, thank God...

He slid back to the ground. Oz the brorilla was still miming his congratulations and asking if Jack needed any help, which he very much did. He was bleeding from multiple places, had lost much blood already, and his hand was ruined. If nothing was done, he would die.

Unfortunately, he'd already used even his last dregs of energy. There was simply nothing left.

"Please help me..." he croaked out before his world turned black.

Chapter 30
Reaping the Rewards

Jack was dragged out of his blissful sleep by burning agony. He woke up screaming.

The last thing he remembered was the black wolf coming for him. He was still in battle. Hell, his entire body burned everywhere the wolf injured him. The pain was immeasurable.

He jumped up with a splash, still screaming at the top of his lungs. Two gorillas were before him, trying to calm him down—or kill him. Rocky walls surrounded him like a coffin, his body was filled with the cold of death, and everything was illuminated by a pale, white light.

Looking down, his feet were dipped in cold, clear water. *Oh.*

It was the ice pond. He was in the ice pond. In his cave. He was safe.

Jack unclenched his left fist, which had almost taken off Oz's head. "Sorry," he tried to say, but found himself exhausted. The next moment, the pain returned at full force. "FU—" Jack bit his lips not to scream.

This agony. The pain of healing. He had to take it.

Still unsure of what was going on, Jack gritted his teeth and sat back in the pond, letting the purifying cold burn his body. He couldn't stifle a few screams, especially when his right fist touched the water. It was completely ruined, with bones sticking out in various locations. How did that happen?

The memories came in flashes, synchronized with the pain. A second black wolf had appeared, determined to kill him. It was strong, very strong. He'd resisted. The battle was fuzzy, but at the end, he'd fused his Dao into the Calamitous Punch skill to create a new skill—a Dao skill—called Meteor Punch that destroyed both his hand and the wolf's head.

He remembered that impact clearly. There was a blinding flash and the roar of thunder, and the wolf was gone.

Despite the pain—which he tried to avoid by thinking—he shivered.

A Dao skill... Is that a skill based on my Dao? Is that why it's so strong? I didn't even know skills could upgrade like that.

It was too much to piece apart right now.

Wait. There was more.

He'd gotten some rewards, then founded a faction, or something like that... That part was unclear.

Thankfully, the two brorillas had also brought his other rewards along. A golden coin and a pear-shaped fruit that exuded violence. Jack didn't know how violent fruit could be, but this particular one was definitely at the top of the charts.

He'd deal with those later.

The pain flared once more before receding, and Jack growled as he stood. He was fine, though terribly exhausted. In fact, he felt something odd, as if his body was still fixing itself even without the pond's assistance.

His thoughts were still slipping through his mind, so he decided to ground them by reviewing some blue screens. He had a bunch.

> **Congratulations!**
> **Pugilist Body (I) → Pugilist Body (II)**
> **Pugilist Body (II):** Your body has adapted to your fighting style. You gain significant flexibility, reflexes, and durability, as well as increased hardness on your knuckles. *You have heightened control over your body, including its natural limiters, and slight regenerative powers.*
>
> **Congratulations!**
> **Drill (I) → Drill (II)**
> **Drill (II):** Passive Skill. By punching straight and true, you carry significant drilling power, letting your strikes penetrate hard defenses. *You can bypass most kinds of armor, including thick ones.*
>
> **Congratulations!**
> **Fistfighting (II) → Fistfighting (III)**
> **Fistfighting (III):** Grants expert knowledge of fistfighting. While fistfighting, enhances your physical attributes, reflexes, and kinetic vision. *Moreover, your brain's wiring is better suited for combat, especially fistfighting.*

Huh.

Besides some adjectives becoming stronger, the System was helpful enough to highlight the main improvements.

He didn't get a new skill at level 30—looks like three was all the class could give him for now—but these improvements were nothing to scoff at.

Pugilist Body looked great. It offered increased control over his body, which was the equivalent of removing his training wheels. And the difference was apparent. Everything felt slightly more complicated, even simple movements like raising his arm. At the same time, it was all done more consciously, granting him far greater control and awareness.

In other words, he had manual control of processes that had so far been automatic.

This skill could be a double-edged sword for most, but for Jack, it was a godsend. He could make up for the complexity by practicing hard, and the benefits would be reaped forever.

Plus, he could now do all sorts of funky things. With amusement, he flexed his intestines—almost getting a cramp—and moved his ears. *Take that, Professor.* She could always do that and used to mock him for being unable to.

He clenched his fist. It was amazing how many little muscles coordinated to achieve such a simple thing. There was still a lot of underlying assistance, but Jack was in conscious control of the movement. Living the rest of his life like that was daunting, and at the same time, massively intriguing. If he could get over the steep learning curve, the sky was the ceiling.

Besides this massive increase in bodily control, he now had regenerative powers, which was excellent. He wouldn't always have the ice pond handy to heal him. Granted, this regeneration wasn't anything great—he could feel it at work, slow as a snail—but it would hopefully get stronger as the skill advanced.

Drill, on the other hand, was a bit underwhelming. Bypassing armor was great, sure, and it had saved his life, but it wasn't anything world-breaking.

Jack shrugged. Maybe that was a good thing. Too much change at once could be overwhelming.

Finally, there was Fistfighting, which claimed to have changed his brain's wiring. Jack couldn't feel anything different. Though being a biologist—and a scholar—he understood how impactful this change was.

Rewiring the brain usually took years of concentrated practice, and it was the hallmark difference between a novice and a master. As you worked on the same field for years on end, your brain adapted to make the most common patterns more accessible. All relative connections were strengthened to achieve superhuman performance in a particular field.

This was the reason why chess masters could analyze a position and calculate three moves ahead in the blink of an eye. To a layman, that was unimaginable. It wasn't because they were geniuses. Their brains were just appropriately rewired after years of concentrated effort.

To be frank, most chess masters *were* geniuses, but that wasn't the sole reason for their superhuman performance.

Jack was shocked that such a feat could be performed by the System. Years of hard work were replaced by a single *ding!* and a blue screen. He wasn't sure how he felt about that.

Plus, his brain had already been wired for something: research. He had a PhD in biology—almost. Were those skills still in place, or had the System wiped them away in favor of combat without asking?

And, if it had, was that a bad thing?

Jack shook his head. There were many things to consider, but now wasn't the time. He moved on to the next screen.

> **Congratulations! Skill Calamitous Punch (I) upgraded into Dao Skill Meteor Punch (I).**
> **Meteor Punch (I):** When meteors fall from space, they cause exponentially more damage than their size would indicate. Your punches can carry the same effect. Overdraw your body's potential and combine it with your Dao of the Fist to unleash a devastating attack.

This skill was insane. Devastating was an understatement. If his hand was hard enough, he was confident in demolishing houses with a single punch.

Are skills split into ranks? he couldn't help but wonder. His other skills couldn't compare to Meteor Punch, at least not in their first tier. Was a Dao skill stronger because of his Dao, or was it just a better skill to begin with?

Regardless, Jack now had a tremendous weapon at his disposal. Based on what he'd seen so far, few things in the F-Grade could take a Meteor Punch head-on—or, at least, few things below level 50. For all he knew, F-Grade extended to level 9000.

He'd also gotten nine level-ups in the fight against the wolves. Done reviewing himself, Jack opened his status screen to take in the spectacle.

> **Name:** Jack Rust
> **Species:** Human, Earth-387
> **Faction:** Bare Fist Brotherhood (F-Grade)
> **Grade:** F
> **Class:** Pugilist (Elite)
> **Level:** 34
> **Strength:** 93
> **Dexterity:** 93
> **Constitution:** 93
> **Mental:** 10
> **Will:** 10
> **Skills:** Fistfighting (III), Drill (II), Pugilist Body (II)
> **Dao Skills:** Meteor Punch (I)
> **Titles:** Planetary Frontrunner (10)

It was shaping up. He'd almost reached 100 points in all his physical stats, which made him giddy. In fact, he was already there, if he included Planetary Frontrunner's 10 percent bonus.

Right now, he could probably match a black wolf head-on, even without Meteor Punch.

Jack spent the next few minutes experimenting with various things. He tried fusing his Dao Root with his other skills, but nothing happened. He wondered why he'd succeeded on Calamitous Punch. Was it due to the skill itself and its connection with the bald man's vision, or was it due to the life-or-death state he'd reached at the time?

Jack had no idea.

He also experimented with his stats a bit. He approached a massive boulder, taller than him, and picked it up.

It must have weighed a ton. Lifting the boulder was strenuous, but nothing too serious. Jack was impressed with himself, and he let it fall back down with a massive bang that rocked the cave and made dust fall from the ceiling.

"Sorry," he told the frightened brorillas.

He then approached his other two rewards—besides the faction-forming permit—and took a good look at them. And, by good look, he asked the System to do it.

> **Trial Planet Token**
> *Can allow one person into Trial Planet.*

Not much to see here. Jack shrugged and pocketed it. He'd find out later.

> **Dao Fruit of the Fist (F-Grade)**
> *Allows the user to enter a meditative nirvana state, where the speed of Dao cultivation is greatly increased. Breakthroughs are greatly assisted. This particular fruit is oriented toward the Dao Root of the Fist. Effects are reduced as the user's Dao gets further away from the fist. Effects are reduced as the user's Dao ascends beyond the Dao Root stage. Only one Dao Fruit can be used per Grade.*

Well, he had his confirmation that the Dao was split into stages, and Dao Root was just one of them.

This reward looked like a great thing for him. He assumed he could advance his Dao, though he was unsure how. Maybe this fruit would hold the clue. Moreover, his eyes lingered on the 'breakthrough' part. That smelled important. Like his Dao would advance from Dao Root to the next stage, which sounded like a crucial and difficult process.

Should he save the fruit until then?

He had no idea. Therefore, he decided to keep it for now. For the first time since the System arrived, he didn't feel the need to get immediately stronger. He could take his time. Now that he could exit the dungeon, he could even ask people. The professor would know for sure.

Speaking of people...

He sat back down. There was one more thing to check before leaving. *Faction.*

> **Faction: Bare Fist Brotherhood (F-Grade)**
> **Leader: Jack Rust**
> **Members: 1**
> **Capital: Milky Way galaxy, Milky Way sector, Animal Kingdom constellation, Earth-387 planet, Forest of the Strong dungeon area.**

Jack hurriedly closed the blue screen. It contained entries for a hundred little things, from resource management to monster status, alignment, a topographical description of the territory, hierarchical structure, buildings, to...

Most of those were null, of course, but Jack was allergic to large-scale management. It didn't matter, anyway. He already had a bunch of things on his plate. He'd deal with the rest later.

The one thing he kept was his faction's capital.

Milky Way galaxy, Milky Way sector, Animal Kingdom constellation, Earth-387 planet, Forest of the Strong dungeon area... Wow. Those are a lot of specifications.

Did it imply that the System stretched over multiple galaxies? That was insane! And how many stages of division were there? Earth—his Earth—apparently belonged to the Animal Kingdom constellation, which belonged to the Milky Way sector, which was a part of the galaxy.

What the hell was the Animal Kingdom constellation!

And just what kind of intergalactic empire had the System shoved them into?

Suddenly, Jack was leery of leaving his little dungeon, where things were nice and simple. He sighed. *Well. If anything confuses me, I guess I can just punch right through it.*

The social equivalent to punching was asking stuff, so he'd do just that. The time to leave the dungeon was nigh. Since the world was so big, he shouldn't linger in a tiny corner for too long.

However, before that, there were two things he needed to do. The first was take care of Harambe and the monkeys. Would they join him? Would they stay here? Could they protect themselves against whatever was out there?

That would be up to them. Monkeys or not, they could make their own decisions. Jack would just let Harambe know of the situation.

The next thing to do...

Then it hit him. He'd conquered the dungeon. He'd escaped. He could return to civilization. He would see humans again.

The relief was so strong he almost fainted again.

Prepare yourself, world, he thought, grinning. *I'm coming!*

Chapter 31
Brock the Monkey

Jack stood in silence. Yesterday morning had been full of tension. Today, grief.

Two brorillas and eleven gymonkeys had given their lives against the black wolves. They were brave. They could have chosen cowardice or half-measures, but every single one of them went forth to fight knowing their lives might be forfeit.

There were many injured, but the ice pond healed them. That wasn't a pretty sight either. Oz had been forced to keep some monkeys in the pond, as their mental fortitude wasn't enough to handle the searing pain.

At the end of the day, they were alive, and that's what mattered. All injured gymonkeys thanked Oz for helping them, while he only nodded stoically. His wide forehead was wrinkled further, and his grumpy eyes were filled with sadness.

Monkeys didn't do much with their fallen brothers and sisters, only dumped them somewhere far away for the parasites and fungi to do their job. Jack wasn't having that. After the injured were healed, he organized a funeral and taught the monkeys how to handle death.

In the process, he'd also taught them the concept of death, which they didn't understand too well.

The morning sun illuminated a forest wet from the night's moisture. Droplets hung from leaves like teardrops, and the light refracted through them to reveal all colors of the rainbow. The birds and critters were quiet today, as if sensing the heavy mood, and the wind didn't dare blow too hard.

Jack stood in a peaceful glade, surrounded by twenty-five monkeys: nineteen gymonkeys, five brorillas, and Harambe. This glade was situated behind the monkey forest gym, close to the edge of the nature reserve. Jack had chosen it for its scenery. There was something about the sparsity of trees and the harmony of foliage that gave this place a serene, holy sensation.

It was also close enough to the monkeys' residences that they could visit whenever they wanted, and far enough that it wouldn't be a bother.

Thirteen graves had been dug and refilled. They didn't have coffins, but they didn't need them, either. The monkeys were part of nature in life and death. Jack stood to the side, facing both the graves and the downcast monkeys.

"We are now brothers and sisters," he declared somberly, the weight of goodbye falling on him. "You are all brave. I'm proud of you. And I am most proud of those who fell, because they were perfect. They gave their lives to protect the rest of us. That is an achievement we, who are still alive, cannot claim. We owe our lives to the fallen."

Nobody dared speak or even breathe loudly. Their gazes alternated between Jack and the graves.

"We will not let their lives go to waste," he continued. "This is a rough, unknown world, and we will carve out a home. We will protect ourselves and our children and create a future. We will be united like the fingers of a fist, and we will defend each other as they defended us."

A monkey shivered. Another sniffed. A few tears rolled.

Jack turned to the graves and bowed. "You have given everything. You are worthy. Now, rest in peace… and we will handle the rest. In the name of the strong primates, Jack Rust, and the Bare Fist Brotherhood, we will lead lives that will make you proud. This, I swear."

As his speech finished, the monkeys erupted into mourning. They cried without fear of where their voices carried, shedding fat tears. Some fell to the ground and punched it, while others tore off tufts of their fur and threw it on the graves. The brorillas left a bunch of bananarms before each grave, then flexed their muscles as tears rolled down their hardened faces.

Harambe, the big bro of the monkeys, stepped before the graves after the brorillas were done. He flexed his large muscles hard enough for his eyes to pop out, then bowed deeply and spread some soil on his face while crying. All monkeys followed.

This was their form of tribute. Jack didn't understand everything, but he let them do their thing. He put some soil on his face, too, to honor their customs. No tears left his eyes, though his heart was filled with sadness. They'd fought together, and they died because he couldn't protect them. Had he been stronger, everyone would still be here.

He vowed to remember this.

It took half an hour before things calmed down a little. During that time, Jack remained still as a rock. When the monkeys began dispersing, he stepped beside the big brorilla.

"Harambe," he said, "walk with me."

Harambe nodded at the brorillas, who nodded back, then he followed Jack deeper into the forest, heading back toward the forest gym.

"What are you planning to do, Harambe?" Jack asked. "The world is large, and there are many things we don't know, many dangers we cannot fathom. I feel that the only way to survive and be free is to get stronger. I plan to leave this place, enter the human world, and see how everything has changed. What do you think?"

The gorilla remained silent for a long time. His thoughts weren't the fastest, but that was okay. Jack waited. They crossed glades and forest paths, stepped over rocks and roots. Finally, Harambe turned to Jack and shook his head. His big knuckles tapped the ground.

"You'll stay here?" Jack asked. "Are you sure? There could be others like you in the wide world, maybe even on this planet. Don't you want to meet them?"

Harambe shook his head again. He pointed at himself, made a scary face, then flexed his muscles.

Jack's eyes mellowed. "You want to get stronger, too..."

The System didn't consider the monkeys sapient, like him. They couldn't level-up or do anything like that. They were simply classified as monsters. To get stronger, they had to toil away at their forest gym, lifting weights and sparring each other.

"You have it right, my friend... but you are *not* monsters. I don't care what the System says. It's wrong. And I swear to you that, when I'm strong enough, I will force it to reconsider. I'll find a way to let you in."

Harambe nodded, then tapped his knuckles on the ground again.

"You'll stay here until then... Yeah. I'm sorry for doubting you. That's a sensible choice. On my part, I'll make sure all nearby areas know not to mess with you—though, from what I imagine, they can't, even if they wanted to. The System won't let you in my faction, but this area is marked as mine. I need you to be the guardians of this place, and in return, everything here will belong to you. Even if more people come, you'll still be the owners of the forest. What do you think? Is that a good offer?"

Harambe nodded, bringing a hand to his chest. Then, he stretched a hand out to Jack.

He looked at the hand, then chuckled. He grabbed and shook it. "You have a deal, my friend. Take good care of your little bros while I'm gone. I'm counting on you."

For the first time since they'd met, Harambe grinned. Jack grinned back. The monkeys were in good hands.

"Then, this is goodbye for now. I'll be back as soon as I settle things out there, whatever they are. Try not to kill humans, if you can, but I'll handle the fallout if they force your hand. Oh, and if you see anyone bearing a"—he looked around, then picked up a jagged stone of peculiar shape—"bearing this stone, know they were sent by me. They'll give you my name, anyway."

Harambe nodded. Then, unlike his usual stoic self, he pulled Jack into a big hug.

"Oof! Dude! This would have killed most people!" Jack laughed as he hugged the gorilla. After bathing in the ice pond, everyone was clean, and the waters remained as crystalline as ever.

Jack had checked the wolf cave for rewards but found nothing. *Fair, I guess. I already got plenty.* He'd also entered the waterfall again but received little benefit. He could sense he'd already reaped all he could from there. To advance his Dao, he needed to experience more things. That was another reason why he was in such a rush to leave. The first was that the System's hints about intergalactic empires had instilled a sense of urgency inside him. Plus, he needed to find out if the professor was okay.

"See you, big bro," Jack said, waving, and made to leave. However, Harambe suddenly shook his head. "Hmm? What is it?"

Harambe pointed somewhere, and Jack turned to look. They'd reached the forest gym, and Harambe was pointing toward its far end, where the bananarm tree stood.

"What is it, Harambe? Do you want to show me something?"

The brorilla nodded and started walking over, slowly. Jack was suddenly curious. Why did Harambe say goodbye before showing him whatever this was? It was clearly deliberate but made no sense.

"Where are you taking me, Harambe?" Jack muttered as he followed Harambe behind the bananarm tree, where he always liked to rest. The vegetation was denser here. Moist bushes with long leaves and vines hanging from the trees above. It looked more and more like a jungle, which had no business being here, in biology's humble opinion.

The analytical part of his mind whispered that this was ridiculous. Everything else reminded him that, after everything the System had done, a little change in topography was nothing.

Harambe led Jack through thick bushes and foliage until they were a couple minutes away from the clearing.

Jack got more and more curious. What could Harambe be hiding?

Another E-Grade resource? His heart sped up.

Harambe approached the base of a large tree. Its roots formed an alcove over the soil, and nestled inside them was a gymonkey that eyed Jack warily. What was it doing here? They were all supposed to be at the funeral—but come to think of it, he did notice one missing.

Harambe said something to the gymonkey, in a tone Jack hadn't heard from him before. It was soft, almost caring, not the sound of a big bro, but of a partner.

Then, the monkey moved, and Jack was left staring at the smaller monkey hiding behind. It was as tall as his forearm was long, had short brown fur, big ears, a long, flexible tail, and looked at him with wide eyes. It resembled a child gymonkey.

A moment later, it snarled and jumped at him. Jack raised his arms in surprise.

Harambe growled. He grabbed the little one by the top of the head midair and growled something in its face. The small monkey flailed ineffectively—it was still airborne—then crossed its arms and glared at Harambe.

Jack looked between the two of them, observing the dynamic, before finally managing to say, "Is that your son, Harambe?"

Harambe nodded. Then he presented the little monkey—still holding it from the top of the head—which stared at Jack as defiantly as it had at its father.

Brorilla, Level 2
A gorilla variant from planet Green. Brorillas usually live with Gymonkeys and train them in the ways of working out. It is due to the

> Brorillas' unmatched pecs that Gymonkeys use poop to fight—they consider themselves too weak for anything else.
>
> Brorillas are usually calm, measured animals. However, if anyone harms their little cousins or invades their territory, they go bananas. This particular Brorilla is a variant that visually resembles a Gymonkey. Though not weaker than other Brorillas, the members of this variant are often shunned due to their lack of bulging muscles.

"He's cute." Jack leaned in. The little monkey tried to claw at him, infuriated at the name. He pulled back. "And feisty."

Harambe nodded with pride. He was so much bigger than his son that it looked ridiculous. The little one could sit on Jack's shoulder, and Jack could probably sit on Harambe's.

"Why didn't you tell me before?" he asked.

Harambe growled, making animated descriptions with his arms. The little monkey flew around, as he still held on to its head, and tried to grab his forearm but failed, making it even more pissed.

"He'd want to join the fight?" Jack tried deciphering Harambe's meaning.

Harambe nodded.

"I see. Congrats, man. And who's this lucky lady?"

He approached the gymonkey, who shook his hand gracefully. Her pecs were more pronounced than most of the gymonkeys—probably why Harambe liked her.

"I'm happy to have met your family, bro," Jack told Harambe. "That makes us real bros. Next time, let's drink together."

Harambe chuckled, then shook his head.

"You don't want to drink?"

More shaking.

"No... it's something else? What are you trying to tell me, Harambe?"

Harambe looked at his partner. Something was exchanged between them that was only too human. Jack saw pain, resolve, and deep longing in those eyes. Then, Harambe brought his son before his face and growled harshly. The little one tried to glare but succumbed under his father's hard stare.

Harambe held his gaze at the little one for a while. Then, he simply turned it around and placed it in front of Jack's feet. Jack blinked in surprise. "What?"

The little monkey glanced at Jack, considering attacking him, then remembered its father's warning and calmed down.

"What are you trying to say, Harambe?" Jack asked hesitantly.

Harambe pushed the little one toward Jack with his knuckles. Then, he took a step back and passed an arm around his partner, who looked at their son with sadness.

"Wait," Jack said. "Are you entrusting your son to me?"

Harambe nodded. The little monkey's eyes widened. Suddenly, it wasn't so wild anymore. It rushed at its parents so hard it tripped. When it got there, Harambe grabbed it and unceremoniously tossed it at Jack, who had to grab it in a hug. He thought it would go wild, but it didn't. The little guy rushed out of his arms without hurting him, then jumped at Harambe who tossed it back again.

"Wait. What is happening?"

Harambe grabbed his child by the head, placed it in front of Jack, and growled sternly. He pointed at it, then at Jack. The little monkey tried to complain, but a second growl, even sterner, cut it short.

"Harambe," Jack said, putting a little bit of force into his voice, and Harambe looked up. "What is happening?"

Harambe then proceeded to mime a long series of things.

"You are entrusting me with your son?" Jack deciphered. "You want him to adventure alongside me? You think I can protect him and make him into a proper brorilla? Let him see the world?"

Harambe nodded.

"Harambe! That's..." Jack was lost for words. He looked down at the little one, taking it in carefully. It had understood its father's words. It was gazing at its parents with longing, but when it looked at Jack, he saw a hidden desire there. The same one he'd felt before the System's arrival. The call of adventure.

"That's such a responsibility..." he managed to say. "You're putting a lot of faith into me..."

Harambe growled in question. He seemed anxious, hoping Jack would say yes.

"It's not about me accepting or not. You have to know that my life will be dangerous," he said. "I don't know what's out there. I might die tomorrow and take this little one with me. I might make enemies."

Harambe's eyes were resolute.

"My adventures could be painful, Harambe, and they might not end well. Are you absolutely certain you want to entrust your son's life to me, knowing you might not see him again soon or ever?"

Harambe nodded. By his side, the gymonkey whimpered, two salty tears appearing in her eyes before she blinked them away. She made sounds of agreement, taking Harambe's hand in hers.

Jack's heart was heavy. "Why would you do that?" he forced out, unable to comprehend.

He wasn't planning on anyone tagging along. He would take the monkeys if they asked him, but a child? What did he know about them? Could he protect it? Raise it?

Should he?

He stared deep into Harambe's eyes and saw the truth. The gorilla wanted his son to become something better than him, to surpass him. At the same time, he couldn't offer that, and not just because this child was doomed to remain less muscular than other brorillas.

Harambe understood the futility of his existence, the hard limits set on him by the System. He'd been created—spawned—as an adult. Even if he was never despawned, there was only so far he could progress. But his son was more fortunate. He was still a child. If life treated him well, he could ascend to heights that Harambe himself had no hope of reaching.

And only Jack had access to the System to offer such potential.

Harambe didn't want to part with his son, give it for another man to raise. Who would? But he steeled his heart and did what was best for it. And he trusted Jack.

Jack had never felt like this before. His heart was filled with equal parts pride, warmth, and weight. He didn't know if he was ready.

But if Harambe could part with his own son, Jack could at least accept it.

"My bro..." Jack kept his voice even as he held out a hand. Harambe grabbed it in a firm handshake, then pulled Jack in for a hug. The two men—one human and one brorilla—held each other tight for a long moment. Then, Harambe turned to the side and pulled his wife into a hug, who grabbed the little one, too.

Their family hug was tighter than Jack's, and it lasted longer. It was a very touching moment. So touching, in fact, that Jack felt guilty, and salt threatened to roll down his cheeks.

Sometime later, the magic was broken. The family slowly withdrew, Harambe pushing the little one into Jack's hands while his partner buried her face in his fur. Harambe's eyes were resolute—and, surprisingly, so were the little one's.

Jack stared at it in wonder, giving a smile whose emotions even he wasn't certain of. "What's his name?"

Harambe made a sound, slowly and purposely.

"Brock?" Jack asked, just to be sure, and Harambe nodded. His partner held on tighter.

"Brock..." he repeated, turning to look at the little one. "What do you think, Brock? Would you like to explore the galaxy with me?" It was a brave one. Not only had it tried to attack Jack when he first appeared, despite the size difference, but when it met his gaze now, it wasn't as grief-struck as a human child's would be.

Maybe it was because animals were less attached to their parents. Or, maybe, this one had a strong soul. In any case, it stared deep into Jack's eyes, pouted its lips to keep them from trembling, and nodded despite the tears rolling freely down its face.

"You are a very brave monkey, Brock," Jack said, petting it on the head. It let him. "I would love to have you along."

Harambe made an odd sound, and his cheeks tightened. It was time to leave.

"We'll go, then," Jack said, holding a fist to his heart. "I promise to come visit you again soon—as soon as I can. And I vow on my very soul that I will keep your son safe, even if it kills me. No matter what."

Harambe nodded, his face spasming with effort to stay still. The gymonkey looked at her son, eyes dripping, then at Jack, with a depth of emotions he never expected from an animal. But, then again, that was an outdated thought. These were people.

"See you both," Jack said. He took Brock by the hand and walked away. Brock kept looking back, but Jack didn't. The sobbing sounds made him think his bro wouldn't want to be seen like that.

And so, a human and a monkey that barely reached his knee walked into the bushes and faded away, each leading the other by the hand.

Chapter 32
Entering Civilization with a Bang

Jack crossed the woods, feeling like Christopher Colombus discovering America. Everything he saw was the same as he remembered, and also different. Being outside the nature reserve—the Forest of the Strong dungeon—was like a dream.

What changed? How had the System impacted humanity? What was the world like?

Was it all real?

Everything was exactly as he remembered. The trees, the broken branches, that fat bush he'd stepped over once upon a time... It made him doubt whether this was all a hallucination induced by some gas in the cave.

He grabbed a thick branch from the ground and easily snapped it in two. Shrugging, he threw it away.

"What do you think, Brock?" he asked the monkey on his shoulder—its short legs made walking side-by-side annoying. "Will we like what we find?"

Brock made monkey sounds. There was undeniable excitement there, though he clearly missed his home, too. He'd looked back multiple times on the way and almost ran away once but stopped himself. He was a brave little monkey.

"Yeah, I think so too," Jack said with a smile.

The System's arrival breathed life into his world. He was strong. Whatever happened, he could take it.

He was just worried about the state of his loved ones, especially the professor, whose old age wasn't suitable for punching monsters.

Jack stepped out of the trees and onto a dirt trail. For the first time, it occurred to him what he looked like: a wild, dirty, bare-chested dude. He was ripped, too. He must have seemed like a savage.

He shrugged and went on his way.

The dirt trail snaked through the forest before ending at a wider trail, where a gray jeep was parked. Seeing a car was completely disorienting. It made such a hard contrast against last week's primal lifestyle that Jack had to stop and stare, unable to reconcile the two worlds.

With a low chuckle, he fished the keys from his pocket—he'd retrieved them from their hiding place in the cave before leaving—unlocked the door and sat in the vehicle. It groaned under his weight. Constitution made him heavier, not too much, but noticeably.

Brock jumped in the co-driver's seat like the experienced monkey he wasn't. He then realized he couldn't see anything from there, so he jumped behind the steering wheel. The windshield was a shock—the poor thing hadn't seen glass before. Thankfully, it was dirty, or he would have headbutted it for sure. It took three swipes

ENTERING CIVILIZATION WITH A BANG

of the wipers to make out the road beyond through a green-brown smudge.

Jack revved up the engine, welcoming the familiar rumbling of the car below him. The seat was soft on his back and a bit scratchy, while the wheel felt like a toy in his hands.

The car jumped a bit as it started, then rolled on slowly. Jack lowered the windows and let his arm hang outside, while Brock was quick to stick out his head and enjoy the faint breeze. He even occasionally put his hand out and tried to resist the breeze. It was nice.

The dirt trail ended on a snaking asphalt road that crossed the forest, and Jack could finally pick up some speed. He stepped on the pedal, eager to feel the acceleration, and the wind buffeted his face. Trees zoomed past him, the occasional stone crunched under the wheels, his body leaned on the turns.

A brief moment of fun. Then, the acceleration stopped, and boredom claimed Jack. He could run faster than this.

Poor car companies...

At least it was comfortable.

The snaking road gave way to a larger one, where the speed still wasn't up to Jack's standards, until small houses began to pepper the countryside. It was Jack's first contact with civilization in over a week. He kept his eyes wide.

By the side, Brock had climbed on the co-driver's seat and couldn't pull his eyes from the forest behind them. His tail curled up in sadness. The forest drifted out of sight, and the little monkey fell on the seat defeated, staring at the empty road ahead.

Theirs was the only car on the road.

The houses were mostly abandoned. The few people Jack saw stared hard at him until he made some distance.

They held guns, bread knives, anything dangerous they could get their hands on to protect their homes. Many were injured. Some wore armor, though he couldn't make out any details.

He also saw a few monsters. There were small packs of goblins roaming the countryside, along with feral wolves, oversized wild dogs, small scaly people, walking mushrooms, and all sorts of nasty things. There were even large maneater plants in the middle of nowhere, where it would take tremendous amounts of idiocy to fall for them.

Right on cue, a goblin stumbled into one of the plants and was summarily swallowed. He chuckled, turning back to the road.

The wind curled around his arm outside the window, making the little hairs wave. His right hand gripped the hard leather of the wheel, while his bare foot stepped on the pedal. Brock screamed in joy as they accelerated, maneuvering around the occasional goblin that littered the road. The poor little fuckers were dumb enough to simply stare at his car as it approached, and a few even dared each other to jump in front of it. One tried, but thankfully chickened out.

Jack only scanned a few of those monsters—they all seemed weak. Only a distant stag with vines on its antlers was somewhat threatening, and that's because everything else avoided it. The monsters were sparse overall, not really grouping together, letting the few farmhouses survive.

With the notable exception of the goblins, they also had the good idea of keeping their distance from the road, which let Jack simply drive through.

Soon, the houses grew denser and the monsters thinner. Neighborhoods appeared, which soon gave way to wide streets and infrastructure. There was an upturned bus by the side of the street, along with a few burned or violently ruined houses. Most cars were just sitting there.

The System's coming hadn't been easy. At the very least, the scenery reaffirmed that Jack wasn't hallucinating.

There were more people, too. Jack spotted them roving in large bands, upwards of ten members each, and attacking any monsters that came within sight. A twelve-person group armed with bread knives fell on a pack of five goblins. After a fierce fight where three of them were injured, they managed to take the goblins down.

Jack shook his head. Their weakness would have been funny if it wasn't sad—or even expected. The leveling speed of such large groups would be atrocious. But who in their right mind would go against the odds to hunt alone?

He didn't stop the car.

As he rode deeper, the people had been growing denser, too. There were guards where the town began, holding handguns. They flagged him down.

"Halt," said one of them, a woman with sharp eyes and a ponytail. "You are approaching Valville, the territory of Henry's Fang. Please enter on foot and surrender any firearms you're carrying."

Brock narrowed his eyes and clenched his little fists. Jack was already getting a headache. Maybe that's why Harambe dumped the little menace on him like that.

"No attacking," he told Brock strictly. "Everyone here is a friend by default. You won't touch anybody unless I say so. Understood?"

Brock released a small holler of protest, only to buckle under Jack's gaze. He was in an unknown place, surrounded by unknown people, and his only connection to his home was this weird big bro. He would listen.

Jack parked at the side of the road and got out of the jeep. Their eyes widened. Whether that was due to Brock on his shoulder or his barbaric appearance, he didn't know.

"I have no firearms, as you can see," he said, approaching carefully. "And I don't mind leaving my car here."

He didn't intend to cause trouble, though he was pretty sure he could survive gunshots. His close to 100 Constitution wasn't for show. As he approached, he scanned them.

> **Human (Earth-387), Level 5**
> **Faction: Henry's Fang (F-Grade)**

The System wasn't too talkative about sapients. Still, Jack got a bunch of information.

The head guard here, on a major road artery, was only level 5. The other four were even lower. Moreover, what kind of stupid name was Henry's Fang? Jack felt better for naming his faction Bare Fist Brotherhood.

As he willed the screens away, he noticed the five guards looking at him like they saw a ghost—they'd obviously scanned him back.

"Welcome to Valville, sir," the head guard said, suddenly way politer. "If I may ask, what is the purpose of your visit? Are you here as a representative of the Bare Fist Brotherhood?"

"Not sure yet. For now, I'm just making sure my family is okay."

"Would you like to arrange an audience with Henry's Fang?"

"Not yet."

"Very well. Please go on, sir."

"Thank you."

For the first time, Jack felt like a VIP. Life was easy when you were strong.

He didn't spare the guards another glance as he entered the town, walking through streets he knew.

Valville wasn't large. With a population of only twenty thousand, its area was even smaller than the Greenway Nature Reserve. Its only notable quality was the nearby town of Tahlequah, which housed the Northeastern State University's Department of Natural Science. That's where Jack studied, and where his foster parents used to teach before retiring.

Valville itself was a dot that didn't even appear on most maps. It was a nice place. The scenery from above the mountain was beautiful, and the streets well-maintained.

Jack liked it here. It was peaceful and pretty—at least, it used to be.

Now, rubble and trash were everywhere. No monster corpses, but he did spot some human bodies haphazardly thrown in alleys. There was no sign of the police.

At the same time, there was new energy suffusing the town. Muscular men and fit women walked around with intensity, doing this or shouting that. The weather was still good, so everyone wore short sleeves—or makeshift armor.

It had only been a week since he'd last seen Valville, and it had changed drastically. Many shops were closed and new ones were springing up like mushrooms. Jack saw a smithy next to a torn-down McDonald's, manned by an older man with a yellow mustache that wouldn't stop grinning through his sweat. He found a tannery on the very edge of the town, where three men worked on the skin of what looked like a deer. He spotted people pulling carts through the streets, as well as merchants loudly proclaiming their wares in a way that wasn't common before the apocalypse.

Jack had to stop and do a double take. *Is this really Valville?*

The buildings were similar, but the town was a mixture between reality and fantasy. Like someone planted a medieval society in the ruins of modern civilization. With their lives on the line and monsters to hunt, people were regressing so fast it was mind-blowing.

Jack got drowned by laughter, cries, shouts, the loud clang of the smith's hammer, the shouting peddlers, children wielding sticks and playing humans versus goblins, the fragrance of food carts, and the heavy odor of blood. The entire street stank of sweat and death—nobody seemed to care. In fact, Jack caught people smiling all around.

That's odd. Are they all like me?

Taking a closer look, he observed a clear dichotomy. On one side, there were people huddling behind windows and shivering, as well as some darting from pedestrian to pedestrian and begging with tears in their eyes. There were crazies shouting incoherently in alleys.

On the other side of the dichotomy were the warriors. Armed with bread knives and armored in pans, they moved with energy and sported clear, smiling eyes. For the first time in his life, Jack realized that people didn't smile on the street before the apocalypse. They were just rushing from place to place full of stress, like zombies. But not anymore.

Jack doubted they all shared his love for battle. However, level-ups and getting stronger had a way to bring euphoria, and life-or-death struggles had a way to make people feel alive.

Jack was stunned. He stood in the middle of street, gawking at everything. The world had turned upside down. It felt like home. He loved this.

A moment later, he shook himself awake. His feet moved by themselves as he approached the smithy; a wide wooden shack with a heavy anvil and a burning oven in the middle, which looked like an electric kitchen adapted to work with wood or coal. The walls were decorated with shitty-looking, uneven swords, as everything better had no doubt been taken already.

Though, to be fair, perhaps proper swords were too much for a week-old blacksmith. Said man was currently hammering away at a glowing lump of metal on his anvil, so focused on the task he didn't notice Jack's approach.

"Hey," Jack said, scanning the man.

> **Human (Earth-387), Level 7**
> **Faction: -**

The blacksmith frowned, then raised his gaze and scanned him top to bottom. His eyes shuddered as he took in Jack's level.

"How can I help you?" he said, abandoning the rapidly cooling metal on his anvil.

Jack raised a brow. "You don't need to do that. I can wait."

The blacksmith smiled under his thick blond mustache, then started hammering again, the metal bending under his System-augmented strength. The clangs were loud enough to be annoying, and the heat of the open oven could be felt all the way to where Jack stood, but he wasn't annoyed. He simply admired the work.

"I can speak while hammering," the blacksmith said, eliciting Jack's chuckle.

"You seem pretty good at this."

"Been doing it for years. Never imagined my hobby would come in handy, but here we are."

He used a pair of long pliers to pick up the lump of metal—it resembled a sword—and stuck it in a water barrel nearby. Steam filled his hut. Brock screamed at the hissing sounds.

"You are enjoying this, aren't you?" Jack shouted over the hissing.

"As much as everyone," the blacksmith replied, wiping his brow. His gaze remained with the blade, weighing it. "I didn't enjoy seeing my best friend murdered before my eyes, but the apocalypse has its bright sides. This is one of them."

He took out the blade, inspecting it through the steam. Jack did, too. This thing was an actual sword. There was an iron handle and a long, straight blade. Tiny bumps riddled its surface, but it at least looked serviceable.

"That's pretty good!" Jack said.

"A piece of shit," the blacksmith replied. "Don't judge by the garbage on my walls, friend. That's just decor."

"Oh," Jack said, looking around. "Don't you think your decor is bad marketing?"

"Doesn't matter. All my blades are bought instantly. The ones I've hung up are unusable, but they were my first efforts. Helps me remember where I came from."

Jack nodded. "Why the iron handle, though?" He pointed at the newly-made sword.

"It just came out of the oven. I'll wrap the leather later."

He left the newborn sword on a counter and turned to Jack, removing his gloves. He stretched a hand.

"George," he said.

"Jack."

His hand was sweaty and hard, but Jack didn't mind. They smiled at each other.

"So?" George the blacksmith asked, wiping some sweat off his forehead again. "How can I help you?"

"I'm just looking, if you don't mind."

George gave him an odd look. "Not with your level, I don't."

"What happened to Valville?"

Another odd look. George grabbed a chair and took a seat. "You weren't in town?"

"Forest."

"Lucky you. Things went to shit at first. Many died before the strong banded together to drive the monsters out. Goblins, mostly, so easy opponents, but it still took four days. Then, we rebuilt with monsters in mind. Most people are warriors or losers now, so we don't need accounting and all that shit. We have plenty of food and water, thankfully, what with many dying and the town's food storage. We also have the farms."

"Losers?" Jack raised a brow. "That's a bit harsh, don't you think?"

"Everything is harsh now." George shook his head.

Jack didn't quite agree, but he could see where the sentiment was coming from.

"And Henry's Fang?" he asked.

At this, the blacksmith raised his eyes. He was clearly deliberating his next words. "They're okay." In a way, that implied the opposite. After all, Jack could have been an ally of Henry's Fang.

A bad omen, Jack thought, nodding again. *I hope the professor is okay.*

Realizing he had nothing else to offer and was just taking up the man's time, he made to leave. "Thank you, George. Happy smithing."

"Anytime, Jack. Come find me if you ever need a new weapon." He eyed Jack's empty hands. "I reckon it will be soon."

Jack only smiled. He walked away to the metallic clangs of Geroge's smithing. At least he wasn't the only one enjoying the apocalypse. *Enjoying? When did I become like that...* He shook his head. *Enough sightseeing. Now, the professor.* He ventured deeper into Valville.

Stares fell on him. He stood out, what with his bare-chested musculature and monkey on his shoulder, so it was natural. He even felt kind of proud when a wave of whispers followed his path as people noticed his level.

He was quite an outlier. Jack scanned dozens of people and only saw one person above level 7; everyone else ranged between 1 and 5. The members of Henry's Fang were rare—most people were factionless—but when he found one, they usually walked around with a swag that resembled his. Others kept their distance from them, looking over with a mixture of fear and disgust.

All members of Henry's Fang glared at Jack before noticing his level, at which point they became subservient. He shook his head and ignored them.

Brock was clearly excited. He tried to jump off once or twice and explore or play with something, but Jack held him back—any random accident could get him sliced to pieces. He was just a monster monkey, after all, and the people of Valville were now warriors. A clear edge shone under their joviality. Jack had no doubt they would have cut Brock to pieces if he came here alone.

Warriors... He focused on that feeling, looking at individual people rather than the general image.

They were different than he remembered. Hardened. Hushed whispers and commanding voices were everywhere under the clamor. When he crossed gazes with someone, most held his gaze for a moment. Groups of people were either going out to hunt monsters or returning, carrying their wounded and seemingly random monster parts—from goblin eyes to brown hearts. The former had clenched fists and set jaws; the latter, empty eyes and palpable relief that they were still whole.

They'd also tried to armor themselves. There were those who wore several thick coats, with pans and pots tied in front of their vulnerable parts as armor, or even holding thin iron plates with jagged sides like shields—maybe that's why most cars lacked a roof. When it rained, they would quickly begin to stink of rot.

Overall, the weapons and armor of these monster hunters were makeshift, and their tactics ineffective, but they were doing their best. Jack could respect them.

The exception to that was the members of Henry's Fang. They held actual swords or handguns as they went out hunting in groups of three to five people, and they wore what looked like real leather armor. They must have had leatherworkers and blacksmiths—like George—working for them.

Moreover, they were relaxed, even cracking jokes as they strutted through the town, shooting mocking glances and pointed comments at those who weren't as well-equipped. Despite their overt mockery of others' misfortune, nobody dared retort. No doubt there would be consequences. This disharmony really ruined Jack's image of the new Valville.

The people of Henry's Fang he'd seen so far were dickheads, but he didn't want to judge too quickly.

After all, he stood out himself. His steps carried confidence, and his gait was wide. His level sent everyone out of his way, including the members of Henry's Fang.

It felt good.

Jack made a beeline for the town's west side. His first priority was making sure the professor was okay—most of his friends were in other towns, and telecommunications were down, so he couldn't contact them. Then, he'd speak to Henry of Henry's Fang. If they were good guys, Jack could work with them to ensure the town's safety. He had much to offer. If not…

His walk through the town took the better part of an hour. He didn't hurry, taking the time to observe the situation.

The areas near the town entrances and close to downtown were as lively as he'd seen them. Everywhere else was abandoned, highlighting the previous dichotomy. There were destroyed buildings and injured people everywhere. Many were obviously sick, too, probably from the dust and grime they carried. Nobody was cleaning or working for the benefit of the town, only hustling from place to place to hunt monsters or procure necessities. There were no ambulances or electricity, either, though the hospital would certainly be filled to the brim.

Seemed like nobody cared for the townspeople. But again, Jack didn't want to judge too quickly. This was a ton of work, and it was the apocalypse. Maybe Henry's Fang was just doing their best—though their many hunting groups indicated otherwise.

At least the town seemed safe from monsters.

A small white house entered Jack's vision as the sun reached its peak. It had a single story and a pink chimney rising from its tiled roof, and the windows were clean. It would have been a picturesque image if not for the patches of blood where the walls met the floor.

Jack's worry mounted. A stubborn knot was in his throat, like when he'd been about to fight the rock bear. There were no sounds coming from the house.

Jack reached the door, mustered his resolve, and knocked.

"Coming!"

His worry deflated instantly. "Oh, thank God," he whispered.

The door opened to reveal a woman in casual clothing. She was short and slim, while her brown eyes remained sharp despite their wrinkles. Jack used to joke that her mind was filled with firecrackers. She kept her white hair short, above shoulder-length, and always spoke and moved around with an energy that belied her old age.

When her gaze met Jack's barbaric form and monkey, she gasped in fear. Then, she scoured his face and recognized the lines. She shivered.

"Jack!" she exclaimed in joyful disbelief.

"Professor!" Jack shouted back, rushing in to hug her—carefully. Besides a suspicious swelling on her cheek, she wasn't injured. Everything was okay.

Except for the unknown burly man standing with crossed arms behind her. That one was not okay.

Chapter 33
Seeking Revenge

Jack raised his gaze to the man behind the professor. His eyes darkened. "Who are you?" he asked.

"This is Hugo," the professor hurried to respond. "He's with Henry's Fang."

"And?"

"I'm here on orders, sir," Hugo said in a deep voice. "We have an agreement with Professor Rust. I make sure everyone honors it."

Jack narrowed his eyes. Hugo was a big man of Slavic descent, with a flat nose and a thick neck. His ears resembled cauliflowers, and his face betrayed a man of stark resolve. Moreover, he wore an overcoat. Before the System, he could have been mafia muscle—they had some in town. Now…

> Human (Earth-387), Level 11

Faction: Henry's Fang (F-Grade)

"Here's what we'll do, Hugo. I will catch up with my mother. You will go take a long walk and return when we call you."

Jack didn't see a threat in this Hugo, and he had zero intentions of letting a nightman linger in his mother's home. Just Hugo's presence was enough to alert Jack that something was very wrong, and he would get to the bottom of it immediately.

When did I become like this? part of him wondered. Maybe it's the Dao of the Fist... I don't dislike it.

Hugo frowned. He'd scanned Jack, hence his respect. "That is difficult, sir. My orders are strict. I am to accompany Professor Rust at all times."

He let his dark overcoat flutter as he moved his hands, not accidentally revealing a gun handle. Jack saw that and nodded.

"Listen, Hugo. I understand you have your orders, okay? I really do. The thing is, I don't give a shit. So take a walk before I make you."

"Jack!" The professor jumped. "What are you saying?"

Hugo's frown deepened. A set of dangerous eyes met Jack's. Jack didn't budge.

Hugo's glare was hard and professional. Coupled with his gun and large body, this was an edge that could intimidate even the staunchest of bar fighters. Unfortunately, he was facing Jack Rust, a man who'd conquered a dungeon by himself.

Jack clenched a fist. A savage aura erupted from his body, burying the room in almost palpable violence. The professor gasped and stepped back, leaning against a wall to stay upright. Then Hugo's edge cracked. His eyes trembled. He looked around, then focused on Jack. Jack's eyes remained calm.

After a moment of tense silence, Hugo ceded. "Yes, sir."

Jack stepped aside, and the Slavic man walked over. Their bodies were very close to each other, and the tension was so explosive it seemed to form sparks. Hugo kept going and left the house, not looking back. Jack closed the door behind him.

"Jack!" the professor shook awake. "What—Do you understand what you did?"

"It's okay. If anybody wants to mistreat you, they have to get past me. How strong is Henry of Henry's Fang?"

Her eyes narrowed. She was catching up. Jack could see all the pieces of the puzzle coming together behind her eyes. "Level 22. A swordsman. He once sliced a bullet in two. What happened to you, Jack? I thought you were dead."

Jack nodded. Level 22 was pretty low.

"So did I," he admitted. "Can we sit? Hugo won't be back for a while."

"Yes, of course. Bring your... monkey... too. It's an unconventional pet, but then again, many things are unconventional lately. I like it."

"His name is Brock." He smiled. "The son of a friend." Brock agreed, reaching out to shake her hand like he'd seen his parents do. The professor smiled, and obliged, scanning him at the same time.

"A brorilla? Son of a friend? You have so many things to tell me, Jack..."

"And I will. Can we go in, first?"

"Of course."

The professor led Jack through a simple, minimalistic house filled with only the necessities—and books, lots of books. There were also a few electronics scattered around the house—a tablet, a laptop, a computer, and various gadgets, all turned off.

They crossed the corridor and entered the living room, where the picture of a smiling old man with a wide mustache stood atop the empty fireplace. The professor sat on a fluffy cushion chair, while Jack chose a simple couch. He looked around as if lost. Brock climbed on the couch next to him and stayed there, watching the professor with crossed arms as if ready to participate in the conversation.

"I can't believe it's all here," Jack said. "Coming back is so surreal... It feels like a dream."

"A nightmare, you mean."

"Depends on how you see it," he replied, eliciting a chuckle.

"No doubt. Many think the same... I'm just tired, that's all. I thought I was over learning new technologies when I retired. Well, guess again, Margaret."

Margaret Rust was a researcher and professor of informatics at Northeastern University, specializing in cybersecurity. When she retired two years ago, she and her late husband moved to Valville, where they could spend their twilight years in peace. Too bad the world had other plans.

"So many numbers, though," Jack said. "Dad would be happy."

"Or distraught."

"Maybe."

Margaret waited but was unable to let her questions go unheard. "What happened to you, Jack?"

"I was in the Greenway Nature Reserve when the System came, which got transformed into a dungeon. I couldn't leave until I beat the biggest, baddest monster around. Long story short, I did, then befriended the native monkey pack, and now I'm back with little Brock here."

"I thought you were dead..." Her eyes watered. "Was it hard?"

"Hardest thing I've ever done. But I made it. Now, I'm strong. Strong enough to protect my mother from criminal idiots with terrible naming sense."

Despite her tears, she chuckled. "They're dangerous people, Jack. They won't let us get away with this."

"Leave that up to me. How was your Integration?"

"Easy. Two goblins appeared outside the house, but a neighbor—you remember Mike—beat them up with a shovel. I just waited inside until things calmed down."

"I see. I'm happy you're alright. Where's Mike? I want to thank him."

"You'll struggle. He died to a wild dog two days later."

"Oh..." Jack digested the information, then nodded. "Keep speaking, Professor. I sense there's much to tell."

"Of course. Three days after the Integration, Henry White's gang formed a System faction and established order. They declared this town their territory. They became the bosses around here. After that, things happened. An alien arrived in the town square; an information merchant. I sold him knowledge on cyber security and got System knowledge in return. I also got an experience ball, which is how I made it to my current level."

She was level 6. Not bad at all, compared to the general population. Jack chuckled. Knowing her, she'd probably invested everything in Mental.

"So, you know things," he said. "About what's happening."

"I thought it was a safe bet. There isn't much an old lady like me can do, even if I learned to slingshot fire at goblins. Information, on the other hand, is my territory. I could help us get a step ahead of the monsters."

He sensed a 'but' there. "But?"

She sighed. "*But*, I miscalculated. Henry White came looking for the information. I don't like that man."

"Who is he?"

"He ran a shady organization downtown, extorting shops for "security" fees. I don't know how he got so lucky during the Integration, but he ended up a few steps ahead of everyone else."

"I see. And then?"

"Then, I miscalculated again." The professor's face turned into a scowl. "I couldn't tell them no, but I tried to hide some things. Unfortunately, the alien merchant traded in information; Henry bought a list with the contents of my transactions. They knew what I had."

"The merchant sold you off."

"Not really. It was my fault. Anyway, Henry's Fang knew what I had."

Jack raised a brow. "You told them everything."

"Kind of. The merchant had given me an information crystal—a wondrous invention, by the way. They store information in the crystal's molecular structure, then read it through the System."

"You gave them the crystal." Jack brought her back on track. "What was it about?"

"Ah, yes. It wasn't much. The merchant didn't deem my lifetime of expertise particularly expensive." She chuckled bitterly. "Then again, they do have a futuristic AI.

Perhaps it could replicate our technology in milliseconds. The crystal was mostly about how to progress through the System. Listen well."

She instantly launched into lecture mode.

"Most people around think stats and levels are the important part; they're wrong. Apparently, the most crucial aspect of progression is something called the Dao. Unfortunately, the crystal didn't mention much besides the name, only some intentionally cryptic things. Then come skills. Those are split into many grades and degrees of proficiency, and they are the bridge between Dao and stats.

"A skill can be enhanced, upgraded, or fused with others. The first option just makes it slightly stronger—it's what usually happens. The other two create skills of a higher-grade, which are exponentially more effective than skills of lower grades. Higher-grade skills channel your Dao better—whatever that is—increase your battle strength, and let you progress further on the path of cultivation—as the System calls its progression."

Jack considered the information. "I think I did that once. Upgrading a skill. It became a Dao skill."

Margaret grinned. "Very game-like, isn't it? Makes you wonder... However, upgrading a skill is tremendous, Jack! Congratulations!"

"Thank you," he replied somberly. "Is there anything else before I get to the important stuff?"

"The System is the most important thing in our lives now, Jack. By far." Margaret's smile turned sad. "There is a lot more information, but... it can wait. Oh! Except one thing. Do you remember what the System said on Integration? About a tournament?"

"No, but I can look it up."

Jack made the first blue screens reappear. Soon, he found the one he was looking for—a part of the Animal Kingdom's message.

> *The first step to that power is the Integration Tournament, which will be held in twenty galaxy days (note: fifteen Earth-387 days) from now. Comprehend even the tiniest corner of the world by then, and endless possibilities will open up for you.*

"I see. What of it?"

"That tournament is extremely important, Jack. You must get in no matter what. Pardon me for asking, but... do you have a Dao Root?"

He nodded and her eyes lit up like a Christmas tree.

"Excellent! That's wonderful! A Dao Root is the requirement to enter the Integration Tournament. You are in, my boy! You're in!"

"What's so special about that tournament, anyway?"

"There are incredible rewards, even for participation. It will put you on the fast track forever—it's like getting a Harvard scholarship. And, if you do well there... Well, that's unlikely. The strongest people from all over Earth-387 will be competing."

"You mean Earth."

"We are part of the galaxy now, Jack. Don't cling to old notions."

He considered it for a moment, then agreed. "Fine. I'll join that tournament and do my best. I'm plenty strong. Which brings us to the main point; what happened to your cheek?"

She looked deep into his eyes. "Jack..." she began, but he raised a hand to cut her off.

"You fought no monsters. Your cheek is swollen. A strongman was in your house. What's up?"

She hesitated. The cogs turning behind her eyes. He even saw her briefly consider lying before she looked straight at him. Jack was inwardly proud.

If there was one thing that stood out about Margaret Rust, it was the speed at which she adapted to new information.

"Henry's Fang left Hugo here to make sure I didn't disseminate the information freely. As for the swelling... Well, they slapped me when I tried to lie. It's not a big deal. The world is far more violent than it used to be. People die all the time."

Jack had stopped listening. "They slapped you."

"It's fine. It was light."

"But they did slap you," he replied calmly. "Who was it?"

She looked into his eyes. "How strong are you, Jack?"

"Plenty."

"It was Henry White."

"Got it. And I assume those guys are bad people?"

"They've been taxing everyone at the gates, and they've been terrorizing the town since they formed. They're tyrants."

"Good."

"Will you be careful? Please. I don't want to lose you again."

"Don't worry about me, Professor. Worry about *them*."

He grabbed Brock and stood. The couch's wooden handlebar was bent out of shape where he'd grabbed it.

"Stay here, little guy," he told the monkey. "I'll be back soon."

Brock, who'd been quiet so far, suddenly protested. His cute little eyes stared fearlessly at Jack. He bared his little fangs. He wanted to come along.

Jack placed him on the table and got on eye level. "Listen. I am *trusting you* with my own mother, okay? You must protect her while I'm away. This is an extremely important mission that only you can complete. Do you understand?"

Brock hesitated. Inwardly, Jack was impressed. Could the monkey actually understand him? However, on the outside, he was stern and earnest, looking at Brock as he would a brother.

"Do you understand?" he repeated, and Brock finally agreed. Glancing at the professor, he jumped at her feet and stood there as tall as he could—which wasn't much—beating his chest and generally doing his best to look threatening. He screamed assertively.

Jack smiled. "Thank you."

"He's cute," said Margaret, sitting back down to pet Brock. He scowled in disgruntlement, as if saying, "I'm a warrior! Do not pet me!"

She laughed.

"Hide in the bunker, Professor. I'll be back."

"Take care, Jack."

They exchanged a hug. Jack watched her climb down to the basement before turning around and heading for the door, which was white and surrounded by flower-painted glass. He turned the doorknob. The door swung open. Three gun barrels were pointed at him.

Jack grinned and cracked his fists. "Hello, Hugo. I see your walk's been productive."

Chapter 34
Ar'Tazul the Merchant

Three men stood at the edge of the yard fifteen feet away, pointing handguns at Jack. Two looked like hoodlums. The third was Hugo, the Slavic mafia man charged with watching the professor.

Jack stared down the gun barrel and didn't flinch. "You found a few more dogs, too."

Hugo's face was still as if cut from stone. "I never got your name."

"See those guns, Hugo? That's called deadly force. If you use deadly force against me, I will use it against you, and you will die. I want that to be very clear."

Jack's fist was clenched, and an invisible, savage aura rolled out of him in waves. The goons by Hugo's side—levels 3 and 4, both members of Henry's Fang—shivered. Their eyes flickered toward Hugo in hesitation, but he remained still as a rock.

"Only one thing is absolute in this world," Hugo said. "Bullets. Goodbye."

His gun spewed fire. The goons yelped—one dropped his gun from the sound, the other emptied his magazine in Jack's general direction.

At the same moment Hugo's finger clenched the trigger, Jack moved. His body flickered with speed, dashing sideways faster than the gunmen could react. Bullets flew left and right, passing by but not touching him.

He wasn't faster than bullets—yet—but he could calculate their trajectories from watching the guns.

The second goon managed to pick up his gun and start firing, trying to catch the blur that headed his way. He failed. Jack reached him, and a terrible slap almost emptied his mouth of teeth. He was unconscious before he even hit the floor.

Hugo was now behind the other goon. Jack didn't care. He grabbed the goon's gun, snapped it in half, and slapped the man hard enough to send him flying like a ballerina. He then stared at Hugo, who stared back.

Only the two of them were left. Hugo had three bullets remaining. He hadn't panicked and wasted them all like his goons.

Excitement glittered in Hugo's eyes. The gun danced in his hand as it spat death. The bullets dug into Jack's chest from almost point-blank, barely penetrating the skin before falling to the ground with a series of plinks.

Jack let himself be shot on purpose, of course. He was confident he could take the bullets, but how much damage would they deal?

Not much, was the answer. They felt like strong finger pokes.

Man... I'm Superman.

Hugo's elation morphed into terror. His clean-shaven face went pale. He looked at Jack in askance and raised his hands, letting the gun hang from his finger. His lips shivered as he tried to speak.

"Sorry, Hugo."

Jack's fist smashed into his face like a sledgehammer. Hugo's head exploded, and his body hit the ground a beat later, covered by its own trench coat.

Jack gazed at his fist. He'd just murdered a man. He could have shown mercy, but he didn't. Was that... bad?

The thing is, he felt nothing. No remorse, no regret, no doubts. His Dao had reinforced his resolve, and so had his multiple life-or-death experiences in the dungeon. Hugo was threatening Jack's mother and tried to kill him. Jack killed him back. It was natural. That was the law of strength, which apparently ruled the world now.

So what if he tried to surrender at the last moment? That shit was fake. He would plant a bullet in my eye the second he got the chance.

Jack looked around. There were people watching from the distance. A few were puking, some looked the other way, and a few were running away. A woman stared at him like he was a monster. Jack only snorted.

If they can try to kill me in broad daylight, with more people and guns, I can at least punch them back.

He shook his fist to get the blood away. *Next stop, Henry's Fang.*

There were definitely safer, more diplomatic options than simply storming in. However, like in the dungeon, Jack had enough of being smart. Now, he wanted to be strong—simple and direct—and he possessed the power to do it. He wanted to strike ahead like a fist and make the world adapt to him instead of the opposite.

That was his life now. And if he died at some point, so be it. At least he had fun.

Heh. Fun. He chuckled, baring his teeth. *I could get used to this.*

After breaking the other guns as well, Jack stepped over the two unconscious thugs and left the professor's front yard. *I should get that cleaned at some point...* he mused. He hadn't considered the issue before, but well, nothing he could do about it now. He was busy.

But where's Henry's Fang? Well, shit. He didn't know. Thankfully, there were people nearby he could ask.

Jack paced to the group watching from afar, keeping his hands high to avoid scaring them. Most ran anyway, but a few remained.

"Hello," he asked politely. "I'm looking for Henry's Fang. Can you tell me where they are?"

"Across the town. They've commandeered the hotel behind the town square. Valville Hotel, it was called."

"Thanks."

The man who replied was in his fifties, with eyes that struggled between respect, hope, and disbelief. His lips were clenched as he watched Jack go. "Hey!" he shouted. "Will you get them?"

Jack looked over his shoulder and cracked a smile. "You bet."

The man shivered, and his lips trembled for a moment. "Thank you! Thank you!"

Jack didn't look back, only gave a thumbs-up.

Let's see now... Valville hotel. It was a nice place. I hope they haven't ruined it. Since I'm going by the town square, I should check that alien out as well. The information merchant.

The streets were rowdy as he passed. The rumors had time to spread, and everyone looked at him with mixed feelings. Some held hope, others, pity, and a few, even hostility.

Jack ignored them all. He walked to the town square neither slow nor fast, letting the town know of his coming. His mind was rolling. Supposing he dismantled Henry's Fang, someone would need to run the town. In other words, he needed reliable people, and thankfully, he already had a plan to find them.

Valville's town square was a large square area surrounded by wide streets. There was a dry fountain in its center and not much else, creating a large empty space where children used to ride their bicycles or run around like the little monkeys they were.

Now, the town square was a far colder place. It was mostly empty, save for a few merchant stands around the square selling knives or makeshift armor, and the alien at its center. Jack's gaze focused there.

This was an alien. *An alien.* Right there in the middle of Valville Square. Just standing around.

The alien was a blue-skinned little man. He sported a short brown beard, wore a turban, and colorful, lax clothes, and generally resembled someone from the merchant cities of Africa or the Middle East if they were painted blue and were only four feet in height.

He was also pudgy, with a healthy belly and a satisfied smile as he lounged on the fountain's edge and whistled a little tune. He seemed to be having a blast.

Jack shook his head, pulling his gaze away. There was nobody trying to shoot him. Henry's Fang probably knew he was coming and waited for him in their hotel, gathering their forces.

A crowd was already forming, but it still wasn't enough for his plan. Jack wanted to get two birds with one stone. He had some time to waste.

As he approached the little blue merchant, he made out more details. A crate was by his feet, which were covered in pointy shoes. His facial features were pronounced. He wore only a light jacket despite the autumn chill, and he seemed completely relaxed in this planet of strangers.

> **Djinn, Level ?? (E-Grade)**
> **Faction: Merchant Union (C-Grade)**

Oh.

There were many new things there. This guy was a djinn; was there a relation to Earth's mythical creatures? His level was question marks, but it was in the E-Grade. Besides the Dao Vision, this was the first creature Jack saw that wasn't F-Grade.

This merchant could probably kick Jack's ass easily. No wonder he was so relaxed.

Moreover, he belonged to a C-Grade faction. That grade was so beyond Jack's current infantile understanding, he couldn't even fathom what it meant. The bald man in his vision and the skyscraper-like beast had both been in the C-Grade as well.

He gulped.

When Jack approached the merchant, he was still lying on the fountain edge, enjoying the afternoon sun without a care in the world.

"Hello," Jack said, making the merchant open an eye.

"Hello to you, my little friend," he said in an eastern accent. "How can I—Oh. You're pretty strong, aren't you?"

"I do my best. I hear you sold information on Professor Rust's transactions. Is that true?"

Though the professor had said it wasn't the merchant's fault, Jack didn't fully trust that. He still felt like blaming the merchant.

However, he was brave, not suicidal. He'd just express his dissatisfaction and begone. After all, this guy was E-Grade. Taunting him would be no good.

"Hmm?" The merchant's eyes twinkled with amusement as he jumped upright. He stood at his full height, barely reaching Jack's chest, and crossed his arms. He smiled brightly. "I did, but she was fully aware of that possibility. The contents of all transactions with me are sellable information. If you want confidentiality, just pay for the confidentiality bonus. It's in the terms."

"The terms?"

"The terms and agreement of the Merchant Union. All transactions are public knowledge unless indicated otherwise. It's even written in the condensed version for non-legally versed sapients."

He whipped out a yellow brochure. It didn't look more than a few pages long, and it was written in big letters. "I gave a copy to the human woman you mentioned; she read it end-to-end, understood it, and when I specifically asked about this, refused to pay for the confidentiality bonus. Here, have one too."

The merchant stuffed the brochure into Jack's hands, who was left trying to process this information. "Okay... Thanks."

If the professor knew about the confidentiality term and explicitly refused to pay it... Hmm. Guess she wasn't lying, after all. It wasn't the merchant's fault.

"No problem. Happy to get that out of the way," the merchant said. "Is there anything else I can do to help?"

"Well..." Jack looked around. Still not enough people. He turned back to the merchant, his previous grudge dissolving as he let excitement tinge his voice. This was an alien. "What *are* you? And how can you speak English?"

"A djinn of planet Bing." The merchant laughed, his voice sonorous. "I don't usually give my name to customers, but I'll make an exception for you: I'm Ar'Tazul, at your service. I know *aliens* seem like a big deal right now, but you'll start seeing a lot more of us soon. Don't get too excited. As for the language barrier you mentioned, the System takes care of that."

"I'm Jack." Jack mechanically shook the djinn's outstretched hand.

"A pleasure. Would you like to browse my stock? I have some things you might be interested in."

"Information?"

"That, too, but I have more. Experience balls, skills, empty crystals, advanced weapons, even Dao Fruits... I suspected there would be high-end customers on this planet, so I brought high-end goods—and you get them at Integration discount, mind you."

Ar'Tazul winked, then retrieved a crystal from his robes. It was rhombus-shaped and pink, and it could barely fit in his small palm. Jack took the crystal. *Now what?* he thought, looking at it. The moment he had the question, a blue screen appeared before his face.

> **Ar'Tazul's Store**
> **Basic Information Package – 500 credits**
> **Advanced Information Package – 3,000 credits**
> **Simple Weapons – 10 credits**

> Small Firearms – 20 credits
> Experience Ball (tiny) – 100 credits
> Experience Ball (small) – 300 credits
> Experience Ball (medium) – 1,000 credits
> Experience Ball (large) – 10,000 credits
> Empty Crystal – 20 credits
> Dao Weapon (F-Grade) (made on demand, delivery times vary) – 5,000 credits
> Dao Fruit (F-Grade) – 10,000 credits

There was also a large assortment of trinkets, electronic devices, medieval weapons, and names Jack didn't recognize. There was even a section about skills, and it included a bunch of stuff ranging anywhere from knitting, to advanced cybersecurity, to swordsmanship. There was the Fistfighting skill, too, but it belonged to the top echelon price-wise, as did most melee combat skills. Skills were expensive overall, starting at a thousand credits and going up to five-digit numbers.

There were no Dao skills, however.

Jack skimmed through the list before returning the crystal to Ar'Tazul.

"Did anything catch your eye, my friend?" asked the merchant, his eyes gleaming.

"I'm just in a hurry. Also, I have none of these... credits."

"Not a problem."

Without batting an eye, Ar'Tazul handed Jack a small plaque made of green, transparent jade. The number 0 shone on its surface in clean white letters. Jack took it and turned it over. It looked pretty.

"Here's a credit card." Ar'Tazul smiled. "It's free of charge; Integration benefits."

"A credit card?"

"Exactly."

"I see... In any case, I still have zero credits. How do I gather them?"

"You sell things for credits, obviously. It's the System currency used in most places throughout the galaxy. For example, we take a selection of monster parts—I have a brochure on that. Additionally, if you have any interesting items or premium information, I could give you a good deal..."

He looked on leadingly. Jack considered it. He did have a few things to sell—expensive ones, too. The Dao Fruit he had was listed in Ar'Tazul's catalog as worth 10,000 credits, which, given the context, was a lot. He remembered the description.

> **Dao Fruit of the Fist (F-Grade)**
> *Allows the user to enter a meditative nirvana state, where the speed of Dao cultivation is greatly increased. Breakthroughs are greatly assisted. This particular fruit is oriented towards the Dao Root of the Fist. Effects are reduced as the user's Dao gets further away from the fist. Effects are reduced as the user's Dao ascends beyond the Dao Root stage. Only one Dao Fruit can be used per Grade.*

Unfortunately, it sounded pretty damn useful and tailored *specifically* for him. Plus, Ar'Tazul mentioned that the prices he saw were after the Integration discount was applied, whatever that was. In any case, selling the fruit sounded like a waste.

Which left the other reward he'd gotten from the dungeon.

> **Trial Planet Token**
> *Can allow one person into Trial Planet.*

Hmm...

Chapter 35
Challenging an Entire Faction

*T*rial Planet Token...

He had no idea what that was. Sounded like a random trinket he couldn't use. Maybe he'd get cheated if he sold it now. Then again, he could at least appraise it and ask what it was. He took it out of his pocket—seemed like an old gold coin.

"I have this. What do you think it's worth?"

"Hmm?"

Ar'Tazul inspected the coin in Jack's hand, then froze. His eyes widened, his professional smile falling, and he released a gasp.

"That's a Trial Planet Token!" he shouted. "How did you get that? Can I see?"

"That's my business, and no." Jack got defensive, stuffing the token back in his pocket. "What is it?"

"Extremely precious, that's what it is."

Ar'Tazul regained his bearing, coughing into his blue hand once and rubbing his beard. He finally took Jack seriously. "I can give you 10,000 credits for that one. It's a useless item to you, but invaluable to many people throughout the galaxy."

"I see. Well, I'll hold onto it for now. Let's discuss it again later."

Jack wasn't a fool. He was absolutely sure Ar'Tazul was trying to cheat him, even though the price *sounded* high.

Ar'Tazul hesitated, then moved a little closer.

"Listen, my friend—Jack. Listen, Jack. I understand you think I'm cheating you; and okay, it's not entirely false. I'm a merchant. I have to make a living, and 10,000 is a good price for me, but we can discuss it. That's not the issue. The issue is that, if people find out that an F-Grade cultivator has a Trial Planet Token, they won't hesitate to kill you for it. Let's try to work out a good deal and everyone will be happy. I'll get my profit, and you'll get a decent profit plus your personal safety, which is priceless. Otherwise, when news spreads..."

Jack's face became hard. "Oh, yeah? And how would *news spread*?"

"Well, I might have accidentally raised my voice before."

Jack blinked, then looked around. A large crowd had already formed, only a few dozen feet away from him. When Ar'Tazul had shouted "that's a Trial Planet Token!" everyone must have heard him.

Blood went straight to Jack's head. He pointed at the merchant.

"You tricked me," he said grimly.

"It was an honest accident. Could happen to anyone." Ar'Tazul shrugged apologetically. "By the way, acting violently against merchants is prohibited by the Merchant Union, a C-Grade faction."

Jack stared with severe irritation. Showing that coin had been a big mistake. He missed his dungeon, where he could punch things with no regard for merchants or unions. Civilization sucked. "Who will they even tell? I'm about to kick the town boss's ass, anyway."

"They won't. But, well..." Ar'Tazul looked to the side. "I am an information merchant, so..."

Jack's eyes narrowed. "You wouldn't dare."

"Hey, it's my job. I told you before, everything I learn is public knowledge unless we agree on a confidentiality term."

Jack was speechless. This guy was trying to con him. Maybe the coin meant nothing at all! But could he take the risk?

If only he could punch this guy... Except he was an E-Grade alien with unknown abilities and a C-Grade organization as his backing. At this point, Jack could only grit his teeth and admit he'd been conned. "How much?"

"How much for what?"

"The confidentiality term."

"Oh, that? Only a thousand credits."

Jack almost exploded. He really was about to punch the merchant, and damned be the consequences. "You know I don't have that much!"

"Sorry, kid. I really want that coin."

"Well, fuck you. I'm not giving you shit."

His raging, bare-chested, muscular form towered over the little merchant, but he didn't seem to mind.

"That's a dangerous call," Ar'Tazul replied.

"I don't fucking care. You can take that confidentiality term and shove it up your blue ass."

"Okay, I understand we got off on the wrong foot here." Ar'Tazul took a step back. "Tell you what. Keep the coin, and I'll keep my mouth shut for a week. Until then, you can buy the thousand-credit confidentiality term whenever you like."

"That's bullshit. Why should I trust you?"

"Because I'm not asking for anything. This is called customer loyalty, kid. That coin is very, very precious, but I see you're determined to keep it. That's fine. Even if I got it, I'd only get a tiny cut of its true value myself. Instead, I'd rather foster a good relationship with you. You're way ahead of the power curve. If you continue like this, you might even do well in the Integration Tournament, and I'm your resident merchant. A good relationship will benefit us both. Maybe even more than a single Trial Planet Token."

Jack peered all the way to the merchant's soul, and saw nothing. "You're lying."

"I can't do much to convince you," Ar'Tazul said, completely calm in the face of Jack's outrage. "But my promise stands. I'll keep my mouth shut for a week—unless you die, of course—but you better hurry. Everyone here heard me, so you never know who the news might reach."

Jack took a deep breath, calming down a bit. This situation was potentially dangerous. He had to handle it well.

When his eyes reopened, they were sharp. "Give me information on the token," he said.

"What?"

"Information on the token. Free of charge. You said you want to forge a good relationship, right? Start by helping me understand the deal you're offering."

Now, it was Ar'Tazul's turn to think. He relented. "Fine." He reached into the crate by his feet and retrieved another information crystal. "Here. This is yours. A gift."

Jack snatched it and put it in his pocket. "Good. I'll consider things again later and come back to you, Ar'Tazul."

"Tazul."

"What?"

The merchant's smile widened, revealing a perfect set of teeth. "Friends and good customers can call me Tazul. No need to be formal, Jack."

"I am not your friend."

"But you *are* a good customer."

"Whatever."

Jack was in no mood to talk. He first wanted to vent his frustration, and coincidentally, the perfect targets waited just around the corner.

Before that, he turned around to survey the crowd. News of him killing Hugo and marching at Henry's Fang had spread already, and throngs of people congregated to watch from a distance. They knew shit was going down. Some supported him, some hated him. He only cared for the former.

"People of Valville," he roared, quieting all murmurs. He wasn't used to such big crowds—he'd only lectured small groups of university students a few times—but the anger helped him overcome social anxiety. "Henry's Fang is a gang of hoodlums. They dared touch my mother. I *will* destroy them, disband their faction, and punish their leaders. I can do it by myself, but I'm aware they've been suppressing and terrorizing you. If you want to get revenge, now is the time. Is there anyone brave enough to join me?"

His speech was short, direct, and shocking. The first rows stared at him with wide eyes—so did the back rows, probably, but he couldn't see them. Behind him, Ar'Tazul had an amused smile.

Jack didn't need help to defeat the gang. However, when the dust settled, he would need people at his side, people who were both capable and trustworthy. People who would join his faction, the Bare Fist Brotherhood, and help him protect both Valville and the Forest of the Strong.

In short, he needed allies. This was a perfect opportunity. Whoever stepped forth now and fought by his side would be both capable and trustworthy.

Jack had hatched this plan on the way, and he was quite proud of it.

However, even after waiting for half a minute, nobody stepped up. Nobody took Jack's offer. Did they not believe him? Even if they didn't, wasn't there anyone willing to risk his or her life for revenge?

Jack waited another half minute. Then, he shook his head, sighed in disappointment, and turned to leave.

"Wait!"

A single man squeezed through the crowd and stepped into the square. He was slim, young, bespectacled, and average in every respect. His messy dark hair and brown eyes would never stand out in a crowd, and his slightly hunched posture didn't scream 'special' either.

He was just your average joe—but his heart was in the right place. He, alone, had accepted Jack's offer.

"Who are you?"

"I'm Edgar!" the man replied, panting slightly. "A wizard."

Jack's smile widened. He inspected the guy.

> Human (Earth-387), Level 11
> Faction: -

That level was enough to pique Jack's curiosity. "A wizard?"

"Yeah. I can shoot fire and stuff."

Edgar whispered something under his breath, then aimed a hand at the sky. A fireball burst out of his palm and flew two dozen feet before dissolving.

Jack's eyes widened. He'd seen System stuff before, but this was real, honest-to-God fantasy magic!

"Damn, man," he said. "You're in!"

Edgar approached and reached out for a handshake. "Cool."

"I'm Jack, by the way. Jack Rust. Why do you hate these guys?"

"They killed my parents."

"Oh..."

"It's not as bad as it sounds. We were on terrible terms." Edgar shrugged. "But they were still my parents, so I have to take revenge. Even if they sucked most of the time."

"Yeah... Okay, hold it. How about we go through the battle first, and you can tell me your personal issues afterward if we both survive?"

"Sure."

"Alright. I'll go on ahead. When I start bashing heads, you come in finger guns blazing and handle the stragglers."

"Works for me." Edgar smiled. Jack smiled back, having forgotten his previous anger.

What an easygoing guy...

"See you there," Jack said, then turned to the merchant. "And I hope I don't see you ever again, Ar'Tazul."

"I'm your resident merchant, friend. I'm the only one here. You're going to see lots and lots of me if you survive." Ar'Tazul waved goodbye. "Take care."

Jack cursed under his breath and took off. He ran to the edge of the square. Then, under the shocked gazes of everyone present, he jumped on a second-story rooftop. Valville Hotel was only a street away. Hopping from rooftop to rooftop, Jack got there in no time, then jumped on the hotel. It had three stories, meaning he stood dozens of feet high.

A wide wooden courtyard stretched below him. It was clean, simple, and filled with roughly thirty people. Most were armed goons, but a few wore trench coats and held themselves straighter. Everyone was busy lounging by a pool, talking to each other, drinking, or playing poker.

In the center of everything, a dark-skinned man in a white suit sat at a poker table, gambling away an obscene amount of chips. Beside him rested a Japanese sword—a katana.

They hadn't noticed Jack yet. In fact, as he watched them from above, they seemed too relaxed. They probably thought he was still in the square—maybe, they didn't even know he was coming. Hugo had done them dirty by not warning them.

It mattered little. He inspected his status screen, taking in all those pretty, pretty numbers.

Jack grinned, bumped his fists together to ramp himself up, then roared, "Henry White! Get your ass out here!"

Chapter 36
Triumph

"Henry White! Get the fuck out here!" Jack roared from the hotel roof, sending his voice throughout the town. Thanks to his enhanced body, his shout was even louder than usual.

The people below froze. Looked around, then up, to find a menacing figure standing over them. Some whispered. Others averted their gaze—the afternoon sun shone behind Jack, hiding his form.

The dark-skinned man at the center of the yard stood up. "I am Henry White," he declared evenly. "Who might you be?"

"Vengeance."

Henry smirked. "You are not a scion."

"A scion of what?"

"Hah!" Henry laughed, hard and loud. "Fuck off, vigilante, before my men fill you with lead. I'll give you a ten second head start."

"Sure." Jack smiled. "How about you start the countdown?"

"Ten—"

Jack leaned forward and fell from the roof. Everyone gasped. No gun fired. Jack landed on the soil of a garden, and before anyone could take in his form, he'd disappeared.

"Fire!" Henry yelled, but his men couldn't react fast enough.

Jack roared like a bull. He smashed a fist into a man's chest and sent him flying. He elbowed another, breaking his ribs. Before they knew it, this crowd of armed mafians had a red-eyed madman in their midst.

Guns rattled. Bangs filled the air, stealing everyone's hearing. Their world turned mute. People screamed.

A barbarian was going berserk on them. He was tall, bare-chested, and lined with muscles, and his hair fluttered by his sheer speed. His eyes shone like twin stars, and his body moved at speeds they couldn't even follow. His every punch was enough to break people, walls, trees, anything that got in his way. People flew away with soundless screams.

He opened his mouth and gave a silent roar, letting bullets graze his hair. Many missed, their wild shots piercing into other gunmen. However, nobody here was too low a level, and their bodies could take a couple bullets.

What they couldn't take, were the punches. Jack smashed a fist into a stomach, holding back to ensure the other man's body didn't explode. He grabbed a man by the head, and tossed him at another, sending them both rolling on the ground and through a wooden column. His bare feet dragged against the gravel as he shot forward, landing between three cloistered together. His fists shot out, sending them flying away like ragdolls.

More guns turned on him in slow motion, and he easily leaned away from the bullets. Most missed due to his speed.

It wasn't just the guns. These people were clumsy, their bodies reacting so pathetically slow it made him feel bad. He held back on purpose, not wanting to slaughter them, but even that was difficult against such frail opponents.

If any die, it's on them. They have guns.

Jack felt vindicated. His ordeal in the dungeon was finally paying off. He was strong! Mid-battle, he clenched his fists, letting the thrill of battle wash over him and show on his grinning lips. For the first time in a long while, *he* was the hunter.

This was like fighting the goblin tribe back in the day, except even easier. His love for fighting shone brighter than ever. The world had gone silent around him from the many bangs, giving the battle a surreal feeling.

His Dao Root of the Fist was a revving engine in his chest. Every punch flew true, his every step carrying him away from danger. It was trivial.

A bullet flew hard into his ribs. Jack stumbled and lost all air inside him. He turned to the side. A man in an overcoat stood behind a knee-high white fence and held an honest-to-God rifle. Jack hadn't expected that, having only seen handguns. He gritted his teeth.

> Human (Earth-387), Level 16
> Faction: Henry's Fang (F-Grade)

Fuck.

Jack ignored the goons and moved in dodging patterns. The rifle bullets screamed by his ears, barely missing him every time. A hint of worry appeared in his heart. Not only were these bullets stronger than the others, able to injure or kill him if they struck at the wrong spot, but the man's marksmanship was superb. He must have had a relevant skill, possibly many.

Jack weaved between the goons like a snake, changing directions and zigzagging as unpredictably as he could. The rifle barrel followed him closely, seeming to have a never-ending magazine. A bullet grazed Jack's ear; another struck his thigh and almost made him fall.

At least his hearing was recovering.

Right then, a loud shout came from a corner of the courtyard. "Yeetus fierus!"

It was followed by screams as balls of fire flew between the goons, hitting some and distracting the others. Some turned to fire on the source.

"Shieldus!"

A blue hemisphere appeared to face the goons, blocking some of the bullets. Behind the shield stood Edgar, hands and eyes blazing with sparkling cyan flames. "Fierus Whipus!" The flames morphed into a long whip that he snapped the air. Any goon it met fell to the ground screaming. "I'm here, Jack!" Edgar shouted over the screams. "I'll handle the little guys. Go get them!"

"What kind of idiot spell names are those!"

Jack's voice came distorted as he still danced around, desperately dodging the rifle bullets.

"They're from Har—Shieldus!" His shield sprang up again, barely blocking a new hail of bullets. "Hurry up! I can't do this for long!"

Jack gritted his teeth. The rifle was persistently on him, eager to reap his life. One bullet in the wrong place would be enough to end him.

Fortunately, there were plenty of human shields around. Jack grabbed one and rushed at the rifle man, still zigzagging at speeds that these low-level hitmen couldn't match.

He leaped over the comically short fence—clearly decorative—and got within a few feet.

The marksman was a short, stocky man with heavy features. He had a scar running from his right wrist to deep inside his trench coat's sleeves, and his eyes were so cold that Jack had goosebumps. This man was a killer—probably before the System.

However, now that Jack was so close, he could—

A sweet smell reached his nostrils, making him stumble. He was violently pulled out of his battle state as more instincts awoke inside him. The smell wasn't exactly sweet, it was also a little sour. Not the bad kind, but like a juicy, mellow lemon. The moment he smelled it, various images sprang uninvited in his mind, and a fire burned his body, starting from his groin. He lost focus.

He looked to the side, where a ravishing woman in underwear stared at him. An urge to drop everything and be with her overcame him—he couldn't afford to miss this chance. A bullet ripped the human shield from his hands, but he didn't care.

His Dao Root roared. A mental fist struck the illusion and broke it like a mirror, snapping Jack free. She was just a woman in underwear.

> **Human (Earth-387), Level 18**
> **Faction: Henry's Fang**

Jack growled, finding the rifle barrel staring at him from inches before his face. He ducked. The bullet grazed

the top of his head, no doubt burning some hair. But now, he was too close.

Jack planted a foot firmly into the ground and smashed a fist into the rifle man's abdomen with all his strength, making his back explode into a shower of blood and bones. The rifle went flying. Jack pivoted toward the woman, who was frenziedly backing away, but she was too slow.

His fist crushed her beautiful face into paste. She was too dangerous to spare. She'd almost developed a Dao Root.

A sudden sense of danger assaulted Jack, screaming out of nowhere. He leaned back, letting a naked blade whistle inches over his nose. He tumbled back. The blade pursued him until he managed to escape beyond its reach.

"Fire, you fools! We almost got him!" Henry White jumped after Jack. He'd let his subordinates scout out Jack, but now, he entered into the fray himself.

From up-close, he was an impressive man. His dark skin cut a clear contrast against his white suit, and his Japanese sword glinted in the afternoon light. His green eyes were incredibly piercing, like he could see through your soul, while his concentration was honed like a blade. He was clean-shaven and exuding an air of transience.

"Surrender!" Henry shouted between swings. "I work for Lord Gan Salin, one of the five scions! Even if you kill me, you'll die too!"

Jack had no idea what that meant, but he sure as hell wasn't going to surrender. He laughed.

"Then, die!" Henry roared.

The blade sang before Jack. For the first time in this fight, he couldn't just waltz in. Henry's strikes were fast and vicious. Skillful. If he just rushed in, even his close to 100 Constitution wouldn't save him.

Fortunately, Jack was faster on his feet. He retreated, observing Henry's patterns. Bullets were still flying, but not nearly as many as before. Many goons had been incapacitated, some were fighting Edgar, and most of the others had run.

Jack's back met a wall. Henry's eyes glinted with excitement as he rushed in for the kill. Jack punched back. Both men aimed for the other, but Henry's sword would reach there first.

Jack's eyes flashed. *Meteor Punch.*

His fist accelerated like a missile, flying so fast that all the bones in his arm creaked. He was pulled forward by the fist's momentum, escaping the sword's trajectory, but it was unnecessary. His punch met Henry's chest and exploded in an incredible display of blinding, ear-rattling force. A fist-shaped meteor had fallen right there.

The world went white for a moment. The katana flew away.

When everyone's vision recovered, they saw a pair of legs flopping to the ground. Henry's entire upper body had disappeared. Some of it incinerated into dust, and some sent flying over the hotel's walls.

Jack's hand remained whole this time, thanks to the level-ups and meeting Henry's soft body instead of the black wolf's fur, but a few bones had cracked. He couldn't control Meteor Punch perfectly yet.

He didn't show that. Instead, he looked at the remaining goons and grinned. "Who's next?"

In hindsight, they couldn't hear him thanks to the multiple gunshots and the meteor's explosion. Even Jack could barely hear himself. But his words had the expected result.

The goons fell on their butts, guns dropped. With their leader dead, what could they do against the natural disaster that went by the name of Jack Rust?

"Fuck off, then," he said. "And Edgar... good job."

"Thanks, man." Edgar adjusted his glasses, nonplussed by the copious amounts of blood and gore around him. He gave Jack a thumbs-up. "You did pretty well yourself."

Jack nodded, ignoring the escaping goons, and jumped on the hotel roof, where he wouldn't be disturbed.

> **The territory of Valville is now unoccupied. Would you like to add it to Bare Fist Brotherhood?**

It didn't take much thought.

Yes.

"People of Valville," he roared, sending his voice over the entire town. "Henry's Fang has been disbanded. From now on, this town is part of the Bare Fist Brotherhood, and under the protection of me, Jack Rust. We will handle things. You can sleep easy."

Of course, he didn't mention that he was the only member of the Brotherhood. *Whoops.*

He then had another thought. System, how long until the Integration Tournament?

> **Seven Earth-387 days**

Got it.

Jack had many things to do, but first, he had to take care of the aftermath. Even better, find someone else to do it for him. He knew just the person.

He also wanted to go through the headquarters of Henry's Fang for any useful items like his Dao Fruit or the Trial Planet Token. He had to find things to sell so he could buy useful skills and items from the merchant, Ar'Tazul. He also needed a lot of information. For example, what exactly was the Integration Tournament? What were those scions Henry had mentioned?

And, most importantly, who the fuck was Gan Salin?